Bob & Sue Jerin
Best wishes
Andy Nixon

THREE LIVES OF PETER NOVAK

Andrew R. Nixon

D1567730

Blue Sun Studio, Inc.

Three Lives of Peter Novak

by Andrew R. Nixon

On the Web at: http://andynixonwordsmith.com

ISBN: 978-0-9890854-2-7

PROLOGUE

The heavy wooden door creaked and groaned as Francie pulled at it. Years of humidity and inattention had skewed the old door, standing as a sentinel, protecting what lay behind from intruders and interlopers. It no longer fit the frame perfectly as it had half a century earlier.

She tugged again at the brass knob and again, this time with both hands, but the door groaned a refusal, still protecting its castle. With one foot placed firmly against the frame and the other on the floor for balance, she clutched the knob tightly and gave it a final yank. The ornate handle came loose from the shaft, and with the knob still grasped tightly in her hands she tumbled backwards across the small room and crashed into the curio cabinet.

Shards of glass flew in every direction as Francie slid down onto her rump, humiliated but happy she was not cut or bleeding. The shaft, stripped of the grooves that once held the handle in place, mocked her. It appeared to be a tongue sticking out, silently taunting and teasing her.

Still sitting, she removed the cell phone from the hip pocket of her jeans, pushed the speed dial button, and after four rings an irritated sleepy voice at the other end mumbled, "What, Francie?"

"You were supposed to be with me to clean out this house so we can list it, remember?"

Maryann yawned. "What time is it?"

"Almost nine. I've been here since seven. You know, the time you were supposed to be here!"

Maryann yawned again. "I'm sorry, Francie. I had a late night."

"Didn't we all. But some of us are responsible enough to get where they're supposed to be on time."

"Ok, ok. It will take me a couple of hours to get ready and drive all the way over there. I'll bring lunch. Ciao."

Francie groaned as she stood and vigorously brushed the shards of broken glass from her flowing auburn hair, sweater, and faded Guess jeans. Of all the times Baba warned the youngsters to be careful near the cabinet, Francie had to break the damn thing as an adult! She chuckled to herself as she pulled the broom and dustpan from the small kitchen closet.

The small residence on Jackson Street had not known the smell of garlic or *sarma* drifting from that kitchen for more than a decade, since her grandfather died at age 102. They had retired in this bucolic community nearly four decades earlier, leaving the belching smokestacks of Clairton behind. It was time to release the house from the family's bonds of ownership.

Gingerly, Francie removed her grandmother's prized knickknacks from the remaining clear glass shelves inside the curio cabinet, wrapped each one in newspaper, and placed them carefully into an empty box. The objects had little monetary value but were of such sentimental value to her grandparents that she could not bring herself to discard them.

Francie made sure the outside property and yard were well maintained, and both she and her sister Maryann stopped by from time to time to monitor and dust the home's sterile interior.

She paused for a few moments. What to do now? Turning on her heel she marched outside, slamming the screen door behind her.

The slanted exterior doors provided quick entry to the storm cellar in the event of a tornado. The concrete stairway beneath them was a great place to lie low during games of "hide and seek." Nobody ever thought to look there. The children had such great times pretending those slanted storm shelter doors were a water slide. Diedo let the hose run at the top as they slid down the incline.

One Sunday each month the family drove to Monaca to visit their retired grandparents. The oversized yard served as a playground for Francie and her cousins while the adults chatted on the porch of the house that seemed so much bigger in her youth.

Francie walked through the yard and yanked the handle on the storm cellar door. The rotting, weather-beaten wood easily gave way, exposing her childhood hiding place. She wiped the cobwebs and debris from the bunker and descended the four steps. The remaining cellar entry door was no match for a determined shoulder. One good heft popped open the remaining cellar door revealing a world of storage.

A naked light bulb dangled from the ceiling, suspended by frayed wires. With a flip of the butterfly switch on the socket, a flickering yellow glow spread throughout the basement. A thick, damp, musty smell surrounded her. As Francie's eyes became used to the dim light she surveyed the contents in the packed basement. *This is going to be way too big a job for the two of us. Hiring a junkman or calling the Salvation Army to haul all this stuff away is a better option.*

She stepped closer to the olio before her and took a deep breath, snapping on the stronger LED beam on her cell phone. Using it as a flashlight she surveyed the piles of items that had been stored and forgotten for decades. She sifted through board games, Serbian record albums, photo albums, garden tools, leftover lengths of lumber, roof shingles, and dozens of odds and ends including a set of studded winter tires and chuckled to herself. *Snow tires? Really? Our grandparents never owned a car!*

A dusty American flag that flew every holiday, now carefully wrapped in yellowed newspapers and sealed with masking tape, lay atop stacks of ancient comic books. "I always preferred Archie and Veronica to Dick and Jane," she mused aloud.

Behind the comic books, one particular object among the well-used items caught her eye; a weathered, expensive-looking valise. Though it looked nearly new, it was an old fashioned style. She spotted an attached card.

Reaching over a host of collectables, she pulled the valise toward her, blowing and wiping the dust with her sleeve, then shined the cellphone light on the card that read, in carefully printed script, "NOT TO BE OPENED UNTIL AFTER MY DEATH" PETER NOVAK.

She carefully lifted the large leather briefcase. It was from clearly from another era, made of fine leather with clasps and buckles protecting the contents. Francie unbuckled and undid the leather straps, opened it, and peeked inside. The contents included a cassette tape recorder and a bulging, sealed manila envelope. She was puzzled. Why would they even have a tape recorder? They listened to their old 78 records on the Victrola. Perhaps they had some favorite songs transferred to these tapes? But if so, why the mysterious card of admonishment on the outside? And what of the envelope? Maybe it contains directions to some hidden treasure or deep dark secret. She smiled at the thought of her grandfather having secrets. Diedo was the least secretive person ever. He spent his days rocking back and forth on the porch swing, smoking his hand-rolled cigarettes, and loving his grandkids. She repacked the satchel and started up the wooden stairs but remembered the recalcitrant door at the top, then turned and exited the way she had come in, carrying her newfound treasure. Once outside, a cool breeze of fresh air replaced the dank heavy stale odors from the cellar. The old attaché case still held the aroma of fine leather and tobacco smoke.

Back in the tiny dining room, Francie removed the tape recorder from the bag, and plugged the cord into an electrical outlet. Inside the manila envelope were three cassette tapes, award medals, and other paraphernalia. She grasped the tape that was labeled "Peter Novak, Tape 1," placed it into the machine, and pressed the "PLAY" button. As the sound began she sat befuddled. The tape contained not music or directions to buried treasure, but clear, crisp speaking that she could not understand. She listened briefly until she heard her sister's knock at the front door.

"Anybody home?" Maryann popped her head in. "I brought lunch. Primanti Brothers sandwiches and diet sodas to make up for my rude behavior this morning. What happened to the cellar storm doors? Why are they opened?" She glanced at the broken glass on the front of the curio cabinet. "What happened here?"

"Shut up. Don't talk to me about the curio cabinet," Francie grumbled. "Or the doorknob. I made an executive decision this morning. We're going to have a professional empty the basement. There's too much stuff down there for us to empty." Her face brightened, "but look what I found!"

Maryann grinned at the object before her. "A cassette player! I haven't seen one of these since high school. Is anything on the tape?"

"Yes, and that's what confuses me. I thought it might be their old music but it sounds like Diedo's voice. And this is really weird… it sounds like he's speaking German!"

"WHAT? Are you sure? It can't be him. He didn't even speak English, only Serbian."

"I know, but listen to this."

Francie rewound the tape to the beginning but it began to unwind from the cassette.

"Oh, Dammit!" She lifted the cassette from the player as the loose tape unraveled like a yo-yo string. Carefully, she used her finger to roll the unwieldy tape back inside the cassette, and then repositioned it in the player. "Now, listen to this."

The speaker began, *"Mein name ist Peter Novak. Ich wurde in Bosnien im Jahre des Herrn 1889 geboren Ich machte ein Versprechen an meine liebe Frau Kata auf dem Sterbebett, dass ich meine Geschichte zu teilen. Dies ist die Geschichte meines Lebens für meine Enkelkinder und deren Kinder zu hören."*

Francie stopped the tape. "It's definitely his voice. You took German in college. What did he say?"

"Wow! I'm not sure. It was twenty years ago that I took one semester of German and barely passed, but I think he is saying Baba asked him to record this for their grandchildren. Let me run this down to the Language Department at Pitt and see if I can get it translated."

"That's just the first tape. There seems to be a set of three."

"He never talked much about his background. He never talked much, period," said Maryann, "We know they met and married in America and they both came from Eastern Europe, Serbia, I think. We know they were dirt poor until Baba became a businesswoman. Mom always said Diedo was unremarkable as a breadwinner but ahead of his time as Mr. Mom. But how is it that he speaks German?"

They locked the house, reset the alarm, and agreed that Francie arrange to have the cellar doors repaired and the house emptied, and Maryann would get the tapes translated and invite their cousins to a listening party.

Three weeks later, more than a dozen family members gathered at Francie's condo to listen to the audiotapes that had been translated into English, transcribed, and re-recorded. Next to the black tape player, contents of the manila envelopes including the original cassettes, a letter personally signed by President Woodrow Wilson, a citation, medals, and other memorabilia were all carefully displayed. Francie placed the first tape in the cassette and turned the switch.

A thickly accented voice on the tape began, "I am Franz Friedrich Volk, Professor Emeritus in the German Language Studies Department at the University of Pittsburgh, and a native speaker of the German language. What follows is a verbatim translation of the audiotapes of Peter Novak, unknown American hero."

Several seconds of hissing followed, then silence, and the professor continued speaking on the tape as Peter's surrogate.

"My name is Peter Novak. I was born ninety-two years ago in Bosnia in the year of Our Lord 1889. I made a promise to my dear wife Kata on her deathbed that I would share my life story with the family. I was reluctant to tell my story and did not want it to be heard during my life. Our children are now gone. What follows is for my grandchildren and their children to hear after my death. I cannot tell of my birth and infancy from firsthand experience, of course, so I will repeat what my father, Nikola Novak told me about his marriage, my mother, Ruža, and my beginnings. From boyhood onward the memories are my own."

FIRST LIFE—BOSNIA

1

ADVICE AND CONSENT

Nikola Novak, hair slicked down tightly to his scalp and smelling of barber's lotion, cleared his throat and pounded heavily on the solid wooden door. He did not mean to pound so hard, but he was nervous. Although the meeting had been prearranged and all participants knew their roles, Nikola worried that they might object, or think him unworthy, or toss him out of the house.

Nikola stood tall on the doorstep, dressed in his best wedding and funeral suit, and with butterflies rising from his stomach to his throat. He hammered at the door a second time. After what seemed like ages, Jelena Stojanović opened the barrier that stood between them.

A flowered apron looped around her neck and tied at the waist accented her plain white housedress. "Nikola, how well you look this morning." She smiled. "Please come in."

Jelena's husband Pavle, half-smoked pipe clutched in his hand, stood and greeted Nikola as he entered. "Come. Sit. Let's have a *slivovitz.*"

Jelena retrieved two shot glasses from the kitchen, wiped them with her apron, and filled each a shot of plum brandy from the clear cut-glass decanter on the wooden table. Raising his glass, Pavle proposed a one-word toast, *"Ziveli."*

Each man downed the first shot in one swallow, then another, as Jelena refilled the shot glasses.

The burning sensation from two shots of liquor crossed Nikola's parched lips and trailed down his throat, calming the butterflies and easing his anxiety. He began, "I am here to ask for the hand of your daughter, Ruža."

His voice trembled. Jelena filled the shot glasses for the third time. Both men took another shot of *slivovitz* then exhaled deeply.

"Ziveli; to your health and long life."

Jelena Stojanović took a seat next to her husband on the well-worn couch. The two sat quietly and waited until Nikola gathered his thoughts, cleared his throat, and spoke again.

"I have a small house that can be expanded as our family grows, and I have a farm and a horse to pull my plow. I will take good care of Ruža, treat her well, and always respect her. With your blessing we will marry in the Serbian church."

Jelena and Pavle exchanged glances. They had hoped for a marriage arrangement for their daughter with a man of some means. Nikola was not only a man of some means, he was known to be a good man and a staunch member of their church. Their families had known one another for generations.

Jelena spoke first. "Our daughter is ready for marriage. She is a good girl and attends church regularly. She cooks and keeps house as well as I do."

The daughter, Ruža, was not quite a woman at the time of her marriage, but no longer a girl. At age fifteen she had barely bid good-bye to her childhood.

"You have our blessing, Nikola Novak," said Pavle as he stood to shake the big farmer's calloused hand. "For her dowry we will give you an iron stove for cooking and warmth, a rug for your floor, and a small sum of money."

Nikola was considered a good catch, though he was twice Ruža's age and just a few years younger than her parents. He had spent the past decade working his small farm in hopes of taking a worthy bride. He had seen Ruža often in the village and at church where she sang in the choir.

As Pavle spoke, Nikola's mind dwelt on the teen's beauty. She enchanted him whenever he looked into the almond-shaped black eyes, deep set in her oval face. He could not believe his good fortune to marry this ebony-haired beauty.

He barely heard Pavle ask, "When would you plan the wedding?"

Before he could answer Jelena called out, "Ruža, come here. We have a guest for you to meet."

The girl appeared in the doorway. Her naturally shaped eyebrows arched perfectly along the curve of her forehead above her turned-up nose that complemented pursed lips, ruby red as wine. Ruža's doll-like features were reflected in her petite body. At barely five feet tall, she was just a wisp of a girl. With eyes cast downward she entered the room and shyly met the man who would soon become her husband.

Nikola shook hands with the parents and left the Stojanović home hurriedly, making his next stop at the office of his mentor and god-father. Goran Jovanović was a businessman and man of means in the village. He related the earlier conversation with Pavle and Jelena to Goran.

The accountant had been preparing documents as Nikola arrived. A pair of worn leather arm wraps prevented ink from soiling his white shirt. His suit coat hung lazily on the chair. As he rose, he set the pen on the desk next to the blotter, and removed the sleeve protectors from his shirtsleeves. He walked around his solid oak desk and hugged Nikola. "Congratulations, my *kumče*. I will pay for the wedding, except the rings, which tradition says must be purchased by the groom."

Goran was twenty years Nikola's senior. He looked like a typical businessman and accountant. Most of his hair was gone and the remaining curly silver locks sat serenely atop his head. His wire-rim spectacles pinched the bridge of his long, crooked nose and at first glance one might think him to resemble Ebenezer Scrooge from the Dickens novel, *A Christmas Carol*. But unlike the cold-hearted Scrooge, Goran was a kind and generous man who was willing to extend credit to farmers during difficult times. In return he was repaid with interest when crops were plentiful.

"Ah my Nikola, I have watched over you since the day you were born. Thirty years seems like yesterday. I am happy that you have chosen the Stojanović girl as your bride and happier that her father agreed. Dragana and I will be honored to take part in your wedding." Goran and his wife Dragana were *kumovi* to Nikola.

Dragana, who had been listening to the conversation from the back of the small office, called out, "You can rest assured that the wedding will be a gala affair, Nik. We will see to that. I can hardly wait to serve as Ruža's matron of honor. The event will be a grand Serbian Orthodox church wedding."

"*Hvala ljepo, kuma,*" replied Nikola, thanking his godmother. He kissed both Goran and Dragana, "I am so fortunate to have you."

The next stop was the home of Nikola's parents and his brother, Pedrag. "Her parents accepted me, brother, so I hope you are ready be my best man. Once I'm married you will become the eldest bachelor in the family. At twenty-eight years you will take my title."

"I watched and learned while you were the family's best man before me, Nik. I learned from the best. I'll greet your guests and offer each a sip of rakija. I know how to work the crowd with an expensive, decorated bottle and make sure each guest is offered a sip. I'll fulfill my duties and make you proud of me." The brothers hugged.

The following morning the two families began planning festivities to unite the couple. My father told me how her best friends, Jovanka and Vesna, received the news. The three girls had grown up together.

Jovanka said, "I will make a tiara of flowers and herbs for you."

"Oh Ruža, I'm so excited for you! You are the first to find a husband," Vesna crooned.

Jovanka added, "Nikola Novak is such a good man. My father said he hopes we could find a man such as Nikola, who already has his own farm. What is the first thing you will do after the wedding, Ruža?"

"Well, after *that* part, you know, is over," Ruža responded as the three teens giggled, "I plan to make his little shack into a nice home for us and our children. I hope you both come to visit often."

"I placed five flowers in your tiara," chortled Vesna "So you will have at least five children."

Jovanka quickly added, "I wove in seven more so you will have a dozen little ones!"

In addition to flowers for the tiara, Jovanka and Vesna picked wild rosemary and made corsages to be sold to guests at the wedding. The money from the corsage sales would go to the couple as a gift to start their marriage with wealth.

The days passed quickly in the rustic village as plans were made. In no time, the day was upon them.

The morning of the wedding a group of friends arrived at the home of Ruža's parents for traditional *Skup* festivities, with food, drink, and song and bartering for the bride's hand. Aromas of traditional foods filled the air.

Ruža's brother Darko served as *Djever*, the bride's guard. "I will stay at your side, sister. Kuma Dragana and I will watch over you this day."

"You are a good brother. The best I could have hoped for."

"Are you nervous, my sister?" Darko whispered in her ear. Ruža shook her head but the chewing of her lip and trembling of shoulders betrayed her.

While the Skup took place at the Stojanović home, the groom's family and friends gathered at his house for an equally festive party of food and drink. The groom's revelry began earlier in the day. Pedrag raised a glass and announced, "We must celebrate, for our family gains a member. The bride's side loses one."

Festivities carried on for most of the morning and early afternoon until the two groups of revelers joined the celebration and strode up the dirt street toward the church.

Jelena, tears running down her cheeks, cried, "I am so happy for my daughter becoming the bride of a man as fine as Nikola, but it is sad to lose a member of my household."

Ruža, meanwhile, was serenaded by a band of local musicians as her guests danced in the street and yard. Amidst singing and dancing, the group drank toast after toast to the couple, who were only allowed to see each other briefly during the toasting. As they passed one another, Ruža whispered into Nikola's ear, "Do you love me just a little?"

The groom grinned and nodded, answering with one word, *"Preko!"*

Nikola was shuffled off to the church ahead of Ruža. Children waved colorful ribbons and ran alongside the procession. Adults cheered the wedding party while the entourage marched from Ruža's parents' house to the church. The cortege entered to the singing of the choir that welcomed them.

The village's Serbian priest, *Pop* Vučen, a giant of a man, officiated. His imposing hulk stood more than six and a half feet tall. His waist-length gray-and-black beard sprinkled with crumbs from several nights' dinners covered a wrinkled black shirt, and most of his three hundred-pound girth.

Pop Vučen carefully crossed himself and began the ceremony.

"I am so nervous," whispered the skittish groom to Goran. "Thank goodness I'll never have to do this again."

Kum Goran patted him on the shoulder and whispered, "You're strong enough to heft a fifty-kilo sack of grain onto your shoulder and carry it to a waiting wagon, why should you tremble before the wedding congregation?"

Nikola smiled. "You are right about the sack of grain. And yet I feel my knees will buckle at any moment."

The betrothal ceremony began. Nikola Novak and Ruža Stojanović, along with their attendants, stood silently at the solid entry doors of the small church.

Pop Vučen met the wedding party at the door then asked, "Do you come to this place of your own free will?"

Both bride and groom nodded and the priest continued, "Have either of you promised yourselves to another?"

The stomach butterflies began to disappear and the couple smiled at each other saying in unison, "No Father. We are here of our own free will and were not otherwise promised."

"Then, my children, please enter this house of worship and take your places before the altar."

The priest blessed the rings, read Bible passages, and again made the sign of the cross while holding the rings, after which he declared the couple betrothed. The ritual was repeated three times to represent the Holy Trinity.

Pop Vučen, with rings in hand, gently pressed his huge clenched fist against the couple's foreheads three times. On cue from the priest, Goran took the wedding bands from the priest and exchanged them between the couple's fingers three times to signify how the weakness of one will be compensated by the strength of the other. The rings were then placed on the third finger of the right hand of the bride and groom, the hand of authority and power, in the tradition of the Serbian Orthodox Church. The couple kissed and the congregation cheered.

After the ceremony guests walked to Nikola Novak's home, a small, humble dwelling made mostly of stones with mud packed tightly between. The thick walls kept the warmth in during winter and the heat out during summer.

Village women from the church had taken over cooking and serving duties, working for hours preparing pots full of traditional foods. The reception took place outside the home in the large, green backyard.

A brook ran through the property and, in the shade next to the house, sat tables and chairs borrowed from neighbors and from the church. Men who had skipped the wedding ceremony and gone directly to the reception were already drinking beer, whiskey, and wine; each one telling stories about his own wedding and, as the liquor flowed, exaggerating his physical and sexual prowess. Occasionally one would take exception or offense to a story and fights broke out. But soon the point of contention was lost and the rivals clasped one another's shoulders and downed another drink.

As guests entered the yard, a trusted cousin of Nikola accepted money and gifts. The new iron stove given by the family of the bride was the grandest of presents for their new home.

Music played and festivities continued well into the night until the last well-lubricated guest, who snored loudly after falling asleep next to the fireplace, was awakened and ushered out the door. The couple soon fell asleep exhausted, wrapped in each other's arms.

2

DYING FOR LIFE

The first year of marriage was a busy and blissful one, as it should be with newlyweds. Ruža transformed their home from a modest bachelor abode into a family nest. On her first day as a housewife, after her husband left for the fields, Ruža removed the dusty, colorless, burlap curtains, and cleaned the windows, caked with several years' worth of Bosnian dirt and grime, thus letting in more sunlight.

As she worked, swept, and scrubbed the hardened dirt floor, just inside the front door, she smelled something foul. Ruža had noticed it earlier, but today it seemed much more obvious. A deep breath caused her to quiver at the rancid miasma. The stench was overwhelming. She followed her nose outside and discovered the source of the offensive odor.

"How could that man stand the smell of this reeking compost heap next to the house?" she asked herself as she wrinkled her nose.

The stink of rotting food and trash brought tears to her eyes and gagged her throat as she made trip after trip from the side of the house to the far corner of her garden. Ruža spent most of that day moving the stinking compost heap to an area where it would not offend. When the job was finally finished, she gathered a basin full of water, brought it inside, and scrubbed herself until her skin was as pink as a baby's bottom.

She finished her work just as Nikola entered the shanty that evening. It had rained and his boots were muddy. "Leave your boots outside. I don't want to ruin our new rug already."

He removed his boots and as he entered the house, was taken aback. "I cannot believe so much light could brighten my, er, our home."

"I removed the curtains from the windows. They are filthy so I put them outside. Tomorrow I'll go to the village to get fabric and make new ones. I hope you like what I choose."

"I will like anything you choose, my dear." He sniffed the air inside the small shack. "Something smells good…You cooked dinner, but there is something else more pleasant…"

"I moved the compost heap away from the house, to the corner next to where I will put in a garden."

Nikola nodded his approval. "I didn't notice the pile of the compost was gone until you mentioned it. No, what I smell is the freshness of a beautiful bride." He folded her petite body into his big arms. "I cannot imagine there is a happier man on this earth today."

She gently pushed him away. "A working man needs his nourishment."

They enjoyed the first dinner that Ruža prepared for him, mutton stew. When Nikola was so full that was he unable to eat another morsel, his bride cleared the table, and sat in his lap. They sat with their arms around one another until he carried her to the nearby bed where they found comfort in each other's arms.

Over the next months, with Ruža's help, the shack slowly transformed itself into a home. Brightly colored curtains replaced the dirty sackcloth drapes. A hand-woven rug, part of Ruža's dowry, lay over the clean-swept hard dirt floor, and a fire of twigs, sticks, and assorted combustibles emitted warmth from the iron stove her parents had given them, keeping away the winter chill that hovered on the other side of the flimsy stone and mud walls.

The couple settled into a routine. At sunrise they awakened and Ruža prepared a breakfast of ham or bacon and eggs. During one such meal Nikola praised his wife for her diligent work. "You have made changes that transformed our house into a home. I could not be happier. I hope you are happy too."

"Marriage is everything I dreamed it would be. You have lived up to your promises to my parents. You treat me very well. And you are a big bear that tends the fields all day and comes home to your den and a loving wife. How could I not be happy?"

"You deserve nothing less than the treatment owed to a princess." He tapped his belly. "Another fantastic breakfast prepared by the hand of my beautiful wife. I would love to spend the day with you, but the fields and animals are calling my name."

"Well, then, you finish breakfast and tend to your chores, Papa," she teased him as she moved nonchalantly around the table.

It took a moment for the comment to sink in. "What? What did you just say?"

"I said...you tend to your chores, *Papa,*" she giggled, and patted her stomach.

"No! Really? Are you saying what I think you are saying? But... how? When?"

"I think you know how," she demurred, leaning her head against his shoulder. "Probably early next fall."

"I'm so happy I cannot speak." Tears streamed down Nikola's cheeks as he kissed her. He spent the day working as usual, his mind filled with thoughts of his first child-to-be. As he walked behind the plow, digging furrows in the rocky soil, he prayed… Please, God, let it be an easy birth for my beautiful Ruža. And God, if it is not too much to ask, I wish my firstborn to be a healthy boy. I will cherish him and teach him to be God-fearing.

Ruža's belly swelled as the baby grew inside her. The morning routine continued with a slight variation. Nikola came to the table each morning, winked, and asked, "What is that belly bump I see at your waist?"

He pulled her closer and rubbed the bulge. She giggled. "Our child is happy in his home. I can hardly wait until he comes out and visits us."

"I can't wait either. Be sure to take it easy while I'm in the fields. I don't want you exerting yourself."

"Oh go on now. I know I must take good care of our child."

In spite of herself, Ruža had misgivings of the looming responsibilities of childbirth and rearing the baby. Concerns weighed heavily on her. She visited her mother often.

"What if I am not a good mother? Already I cannot sleep and my body aches. One minute I feel fine. The next, I'm exhausted, like I've run to the next village and back. Some days I feel like I haven't slept in a week.

"Suppose it is not a boy. Nikola so wants a boy as his firstborn. What if I do something wrong and the baby is born unwell?" She continued, working herself into frenzy. "Mama, I don't know what to do when the baby comes. What if…."

Jelena, folding the laundry she'd just taken from the line, interrupted her daughter gently, "Hush now, Daughter. Women have been having babies for a long time. You have little say over those things. God will decide if it is to be a boy or girl. You will be fine.

The midwife Dženana Ibrahim will be with you to help when the baby comes. She has delivered more little ones that I can count. She brought both you and Nikola into the world. You must not worry yourself."

As the pregnancy progressed, Jelena told Nikola of Ruža's worries. "You must be gentle with her, Nik, now more than ever. She worries about not pleasing you if she does not have a son. She worries if the child is born unwell. She has all the worries of a woman giving birth to her first child. It is something many women go through but you must help by reassuring her.

"I do, Jelena. I try to calm her each night, but I'll be sure to do so even more often."

Ruža's body continued to ache and all things physical became more difficult. She strained bending over, and reaching up to hang clothes was nearly impossible. But Jelena and the other mothers in the village recounted stories of similar troubles during their first pregnancies. The stories eased Ruža's mind some. She wondered if she really had cause to worry, or was she just being a little girl. Something inside her felt very wrong..

The day of the birth began like any other in the small village nestled in the harsh mountains of northwest Bosnia. Nikola left to tend the fields and a cacophony of color fell across the mountains as trees shed their leaves on the crisp, blustery autumn morning. The cycle of life was evident outside as well as within the small house where the midwife Dženana Ibrahim, straight-faced and dour, walked to her station. She examined the patient, then left. "I'll return in a few hours."

The midwife returned to her own home, made strong tea and fortified herself for what she was certain would be a long night.

Shortly after Nikola returned from the fields, he answered a sharp rap on the door. The elderly, petite woman clad head to toe in a well-worn black outfit and clutching a satchel spoke, "I am here to check on Ruža." Looking at her patient she added, "I think her time is near, Nikola. I will take care of your bride as I took care of your mother when you arrived. Do not be a nuisance. Wait on the bench outside. I'll let you know when you become a father."

From across the room came a small voice. "Welcome back to our home, Mrs. Ibrahim," Ruža muttered as she leaned heavily on the table, hunched over with one hand massaging her huge belly.

The couple received the Muslim midwife into their home without hesitation. Serbians, Muslims, Jews, and Croatians populated the Bosnian village, and though they worshipped separately, the village had a strong sense of community. Rarely did issues of religion arise among neighbors.

Nikola stepped outside and paced, wondering how long it would take until he heard the cries of a new life.

"I will prepare the dining table as a bed for you," the midwife told Ruža. "It will be easier for you and for me. The bed is too low."

She carefully took well-worn but thick sheets and blankets from her bag and set them atop the dining table. "You relax in the chair for a few more moments. Not to worry my dear, this is your first delivery, but it is not mine.

"These woven sheets are for your comfort and will absorb body fluids once the child arrives. The heavy sheets and blankets will give you all the comfort of a bed of roses. Once your baby arrives I'll clean you both so you look nice for Nikola."

The old woman waddled to the stove and made sure enough fuel was available to keep hot water coming as she needed it. Returning to the table her staccato voice calmed the patient.

"Did you ever wonder why the flowers and my garden are so

robust?" Dženana asked Ruža as she prepared the table, "I use these sheets to wrap the afterbirth and blood, then take it home and spread the contents over my garden. It makes great fertilizer. I wash the bedclothes and put away until they are next needed."

Nikola knew of this trick. He used the residue from newborn sheep in his own fields to boost the harvest.

Nikola listened and paced outside until the door opened and the midwife announced. "You can come inside now and lift your bride to the throne where she will have your child."

Nikola entered the house, sweating profusely despite the cold. Ruža's belly appeared larger than it had been when he left the house, and her complexion had paled. He lifted his bride from the chair and gently placed her on the table. She held him tightly around the neck and grunted as she tried to help.

The midwife explained, "The birthing process here is not much different than the field with your sheep, except this is your wife and you cannot be present until you are called. Now you wait outside. I will call you when your child has arrived."

Again the anxious husband went to the door but did not leave for a moment leaning on one leg like a boy who had just been scolded.

Dženana turned her attention to Ruža, patted her patient's hand. "Things will be fine."

The sixteen-year-old expectant mother lay in a weakened state, doing her best to prepare to bear her first child. Pains shot through her body but Ruža willed herself to be brave and not flinch. "I will think of something other than the pain—something less foreboding, more pleasant."

She thought of wildflowers that grew among the gravel stones outside the humble shanty and said to the midwife, "I am not alone. The flowers also struggle their way into the world. They fight and tunnel a path up through the hard earth and rough pebbles with their tiny buds testing the spring air like blind mice. First they poke through and feel for an open surface. They grow and push and finally pop open with painted leaves. Their bright tints liven the yard and the home during their life, a length of time that seems but a heart-beat to humans. Then the flowers are picked to make room for their offspring.

Ruža was a romantic. She focused not of the end of the lives of the flowers as they withered in a makeshift vase near her bed, but of the bountiful array of colors that welcomed her each time she left the house to pick another garland.

She told Dženana that the previous day that her dear neighbor Milica brought a bouquet picked from the edges of the farmland, and expressed how the blue tint complemented her pale blue dress! "The flowers smelled fresh and are a feast for the eyes. If I'm able I'll pick some every day for the baby and for Nikola. I'll wear them like the crown I wore on my wedding day."

As the hours passed, Ruža drifted in and out of that netherworld between sleep and consciousness. Dženana Ibrahim sat next to her on a heavy wooden chair and leaned back, away from the young girl, to ease the tension in her aged neck and shoulders. A flicker of orange and yellow light from the lantern, propped on the wooden table next to the bed, fell across the room. Outside, slices of light from bright sky and full moon, peeked through the crevices where the curtains didn't meet. Rays of light fell across Ruža's face and stomach, highlighting the pain on her face.

Ruža moaned and Dženana shook herself from a trance back to reality.

Nikola thought he heard a moan and ran to the window. He saw the midwife's faded, hand-woven bag sitting on the floor. The bag matched her drab dress and black shoes. Ruža lay still on the table. She looked to be at peace so he retreated.

The elderly midwife lost track of the time. Day was night. Night was day. Had it been minutes or hours since the ordeal began? She pulled the old, hand-crocheted shawl more tightly around her aching, frail shoulders and exhaled a long, deep breath.

Only then did the chill of the predawn darkness pierce her back and shoulders. Dank stale air, peppered with foul-smelling vapors rose from the bed, and clung to the old woman's hair. Musty walls, soiled bedclothes, and the cloying smell of death also hung in the air. Yet the room also promised life, a new life that was fighting to enter an unforgiving world full of poverty and hardship. "Too late life, too soon death," she mused as she surveyed the harrowing scene.

"I feel something moving inside me," Ruža called out. Her small size made the pregnancy difficult, but the baby was finally on its way out of the oven and into the world.

The midwife held Ruža's hand and soothed her as a mother would a child. "This part will soon pass, little one, and your baby will come out of its shelter to greet you."

Outside, the cabin stars glittered and the night was bright above the mountain. A ray of moonlight fell across the hump of Ruža's protruding belly. But Dženana did not need the light to see the pallor of her patient's cheeks, nor did she need the light to see the frail elfin body that carried another life within. "I have had many deliveries, my child, and I know you are in pain, but you are the bravest mother I have ever known. You bear the pain like a soldier. Relax now. The process of birth has begun and will now move quickly."

Blood ran in rivulets from between Ruža's slender legs and soaked the sheets. The patient gritted her teeth and looked straight ahead, as though in a daze. "Mmmmmph," she grunted and bore down onto the table.

Dženana Ibrahim positioned herself between the girl's legs and began to mumble to herself. "Too much blood. I can't see."

The elderly midwife perspired as she swabbed and dabbed the blood. Still unable to see any part of the baby, she tilted her head for a better view of the birth canal.

At last, a head came into view. Uterine contractions continued, and though the massive bleeding obscured her view, the midwife felt Ruža's belly and determine my continued progress.

As the baby left the safety of the mother's womb, all movement from Ruža ceased. The midwife, drenched in sweat and blood, hovered, straining to hear an utterance or sound from the young girl, but none came.

3

Burying and Marrying

Nikola sat on the bench that cold winter night, shivering and waiting anxiously as the heavy wooden door opened and the exhausted midwife appeared. Her sad eyes told a tale that Nikola was unwilling to hear, "I'm sorry, Nikola. It was a very difficult birth. Your Ruža is gone. The flame of our darling Ruža had gone cold. Thank God, you have a healthy son."

The burly farmer's mind refused to process the words of the woman. "Ruža, dead? It cannot be. I hear crying inside the house. You are mistaken."

He tried to push his way into the house to see for himself but the diminutive woman in black blocked his path. "The crying you hear is from your son. There is nothing that you need to see inside the house right now. You must fetch your priest. Let me tend to your son and your wife.

He did not accept the loss of his beloved, but as a farmer his sense of smell was attuned to the aromas of birth and death. He knew that the essence of death passed from the cabin to his nostrils and throat, but refused to accept reality.

The big man, shaking and with reddened eyes, turned and stumbled toward Pop Vučen's home, mumbling to himself. "My beautiful Ruža. She cannot be gone. Dženana must have made a mistake."

His mind wandered and he walked slowly, perhaps hoping the more time he spent walking, the longer Ruža would be alive.

A gust of foul wind slapped his face as he opened his mouth to lick his lips. It tasted like dross from an empty wine barrel, as it swirled. The leaves gossiped loudly enough to mask his own screams. The shrieking wind, called *burra* by the villagers, surrounded Nikola, mercilessly biting anything in its way. It seemed to carry an unseen pack of wolves that howled and lashed at Nikola's face and cheeks turning hot tears into ice crystals.

As he stumbled toward the priest's house his mind began to imagine Death thundering across the sky. He thought he heard the Dark Angel shouting, "I'm coming for your wife." He envisioned Death tugging at the reins of six huge black horses pulling a chariot. Tall and regal, hooves glistening and heads held high, their silky black manes rippled down their necks like ebony waterfalls.

With an earth-shattering snort they turned as Death beckoned them. The chariot blazed across the sky, sparks from horse's hooves flying and fire flashing in Death's eyes. Nikola was certain he saw Ruža inside the chariot, where she lay limp as a rag doll.

The scene in his mind disappeared when he realized he had arrived at the home of the village cleric.

The priest's wife, Iva, answered the hammering at her door and immediately read Nikola's grief-stricken face. He could barely speak as he stammered, "She is gone, Mrs. Vučen. My Ruža. She is dead! My son lives but my beloved wife does not."

Iva led the shaken parishioner into the house and attempted to calm him. "Sit, Nikola. I will make some tea while my husband dresses."

She placed the kettle on the stove, lit a fire, and soon the rising steam announced the hot water was ready. She brought a piping hot cup of tea to the shaking shadow of a man. He let it steep as he sat trembling, clutching the hot cup with both hands as though trying to squeeze the life out of it, hoping it might somehow bring Ruža back.

He rambled, "How could this be? How could God let her die? She was so young. So full of life."

The priest's wife patted his shoulder. He gazed blankly through the open bedroom door and saw sleepy-eyed Pop Vučen pull on his well-worn black trousers and tuck the wrinkled shirt into his pants.

"I'm sorry to wake you at this ungodly hour, but please, you must come to my Ruža." Nikola managed to offer a hint of civility as the tea calmed him.

A sleepy Pop Vučen entered the front room. "Do not worry about me, my son. Being awakened in the middle of the night is part of the priesthood."

The priest stood in the kitchen until both men finished their tea, then slipped on his shabby jacket, kissed Iva, and the two of them left the house together.

As they walked, Nikola prattled on, "I knew Ruža wasn't strong. I prayed. I treated her well and did my best to help her. What else could I do?"

He began to rave, "I'm a religious man, Pop Vučen. You know that. During the pregnancy I spent many hours on my knees begging God that the birth would be an easy one. Why has He forsaken me?"

"God works in mysterious ways, my son. He has His reasons. It is not for us mortals to know His mind. Perhaps he needed Ruža to be the brightest star in the heavens. She gave her life so God could give you a great gift, a child. It is His will and the blessing of a new life will remind you of the child's mother each time you look at him."

Overcome with confusion and grief, Nikola barely heard him. The cleric put his arm around the farmer's shoulders and they walked the rest of the way in silence as the sun began to peek through the mountain passes.

Dženana greeted them at the shanty door. "The dairyman passed by a while ago. I sent his boy to fetch Jelena. She should arrive soon."

As she spoke, Momir the village carpenter arrived at the open door carrying a wooden casket. "I am sorry to hear of Ruža's death, Nikola. The dairyman's boy told me of your loss. I know you need this now. We will talk later."

The two men hugged and Momir left to return to his shop.

"Ruža has been bathed," the midwife said to the clergyman. "I can wait outside if you prefer while you perform your religious rites."

"No. You are welcome to stay, Dženana. I am certain Nikola has no objection nor will Jelena. We have some different beliefs but we all worship the same God."

Nikola stood and nodded in silence.

Within minutes the sun had fully risen. Peter's grandparents, Pavle and Jelena arrived and entered the small house. Jelena had shed tears in her own home but now, without any outward emotion, she prepared to follow a long-held Serbian Orthodox religious routine with the help of Dženana, despite her Muslim faith.

Jelena hugged the burly farmer. "Oh Nick, she loved you so much and was happy and excited to have your child. I cannot believe she is gone. Part of our heart has vanished."

Pavle and Nikola hugged and kissed each other on the cheek, but neither spoke. They both shed tears of sadness.

"Thank you for your help, Dženana, and you, Father," Jelena managed to say, "I brought the clothes our Ruža will wear in heaven."

Carefully, sadly, and with loving tenderness, the two women quietly proceeded with the reverent tradition of bathing and dressing the mother/child in her final resting clothes while Pop Vučen chanted Bible verses.

The priest spoke religious passages as he sprinkled holy water on all four sides of the casket before Ruža's body was placed inside. "We pray for the repose of the soul of Ruža, the servant of God, who departed this life too soon. May our dear daughter find herself in heaven where the just repose." He continued chants and blessings for nearly an hour before the ritual ended.

As the priest spoke, Nikola stared blankly. He was so distraught. Tears blocked his vision. "What will become of our child? What will become of me? I am not equipped to raise a child alone."

"You will not be alone, Nikola. The church and village will help you. God has a plan for you. We do not know what the plan is at the moment, but God will provide. You must have faith."

Nikola's tears continued to flow, as he looked toward the basket with the baby inside. He walked over to basket, watching as the infant seemed to have not a care in the world, sleeping quietly an innocent cherub. He wiped the tears from his eyes with big ham-hock fists, and whispered, "I do not have much to give you, my son, but will give you all the little I have. I will love, protect, and care for you. It will not be easy, Little Man, but somehow we will survive—together."

Once Ruža was dressed, her husband and father together lifted her from the bed and carefully placed her in the casket. She looked like an angel who had fallen asleep.

Dressed in a snow-white frock from her ankles to her neck, Ruža lay at peace in the casket. Knitted slippers covered her tiny feet. A pale blue scarf, the color of the noonday sky, wrapped her waist and a soft blue blanket covered her legs. A tiny gold locket draped from her neck, held by a thin chain. The locket, a gift to Jelena from her mother, had been in the family for generations.

A three-day wake followed. Family and friends recited passages from the Book of Psalms as Nikola sat in a trance next to his dear wife. Despite the efforts of Jelena and family members to console him, he remained in a pathetic stupor.

When the wake ended, Nikola's godfather, Goran Jovanović, carried a cross and chanted Psalms leading the congregation to the church for the funeral service. Pop Vučen waved a censer back and forth and walked ahead of the coffin, carried by six pallbearers. The fragrant smoke wafted through the narrow street while the procession moved slowly into the church and up to the altar.

A bowl of *koliva,* boiled wheat with honey, symbolizing the seasonal nature of life and the sweetness of heaven, and a lit candle representing the frailty of life, both sat near Ruža's head.

She wore a crown wreath of laurel leaves and flowers and held a small beaded chain with an ivory icon of Christ on a cross, wrapped around her hand. Candles burned throughout the funeral service.

Mourners and worshipers stood during the service then approached the casket to bid Ruža farewell. Words of comfort, "I'm sorry, Nikola" and "She was taken too soon" did not reach him. With tears flowing he was in the depth of despair and wondered what would become of himself and his son..

The priest closed the wooden casket and pallbearers took Ruža to the village cemetery. After another short ceremony she was committed to the earth.

Members of the congregation, friends, relatives, and neighbors moved on to the Novak house for a traditional mercy meal prepared by the church women's auxiliary.

Nikola sat, still dazed, a conversation with Ruža pressed into his memory. He mumbled, barely audible, "My son does not have a name. We said that if our first child is a boy, we will call him Peter after the patron saint of our family. We will celebrate St. Peter on our Slava, and teach him that Slava is the most important holiday in our household, equal to a marriage. As it was passed from my father to me, so shall my entire family celebrate the protection of Saint Peter over our household."

~

At the Mercy Dinner, "What will you do now, Nikola," became a question oft repeated by friends and family. He did not respond; just shrugged and shook his head in anguish.

When he did speak, he worried, "Even before Ruža's death, finances were lean. The farm, goats, and sheep earned barely enough to keep us fed. Now there is a motherless infant to feed and clothe. What will I do?"

That first evening, alone, Nikola tucked Baby Peter in the basket after he had been fed and changed. Enough rags were strewn around the house to keep him clean for the moment, and Nikola didn't have the energy to think about tomorrow. But he knew he must force himself to continue living if only for the sake of his son.

Early the following morning Jelena knocked on the door, awakening both Nikola and Peter. "I brought diapers and clothing for Peter. They haven't been used since Ruža was a baby."

"Thank you, Jelena. I've got to get back to the fields sometime and I don't know what to do with Peter. I can't leave him. He must eat. He needs, um, you know, feeding. I just don't know what to do."

"I can come by each day and tend him here while you work or bring him to my house until we figure a plan for the two of you. But he needs a mother's nourishment and I can't help you with that."

A knock on the door startled them as they hovered over the baby, watching him sleep, tiny arms raised as though he were a priest beckoning the congregation.

Nikola opened the door to a neighbor, Danica, who had recently given birth to twins.

"Hello Nikola, Jelena. I knew you would need help with your baby so I brought clean diapers to you. I don't mind washing them when I do laundry for the twins."

Jelena spoke up. "We're in good shape with diapers, Danica. I just brought all Ruža's old nappies, and thank you for your offer to launder them. That will be a big help. But what Peter really needs is a wet nurse."

"I can be his *dojilja* if you like." She looked at the baby, lying quietly, with eyes open wide. "Let me feed him now. I can see the poor boy is starving." Danica gently lifted him from the crib, undid her top, and placed a firm nipple to the hungry, waiting mouth. Peter preferred to dine with Danica rather than drink the goat's milk that had been his staple since birth..

As Danica fed the happy baby, the entry door was again assaulted. This time another parishioner and neighbor, Saša, arrived for a visit. "Can I take that beautiful boy with me on Monday? I do my wash, and when my twins were babies they loved to curl up in the basket while I hung the laundry to dry."

I didn't know what to say except, "Thank you, Saša. That would be a big help."

For weeks then months, neighbor after neighbor arrived at the house bearing food, clothing, and offers of help. The village rallied around the father and son and together they raised the lad through the early months of life. The entire village became Peter's godparents.

Thanks to friends, neighbors, and church members, things improved beyond Nikola's wildest hopes. Still, he continued to brood as he went about his daily routine. He appreciated the help but remained inconsolable for months over the loss of Ruža. That was, until Little Peter uttered his first word. "Dada."

Villagers said of the infant,, "Peter is such a good baby. He rarely cries and often smiles. He loves the attention from the neighborhood women as much as they enjoyed fawning over him."

Once Peter progressed beyond suckling, he was fed goat's milk and pap that Jelena taught Nikola to prepare. On days neighbors weren't unavailable to tend the boy, Nikola placed him in a basket and took him to the fields. Peter became a farmer before he was able to walk.

Another neighbor and farmer, Jozo Pacić, and his wife, Miloška, were regular visitors to the Novak house. "Look how cute he is," cried Miloška. "I just might take him home and keep him." She loved to fuss over him. The Pacić family had not been blessed with children although the couple had been married more than a decade.

While playing with Peter Miloška suggested, "Let me make some tea for you men." It was an effort an effort Nikola appreciated, as he enjoyed the beverage but rarely made it for himself after Ruža died.

Peter continued to grow, Jozo and Miloška continued to visit, and Miloška continued to make tea for the men. Peter enjoyed tea licked from the tip of Miloška's finger.

Jelena watched as Peter took his first unsteady steps on the same day Jozo Pacić's accident happened while tilling his field. Row after row of poor soil turned over, as had been done for centuries by village farmers. Jozo's thoughts were certainly those of a typical farmer, *how much will this meager crop bring? What will I do with the profits? Will the weather allow for a healthy crop? Should I buy the farm next to mine?*

Perhaps his mind drifted to his wife... *She is as beautiful now at twenty-five as she was when we married.*

With her long golden hair billowing in the breezes, her perfect face and ice blue eyes, and his handsome face and strong body, they made a striking couple. She had never held milk for an infant, and her round hips, ideal for carrying children, were barren. It was clear to see how much they wanted children when they visited .

Jozo asked Nikola many times, over cups of tea, "So why are we still childless? We make love passionately, but no babies are come. Tonight I will try again with every ounce of passion in my body. She is so good with your little boy. We must have a child soon!"

Jozo told Nikola he thought about Miloška and their childless state nearly every minute while plowing his field. He performed his farming routine so many times that he could do it with his eyes closed and his mind on other things. But one time, one single time, the plow struck a rock at an unusual angle. At the exact instant Jozo leaned forward to free the rock, his horse stumbled and lurched forward, causing the plow to jerk and toss Jozo over its frame. His head and neck came down on the sharp blade, slashing the skin on his cheek and forehead and severing his carotid artery. Jozo most likely bled to death within minutes, slumped over the plow.

Miloška cooked mutton for dinner as usual that evening and waited patiently for her husband to come home. She began to worry when she didn't hear the plodding of the old nag as usual when he arrived home, and did not hear Jozo whistling a happy tune. Where could he be?

The sun began to set with Jozo still not home. Miloška pulled a shawl around her shoulders and left the house to look for him. The field came into view. She was puzzled by her first sight, two boots and pant legs sticking up toward the sky. As she ran toward the field, the rest of the horrible scene unfolded before her, though her mind could not process what she was seeing.

"Mužu, mužu," she called to Jozo as she approached. He did not move. Getting closer she saw the red-stained earth beneath the blades. The horse had repeatedly tried to pull forward but was restrained by the rock-stuck plow and Jozo's head and neck caught between the blades. The tugging back and forth left Jozo's face unrecognizable.

Miloška's knees buckled. She screamed nearly loudly enough to wake her dead husband, but her voice went unheard over the vastness of the farm and distance from the village.

She steeled herself and unhitched the horse from the plow. Then she tried unsuccessfully to free Jozo's head and neck.

Unable to free him, Miloška walked toward the village, leading the horse, until she came upon a house. She was too dazed to realize it was Nikola's house as she pounded on the door.

"What is it, Miloška? What has happened?"

"My Jozo. He had a bad accident in the field. Please help."

"You stay here with the baby."

Nikola ran to gather a few neighbors, and together they rushed to the field. It was late before Jozo's body was separated from the plow and taken to his house to be cleaned and set up for mourning.

Nikola and Peter were among those who came to Miloška's house to express condolences during the wake. She was still in shock, her eyes red from crying.

After the wake, Jozo's body was taken to the church for the funeral service just as Ruža's had been.

At the mercy dinner following Jozo's funeral, two portly women,

Zora and Andjela, the village gossips, chatted as they sat in the corner on the only two cushioned chairs in the room. While stuffing themselves with food, they planned what might lie ahead in the life of the widow Pacić. Zora began, "So young, so pretty. She should not have a difficult time finding another husband."

Andjela answered, "She will bring a nice dowry to the new husband. I hear Jozo did very well on his farm."

"She is lucky she doesn't have any brats to drag around. You know, many men might not mind used goods, but they don't want somebody else's brats to raise," added Zora.

"Do you think she will leave the village?"

"Maybe. But I'll tell you what. With that pretty face and long golden hair she better leave or get married in a hurry. If she comes shaking her cute young widowed behind around my man, she'll be sorry."

"Remember that Milinka tramp? Her old man left for America. Told her he would send for her and she never heard from him again. Screwed every man in the village. I told my Momir, if I ever catch him around her, I'll make him a eunuch."

The two toothless old hags giggled like schoolgirls and did not notice Pop Vučen standing behind them until he said, "Hello, ladies. Anything I could add to your conversation?"

The busybodies turned as red as out-of-season wine. In unison, they said, "No, Father, we were just leaving."

"Well then, be sure to express your condolences to Mrs. Pacić on your way out."

Zora and Andjela waddled to the door but did not exit before each loaded a plate with food to take home.

When the sad widow spotted Peter tucked under Nikola's arm she smiled for the first time since the tragedy.

"Come to me, Little Prince," said Miloška as she extended her arms. He giggled and cooed for Miloška, then walked on unsteady legs to her outstretched arms. She lifted him and he nuzzled her shoulder.

Pop Vučen approached and asked Nikola and Miloška to follow him into the kitchen. He ushered the few remaining cooks out of the kitchen and said, "Please be seated."

Miloška, still holding the baby in her arms, took a seat at the table. Nikola sat across from the two of them.

Pop Vučen began, "I must first tell you how sorry I am for both your losses. It is not up to us to question God's way or why one must die and another lives. Neither is it our right to question why some who seem to be evil are allowed to live while those who have so much to offer are taken.

"I cannot tell you why your Jozo or your Ruža were taken. Perhaps God had a greater calling for them with Him. I do not know."

They sat in silence, while Peter's eyes darted back and forth surveying the room.

"I do know this. It is God's will, and in the best interest of infant Peter, the village, and both of you, that you marry as soon as the forty-day mourning period ends. I will leave you now but if you have anything you want to talk about, I am here for you."

There was no discussion. Once the huge bearded priest finished speaking, he stood and left the room. The 'engaged' couple both blushed beet-red and looked blankly at one another. Nikola's heart ached for his wife's company and counsel. He realized that Miloška's heart must be aching as well.

Nikola attempted to take charge and speak, "I... er... ah.... uhm... Pop is... I mean..."

The bright red color began to recede from her face. Miloška, still holding the baby in one arm, reached out the other to Nikola and took his hand. "Thank you, Nikola. You have been very kind. We both have much to think about."

She stood and handed the boy to his father, and then they both awkwardly returned to her guests.

≈

Before the wedding the priest counseled the couple. "It is natural for you to be nervous," he began. "But you will be nervous this wedding night for a different reason than your first."

"Miloška, you were married for more than a decade and I'm sure you never imagined being with another man." She blushed as Pop Vučen added, "Yet you are about to lie with a near stranger."

"Nikola, as a man I am sure you are less anxious about sleeping together, but your feelings of guilt and anxiety are natural, for your year of marriage to Ruža was still in the throes of your honeymoon when she was taken."

He nodded in mute agreement.

The priest was right, of course. They both had feelings of desire, desperation, guilt, disapproval, and fear associated with sleeping with one who was not their spouse.

He continued, "You must abandon those feelings of anxiety and have a legitimate intimate relationship. If it takes a while to become accustomed to one another, be patient. Be considerate to one another. You will have a long and happy life together."

Miloška's grieving period lasted the traditional forty days as dictated by the church. She sold the farm as well as the horse that had been present during Jozo's death. The money was used to pay debts that both Jozo and Nikola had accumulated over the years, allowing them to begin their lives debt free.

Pop Vučen had officiated both of their first weddings and performed this second wedding as well. It was neither a typical Serbian fete nor as big a deal as the first ones. Conducted at home, it was a small ceremony with only a few family and friends in attendance.

Nikola took the priest's advice to heart on their first night together. With Peter in a basket on the floor next to them, Nikola turned his back as any gentleman would while the new bride changed into her nightclothes, crawled into bed, and pulled the blankets up to her chin. Then he cautiously entered the bed from the other side. It was an awkward beginning, neither found much sleep until nearly dawn.

Miloška arose first, and remembering his desire for tea, brewed a pot. As she was about to remove it from the stove, he came up from behind and wrapped his arms around her shoulders. With voice cracking, he said, "I will do my best to be a good husband to you."

Miloška turned to face him, and still cradled in my arms, wrapped her own arms around his neck. "And I will be a good and faithful wife." They stood and embraced for a long time, then hand-in-hand, walked over to the basket where Peter slept, and held hands silently as they watched him sleep.

4

Coming of Age in Bosnia

I was eight years old when I visited Dženana Ibrahim for the last time. She had withered after the death of my mother and had not tended a birth since that time. In a halting voice she recounted the events surrounding my birth and the death of my mother. She had a recurring dream from that horrid night. It began when she stepped away from the sleeping baby to clean the makeshift bed where Ruža's body lay still. She said the scene in her dream was set exactly as it had been at my mother's bedside.

In her dream Dženana wrapped the lifeless corpse in a sheet and carried it to the bed. She scrubbed the blood and residue from the table where the birth had taken place. It took several trips to the stream behind the house to empty the basin of brackish red water and refill the basin with clean.

After washing her own hands and arms with lye soap, Dženana gathered one more bowl of water and placed it on the stove. Sliding the sleeves of her well-worn sweater farther up her arms, she dipped a cloth into the hot water, rubbed it with soap, then began to wash my mother's body. She first removed the sheet and then, starting at the hairline, gently washed Ruža's face. She removed the soiled dress, cleansed her body, then rewrapped her in a clean white sheet.

When the task was completed, the midwife finally paused. The impact of the scene took hold and she drew in a long, sharp breath.

The dream ended quickly. Dženana felt nauseous, knowing what she next faced —a mourning husband and Ruža's shattered parents asking God "Why?"

She told me that when she awakened from the dream she fell into a state of sadness that has remained to this day. She knew it would not be long before her own cycle of life would run its course, but said it seemed so unfair that Ruža's ended too soon.

"I decided at the moment of your mother's death and the beginning of your life that I had delivered my last baby. I'm sorry for your loss, Pero."

She always called me by my boyhood nickname.

I sat with her in silence for several minutes, then she spoke again, "I have been a midwife nearly fifty years. I chose this profession to bring happiness into the world. I brought Ruža into the world sixteen years before her death, and her mother Jelena eighteen years earlier. My heart can no longer endure the grief that comes with the loss of a young mother."

Her dark eyes, sunken into their sockets, were moist, but no river of tears flowed from the old woman.

"Perhaps the body can create only so many tears and my supply was exhausted the night you were born," she whispered.

"I can see you Baby Pero, still sleeping peacefully across the room, unaware of the tragedy that marked your birth. I don't know why a young one must die and an old hag like me continues to live. It isn't fair!"

The lips of the elderly woman barely moved as she drifted to off sleep. "It's not fair. Not fair. I did the best I could for your mother, my child. I can see her now."

Dženana Ibrahim did not awaken.

My father and stepmother also called me by my nickname, Pero. I was not quite two-years-old when my first half-sibling arrived, a boy they named Jozo, in memory of Miloška's deceased husband. Over the next five-year period, Miloška and my father had two more sons and two daughters bringing the family count to eight. My stepmother treated me as kindly as if I had come from her own womb, though I always felt I was different from the other children in my family. With my dark skin, brown eyes, and black curly hair I stood out from my blond-haired blue-eyed siblings.

The eighth year of my life saw major events that shaped who I was and who I would become. Like many eight-year old boys I had an inquiring mind. My best friend Mijo and I considered ourselves to be great explorers. We were inquisitive about everything from anvils, "Why are they so heavy?" to zoology, "Why do dogs run in packs?" Although neither of us had ever been out of our village, we sat in awe and listened with great interest to tales of the outside world, and wondered how different things really were from life in Stabandža.

Mijo's father owned a tavern where we two pals often sat wide-eyed next to the bar, listening to stories told by men who returned from other parts of Europe, America, and beyond. One day a bar patron named Bobo regaled us with tales of huge ranches in Texas, larger than our entire village.

When we left the tavern to explore our little corner of Bosnia, I spat on the ground as I had seen the men in the tavern do, tongue against teeth. Spittle made a hissing sound as it passed my lips, and some dripped on my chin. I wiped it with the back of my hand then wiped my hand on my pant leg and asked Mijo, "Do you think one person can really own more land than our entire village?"

Mijo spit and scratched his crotch as men do when contemplating. "My cousin went to Australia and says it's so. Houses there are larger than churches. And there are animals that stand on two feet, like a man, and hop. They keep their babies in a tummy pouch. "

"I don't believe it," I said, kicking a clod of dirt with my bare foot.

"It is true! And that's not all. One of the men in my father's beer garden said he knew a sailor who had a steel hook for a hand!"

"A steel hook for a hand? No way." But I thought for a moment and then added; "I'll bet he has to be careful after he uses the privy."

We both laughed and continued the discussion. Mijo swept a bug into his hand then tossed it back into the air, "A Russian man told me that in France they have wagons that don't need horses or mules. They move by themselves."

"Where's France?" I asked

"I don't know, maybe in America. But can you believe it? How is it possible? A wagon that moves by itself?"

"Moves by itself? Ha! I could make a wagon move by itself. Just push it down a hill!"

Mijo confessed, "I never thought about that. Maybe all the hills in France go down and none go up."

We laughed again and continued the conversation while exploring the village. We knew every nook and cranny of Stabandža and the surrounding area, and found it difficult to believe that the outside world was so different than our bailiwick.

We whistled and skipped and sauntered down the dirt road that was more of a wagon path than a street. "I am the great Serbian inventor Nikola Tesla," I boasted. "I will change the world!"

"I am Archduke Ferdinand and I rule your world," answered Mijo. "Since you are my best friend you can have anything in my kingdom. Anything you want is yours."

We both scanned the ground hoping to spot a prize; an errant reptile, coin, or any other object that boys find fascinating.

Finally I saw something. "Oh ho, what is this?"

Neither Mijo nor I had ever heard of Charles Goodyear, the American who received a patent for his invention a process called vulcanization. Mr. Goodyear's invention led to improvements in tires, shoe soles, hoses and conveyor belts and would lead to a discovery that shaped my destiny.

A black object lay on the edge of the wagon path. I leaned over to pick up a section of a discarded rubber tube. "What is this strange material? What would Mr. Tesla make of this?

"Look Mijo, it bends like a green twig but doesn't break or tear. But I don't have the strength to rip it apart."

Together we pulled and released the material. Each time, the black pliable stuff snapped back to its original form.

Fascinated by the elasticity of the material, we became rougher with it.

"Ugh," I grunted, pulling and tugging, but upon its release the stuff always returned to its original shape. "I WILL rip this thing," I grunted as I pulled harder, but the item did not break or tear. It simply snapped back.

Frustrated and excited, I asked Mijo, "Have you ever seen anything like this?"

"No. What do you think it might be?"

"I don't know. Let's see what else we can do with it."

"Watch," I said as I pulled it down over my head like a hat, and then released it again. We both laughed as it snapped back regardless of how it was pulled. "Let's take it to a field at the edge of the village. I am determined to split this thing."

We raced to the edge of an abandoned field where we could play and not be a nuisance to the owner.

"Watch this," I said as I hooked the material around a fence post, braced both feet against the post, and pulled with both hands. I pulled and yanked hard as I could until it slipped out of my hands and flew into an adjacent field and I fell backwards with a splash into a mud puddle, landing on my behind, and adding one more large round spot of dirt to my filthy, bedraggled clothing.

"I'll get it, Pero," cried Mijo. He raced into the field, leaving me to wallow in my own humiliation and the mud puddle.

Once we retrieved the object we tried different approaches to rend it. "Let me tie this end around a post," Mijo grunted as he lashed it as tightly as he was able. We held onto the other end and pulled as we walked, grunting and straining with all our might until it would stretch no further.

"We're just about there... ugh, mmmph."

Digging our heels into the dirt, together we gave it one last hard tug, then... CRACK!

The top of the rotting wooden post snapped and broke with the wood still attached, flying back directly at us, and slapping me hard across the cheek, raising a welt.

"Ohh, argh, ouch," I cried, clasping my hands to my cheek and face, rubbing, trying to ease the sting of the wood that came within a fraction of an inch of my eye.

Mijo laughed loudly as I cursed, crying out *"Stupid jackass stuff!"* and rubbed my throbbing cheek until the sting left and I became even more determined.

Finally, I tied the thing around my waist like a belt and turned to Mijo.

"Let's go ask Vasie. He knows everything,"

We took the find to Vasilije Božić, village blacksmith and an ex-sailor who had been around the world several times. He was considered the local walking encyclopedia.

"Vasi, look what I found. Do you know what it is?"

The huge man, whose tattooed arms were bigger than my chest, examined the material for a few moments. "This is called rubber. It is grown on trees… in Brazil, I think. An Irishman or American, I don't remember which, invented what you hold in your hand. It has many uses. Your piece looks to be the type of rubber used inside tires." He paused then added, "From all the repair work I've done, I'm sure what you have is part of an inner tube."

Excited, I asked, "Can I make a tire from this piece? If it comes from a tree will it grow if I plant it or place it in water?"

Vasilije laughed. "No, it repels water, but you should keep it. It will make a great toy, and you will have the only inner tube in the village."

"Thank you, Vasi." I gave the big man a hug as we left the blacksmith shop. "Now, Mijo, let's figure out what to do with this."

We brainstormed for a considerable amount of time trying to figure what use this toy might have. Suddenly an idea struck me.

"Watch this, Mijo." I stopped along the path and tied each end of the rubber to a post, then pulled the material from the center. With Mijo's help we strained to pull it back as far as we could, but again one end became untied, snapped back, and this time slapped Mijo hard across the shoulder.

Mijo yelped in pain. "If this keeps up we will be as marked up as the stubborn mules in the village!"

For several minutes I was quiet. Then, "I have another idea."

"I hope this one doesn't knock us out."

"Watch this," I said. "Vasie taught me how to make some sailor's knots.

We tied each end of the rubber more tightly on separate posts, using a self-tightening sailor's knot. We also remembered not to pull quite so hard.

I held the rubber strip taut. "Hand me a pebble, Mijo."

He reached to the ground and found a smooth one about half the size of a small chicken egg. "Here, try this."

I slipped it into in the center of the rubber. After one more tug I released the rubber. It recoiled with great force but the rock soared far into the adjacent field. We laughed at our discovery. Then we tried again.

This time Mijo pulled back on it and aimed at a corn stalk in the field. The rock soared, overshooting the target. We took turns but found the invention was too big and cumbersome to control accurately. After a while, Mijo became bored and went home, but I remained, content to pull, play, and ponder alone.

There is something about a young boy pondering. His mind is not cluttered with thoughts of how things should be, like an adult's mind. A boy can see lots of possibilities that adults find silly, if they find them at all. Children lose most of their creative ability as they grow into adulthood. Fortunately, I had not yet grown up so I was able to visualize other possibilities for the rubber.

And then the vision came to me. "Aha! That's it! I know what I'll do with this!"

I raced into the wooded area and snatched up stick after stick. "This one! No, not that one. Oh, that one might work. No, too uneven."

After nearly an hour, and ignoring scratches on my legs from the prickly brush, I found several of the pieces that I wanted. Holding the treasures tightly, I carried them home to my father's tool shed. There I examined the hanging tools until I found a pair of cutting shears. "Aha! This is exactly what I need."

Taking the rubber from my pants pocket, I sat on a stump, then picked up one of the items from the woods, a small limb that had grown in two directions in the shape of a "Y."

Carefully I cut a strip of rubber and attached one end to each arm of the "Y." Grasping the tail, I pulled back on the rubber with one hand, holding the tail with the other. The prongs of the stick strained until the wooden tail snapped and split just below the confluence of the arms.

Too green.

I tried several more Y-shaped sticks and discovered dead limbs work better than fresh ones.

A small hole, bored through each arm provided an opening. I laced a thin strip of rubber through, wrapping and tying it using a sailor's knot, so when I pulled, the rubber tightened around itself.

Next, I found just the right stone for the best range and velocity, and returned to where we had been earlier.

Back at the edge of the forest I stood about twenty paces from the nearest tree. My right hand held the "Y" as my left hand pulled back on the rubber, resting it against my chin. I placed a pebble in the center of the rubber, aimed at the tree trunk, released the rubber and swish! The pebble sailed past the tree.

I tried again and again and again until one stone finally hit the tree. I tried again. Another hit! I aimed at a fencepost, hitting it square. Several additional shots found their marks as well, and I smiled a smile of accomplishment to myself.

I did not realize it at the moment, but Peter Novak, the illiterate farm boy, had just invented a mala praćka or what you call a slingshot.

It was nearly dusk. My arms ached but I sauntered over to Mijo's house to show him the fruits of my labor. "Let me try."

We took turns practicing with the device until it became too dark to see the targets. Then I went home and dreamed about how the world might be conquered with my invention.

Mijo never did master the weapon but I became an expert marksman, using the slingshot to shoot game and help feed the family. As time passed I refined my technique and the device, with an eye toward maximum accuracy. I did not realize it then but my invention would play an important part in the rest of my life. Not only did it protect me, it almost made me famous, although that remarkable incident lay far in the future.

5

PERO THE HORSE WHISPERER

My reputation grew not only as a marksman with my sling-shot, but I also had a natural way with animals. I took care of the old nag that pulled my father's plow, and whenever a neighbor's dog became sick or a barn cat ceased to be a mouser, it seemed like the villagers asked me to take a look at their animals. I'm not sure how this got started, but it is true that I have always had a kinship with animals. I find them to be much more gentle and civil than humans.

One incident stands out in my mind. I can't remember exactly if it was before or after I invented my slingshot, but it was in that same year. As I look back, my reputation for helping animals might have come less from my skills as a boy-veterinarian and more from the fact that poor villagers were unable to pay for a real vet and my fees were based entirely on donations and good wishes.

A farmer's reliable old plow horse became unruly. Andrij Babić told his wife, "The horse refuses to wear the harness. It reared and bucked, bit at me, and kicked at the boards of its stall. I've tried everything. I fear the animal suffers from some sort of mental disease. I hate to do it but I might have to put it down."

"But that would be terrible. You know we can't afford to buy another. Why don't you ask Nikola Novak if his boy will come to the house and take a look at him. What can you lose?"

Andrij Babić became an instant celebrity several years earlier when a traveler stopped in at a local bistro to relax and enjoy a beer on his way back to France. He sat in on a card game with several locals, including Babić, who had an unusual run of good luck just as the Frenchman had an equally unusual run of bad luck. The final hand saw all the gamblers drop out except Babić and the Frenchman.

The Frenchman believed he had the winning hand and wanted to call but was out of money, so he offered to include his fine Percheron horse as collateral against the entire pot of money. Babić accepted the challenge, for he had entered the game with only a few *krone* in his pocket. If he lost the hand he would not be much the worse for it.

The bet was made, the cards shown, and Babić became the proud owner of the entire pot as well as the finest Percheron horse in all the surrounding villages. Local men would come to the Babić farm just to watch the mighty steed pull the plow with ease, while their old nags struggled against the rocky soil.

When the Percheron stopped working, Babić whipped and scolded the horse in an effort to get it to return to its old self, but nothing worked. The farmer finally yielded to his wife's pleadings and agreed to seek me out and see if I could do anything with the beast.

Babić walked to my father's farm and waved as Nikola waved back while moving up and down furrows, planting seeds in the freshly plowed field as he went.

"Hey Babić, what you doing here? Why aren't you putting in your crop? I walked past your field yesterday and it isn't even plowed. Are you so rich you can afford to skip a planting season?"

"You make jokes, but I have troubles."

"What kind of troubles can you have? You've got the best horse in three counties. Your fields are always the finest in the area."

"My Percheron is the problem. Something is wrong with him. He has gone crazy on me. Won't work. Acts wild. He behaves more like a wild stallion than a plow horse. I am worried I might have to put him down. I could never afford to buy another one like him and there don't seem to be many Frenchmen looking to lose another one in a card game."

"I'm really sorry to hear that, Babić. Is there anything I can do to help you out? My boys can help you dig furrows if you want."

"Well, there is something," he answered. "Your boy Pero is said to be gifted with animals. Do you think he can come over and have a look? I can pay him a little something."

"Of course. He just left from helping me plant. I'll send him over this evening."

"Thank you, Nikola. I'm sure it will be wasted time, but my wife insisted. I think the horse has gone mental, but who knows? Maybe your kid will be able to talk the nag back to being its old self, God willing."

When I arrived home that evening, my father told me that Babić had come to see him in the fields that afternoon and why. "I know that horse has a very calm manner. If it is acting up and refusing to work, my guess is that the big boy is in pain."

"That was my thinking too, Son. The horse is too young to be senile. You look it over and do it your best. I know you will."

"I will, Papa. Don't look for me tonight. I'll have to make friends with the horse and sleep in his stall so he thinks I am a member of his family. I'll take some salve with me in case I find an infection. It could be in his foot or his teeth. I just don't know. But I'll find out."

"I'm sure you will, my boy."

After dinner I walked to the farmer's home, stopping at a pile of fresh horse manure at the side of the road. I scooped a handful and rubbed it on myself. The odor would give the horse a feeling of kinship with me.

I rapped at the door of the farmer's house. Mr. Babić opened the door and smiled as he looked at me. My clothes reeked of fresh earth and horse manure.

"Would you like to come into the house?"

I shook my head.

"No? We can talk here then I'll take you to see the horse-turned-monster."

Mrs. Babić came to the door momentarily took a whiff, then turned and walked back into the house and I spoke to the husband. "Please, Sir, do not come with me. Let me spend time getting to know the horse by myself. If he allows it, I'll spend the night with him. I'll try to stay in the stall. If not, I'll sleep in the barn, next to the stall."

Andrij Babić had some concerns about my suggestion. He worried for my safety, but he shrugged and agreed.

"Thank you, Mr. Babić. I'll go to him and we'll talk. The big boy will tell me what ails him and I'll try to help."

I turned on my heel and walked toward the old barn. Gaps between its warped planks were wide enough to peek through and glimpse the Percheron, but I didn't want him to think I was sneaking around him so I walked straightaway into the barn. There were several empty stalls but his was the only one occupied. Mr. Babić must have recently cleaned because there was little manure or urine on the hard floor. Fresh straw had been placed in the stall and a pitchfork of hay had been provided for his dinner. I just gazed at him for a while. This was the closest I'd ever been to such a royal animal.

"So, Big Boy, how are you doing tonight?" I asked. Farmers in those days did not name their horses so I just called him Big Boy. He needed a better name.

"I think I'll call you *Kraljevstvo.*'"

The huge Kraljevstvo stood nearly nineteen hands tall, and despite having pulled a plow for years, still had the graceful lines of a young stallion. His color was pure black with white markings around two hooves. This Percheron was a finest horse I'd ever seen.

Kraljevstvo did not appreciate an interloper in his stall and at first bit at and tried to kick me, but I spoke calmly to him. "Oh, you beauty. You don't need to be cross with me Kraljevstvo. I'm your friend."

I began to softly sing a made-up song. "Mighty, mighty Percheron, tell me boy, what ails you. We'll be friends, you handsome man. I will make you better."

My singing continued and my voice seemed to calm the huge steed. I hoped it would eventually allow me to curl up inside the enclosure.

My song resumed, "Oh you big baby. I can see you are in pain. Can you tell me where it hurts? We will find out and I will make you better. This I promise you Kraljevstvo, although you are slow to become my friend, before the sun rises you will let me into your heart."

The Percheron snorted and moved aside, and I nestled in the straw and pretended to sleep.

It was well past midnight when I stood up from my bed of straw, and the Percheron allowed me to stroke him. I ran my hands gently over the entire surface of the animal, from nose to tail, from mane to hoof, while the horse shimmied and sighed, nickered and groaned. He allowed me to gently massage his entire body. Eventually the animal snorted and nickered, letting me know that it trusted me.

The hooves were the first to be inspected to see if a splinter or stone had caused an irritation, but I found nothing. Picking up a large horse brush, I ran it over the the beast's entire body. Nothing. I did it again. Finally, as I brushed for the fourth time, the Percheron flinched and groaned when a brush bristle slid over a spot on its flank. I rubbed the spot again, this time with my bare hand, and again the horse flinched. With that, I set the brush aside and curled up on the straw. But this time I went to sleep next to the mighty Percheron.

As the first rays of sunlight broke through the sky and slipped between the slats of the barn walls, I awoke and stretched, then turned the horse so the area that seemed to be the cause of distress was visible. Sure enough a tiny hole had begun to fester.

While calming the horse with my voice, I worked the wound, gently rubbing and stroking until a splinter was ejected, followed by pus and dark blood. The splinter or thorn tip had gotten under the skin and remained there, causing soreness and damage. The offending item burrowed into the flesh in such a way that it was nearly impossible to be seen.

After removing the splinter I squeezed out as much of the infection as I could, cleaned the wound and covered it with salve to help it heal.

When Andrej Babić arrived at the barn from the house that morning, I told him what I'd discovered. He looked skeptical. "Wait and see," I said. "Let the big workhorse rest for the weekend. Give him a holiday, Mr. Babić and by Monday you'll once more have the finest plow horse in the village. I named him Kraljevstvo."

I knew the farmer was skeptical that the horse would be fine. He tried to pay me for my services but I refused and told him to wait until Monday. If he was satisfied with my work, perhaps he could bring some of his harvest to my family. We shook hands and I left the Babić farm.

Monday afternoon Mr. Babić came to our door. He hugged me and handed me two krone to show his gratitude. "My boy," he said, "it is true what they say of your skills in the village. I am so happy that I listened to my wife and didn't shoot the animal. One day you will be famous for your skills."

The compliment made me blush and I refused the money. "Instead of the money," I asked the prosperous Babić, "Would you send food to my family?

"Outside on the wagon is the best of my harvest for your family. But take the money as well. What you did for me this day is worth more than these few krone. Thank you, my boy."

My reputation at being skilled with horses led to the third venture that would change my life forever.

6

PERO'S CONTRACT

Harvest season was over and I was nearing my ninth birthday when my next life-changing event took place. With the birth of each additional child, Nikola and Miloška faced an even greater struggle to get by on the small farm whose rocky soil yielded barely enough to survive. The shanty had been expanded and bedrooms added, but it still offered too little room for a family of eight.

Feeding eight from my father's farm left little profit, and taxes continued to increase. Nikola and Miloška had initially pooled their resources, but the nest egg was long gone and a recent poor growing season left the family in debt.

Despite the difficult times, the couple did not argue. When Nikola worried that he didn't know how they would survive another winter, Miloška calmed him. "God will provide," she would say. "He always has. He always will. He brought us together, right? And look at our beautiful family. We are truly blessed."

Nikola smiled. "You are amazing. My rock!"

While killing time at Mijo's father's beer garden, we listened to tales from a bar patron, Nenad Mikulić. The merchant climbed onto a table and told of a flea market. "Yes, all these things take place within a day's travel from your village. You think of farming for your livelihood, but besides farming, there are many other ways to make a living. I travel to bazaars, open-air markets, and fairs and see huge displays with many merchants selling and trading their wares. The French call them 'marché aux puces.' That means 'market of the fleas.' I speak many languages. That's why I'm successful.

"For years farmers, tinkers, tailors, butchers, bakers, and every type of craftsmen with something to sell, trade, or need to buy, have come to the flea market. We drink wine and beer and watch singers, dancers, jugglers, fire eaters, and other entertainers."

Mijo and I sat wide-eyed as we listened to the merchant Nenad tell of this exciting event. The rural flea markets last several days and are held semi-annually after harvest.

"Some merchants come from faraway lands to sell or trade Persian rugs, Asian silk, perfumes, fine Arabian horses, and nearly any product you can imagine. It's the commercial and social event of the season and this one will be no different and held nearby so you can take advantage."

I longed to visit one of the flea markets but the idea was far beyond my reach. I would have to be content to play in the village with Mijo, and listen to tales by men more fortunate than me; men of adventure who visit such exotic places. Men like Nenad Mikulić.

Once Nenad was certain he had the attention of all the bar patrons, he announced, "I'm in your village to select consigned goods from you. Please ask your neighbors if they have goods to sell or need items. I will do my best to buy, sell, and trade at the flea market for you, your neighbors and my other clients. If your product sells, I will collect a commission in the bargain. If not, I'll return your goods to you and charge no fee. A good week at the flea market can mean a handsome profit for you."

Word spread quickly throughout the village and Nenad soon had his wagon packed with local goods, some purchased, some consigned, and prepared to make trades and sales.

With his wagon ready to go that evening, Nenad approached my father and asked, "I have a full wagon. Tomorrow morning I could use some help on this trip. Do you think your boy would like a job for a week or so? For the most part, once we get there he will be free to gawk at all the sights, sounds, and smells, but he will also be company for me. I'll pay him half a krone to help load the wagon, groom the mule, fetch water, and do other chores."

My father's response was sad but straightforward. "It has been a difficult year, my friend. See how thin the boy is. Take him. At least I will know he will eat well for a change, and to be honest, one less mouth to feed while he is gone will be a blessing."

Nenad Mikulić nodded. "It will be good for the boy to get out of the village. I know a German fellow who buys goods and sells horses. He usually looks for somebody at the market to tend his horses. I've heard of your son's way with animals. If the German attends, perhaps the lad will come home with an extra Austrian krone or even a German gold mark in his pocket.

"There is another possibility. Wealthy landowners sometimes buy young boys to work on their land. If I can put such a deal together you will be paid for the boy's labor. Think on that.

"We will leave at sunrise. Have him here by then."

"Pero," my father called. "Come here. Would you like to go to the flea market and work for Mr. Mikulić?"

With the childish innocence and enthusiasm that can be found in an eight-year-old boy, I answered, "Are you kidding? I will work my fingers to the bone if he gives me a chance."

"Good. You will travel with him to the flea market. Work hard and do what he tells you and he will pay you for your services. "

My father did not seem as happy to see me go as I was to go. I could not believe my good fortune! Mijo and I had listened to tales of the flea market all year in the beer garden. We played, pretending we were vendors, or actors, or even wealthy horse buyers, but I never imagined I would get a chance to actually go to the market. This was a dream come true. I could hardly wait to tell Mijo.

I didn't sleep a wink that night. I imagined myself at the fair, buying and selling horses. Perhaps I'd find a way to buy a plow horse for my father. Such thoughts are what dreams are made of, especially when a lad is unable to sleep.

I was awake and ready to begin before sunrise. My stepmother, who I affectionately called Mila, insisted I eat a hearty breakfast like any workingman before I started my job. I quickly gobbled down the morning meal and raced to the spot where the wagon stood. Scampering up the side like a little monkey, I grabbed the spokes of one of the large wheels to use as stairs and bounded over the upper layer of the wares, piled high atop the buckboard.

Despite the early hour, a crowd gathered. It seemed the entire village came to see us off. By seven o'clock that morning Nenad and I embarked on a journey into my future aboard the rickety wagon, whose contents jingled and jangled. Hanging lanterns, pots, pans, and utensils clashed together and I bounced atop the pile as the old mule pulled the wagon's wheels over the corrugated red mud road that exited the village.

Feeling like royalty, I waved to my family and neighbors. "Goodbye, family. Goodbye, Mijo. Goodbye, friends. I'm off to parts unknown to make sure the merchants don't cheat Mr. Mikulić."

As we passed my father and mother, I waved to them. My mother smiled broadly, but I thought I saw a tear glisten in Nikola's eye.

The overloaded wagon creaked its objection, and the mule brayed stubbornness as we lumbered along. Nenad made up a song to a tune inspired by the back and forth motion of the wagon's contents, piled halfway to the clouds, "Ho ho ho where we go, girls await the wagon ho."

We two adventurers left the cobblestone streets of the village and turned onto a dirt path that led me away from my home for the first time in my young life, my slingshot tucked into ill-fitting pants. The rhythmic rocking of the wagon might have put a normal boy to sleep, especially one who had not slept the previous night, but my eyes were wide open as we crossed mountain passes, hills and dales that were much as I had imagined. Nenad talked to the mule, the wagon, to himself, and to me, but none of us could make out much of what he said over the din of the creaking wagon and its clanking cargo.

As the noonday sun smiled from the above the clouds, two vaga-bonds, man and boy, stopped at a roadside kiosk called a *krchma*. Behind it, fresh spring lamb roasting on a spit sent its sweet smell to tease my nostrils. I suddenly realized I had no money and wondered how I would pay for the delicious food that made my mouth water. My anxiety was soon soothed as Nenad pulled a few coins from his purse and treated me to half a kilo.

"Work like a man, eat like a man."

We enjoyed the warm meat pulled right from the spit and washed down with red wine from a bota bag my employer had slung over his shoulder. The mule had a large drink of water and some food Nenad had stashed in its nosebag. The mule bellowed and relieved itself on the side of the road, away from the kiosk.

As we resumed our journey, the combination of a full stomach, warm wine, and a sunny afternoon, made my eyes grow heavy. In spite of myself, I curled up in the back of the wagon, on top of some furs, and drifted off to dreamland.

By late afternoon I was jostled awake by the wagon stopping and restarting. The mule, our goods, and we two nomads had arrived safely at the flea market fairgrounds, located in a large clearing. Nenad staked out a good spot for the wagon, in the shade of a large tree and in the path of the fairgoers. He unhooked the mule to graze. "Take care of the animal first, then you can walk around the grounds."

After climbing down from my perch, I watered and fed the trusty beast, and made sure she was comfortable. "Okay, Mule. You worked hard today. Here is your reward. You have your dinner and I'll brush the sweat from your hide. Then you can relax for a few days."

I continued talking to the mule while brushing and feeding her. The beast stuck its face in the nosebag and devoured the contents. When the animal finished dinner and was properly brushed, I said, "You had your feast. This evening I will find food for my boss and me. I want to show him I appreciate the lamb we had for lunch."

Meandering through the area I gawked at sights such as I had never before seen, but heard of at the beer garden. Hawkers, actors and other performers held my interest for a time. But it wasn't the jugglers, acrobats, or even the fire-eaters that captured my deepest attention, it was a stable with seven of the most beautiful horses I had ever seen.

My imagination could not have perceived such fine horseflesh standing before me. A few of the more well-to-do farmers in the village owned horses, but most, like Nenad, either used mules or, like Nikola, pulled the plow themselves. Farm horses that I'd seen and worked on were usually broken-down nags that could barely stand or pull a plow. The horses before me were tall and strong and beautiful, much grander even than Andrij Babić's Percheron in its prime.

My father's plow horse was old and tired during its latter years. To give it an occasional rest, Nikola sometimes pulled the plow himself with Miloška guiding it. The old nag eventually died despite my best care, although it lived and worked years beyond its life expectancy.

As I grew bigger and stronger, I often replaced Miloška on the plow. While away, my younger half-brothers Jozo and Džordž took over my duties. I could hardly wait to return home and tell all who would listen about the beautiful Arabian steeds at the market. If only there was a way one of these beauties could be brought back to the village…

I had never seen Arabian horses before and was so taken by them I picked up a brush that lay near the stalls and began to talk to them and brush one of them.

"Hello, you beautiful beast. Can I touch you? Let's see how well this brush feels against your flank."

I was soon lost in the atmosphere of the corral with stunning animals.

Herr Friedrich Richter, a wealthy German aristocrat and owner of the horses that I ogled, petted, and brushed, had gone from the stalls to walk the grounds and gauge the possibilities of selling his horses. He returned and watched me, an interloper, unnoticed and amazed. I brushed the horses and spoke to them in a tone that they seemed to understand, "Look at my big babies. You like the brush, don't you?" A mare whinnied. "Be patient, pretty girl, I'll get to you next." They nuzzled me as I gave them treats of leftover lamb dug from my pockets.

Nenad arrived to retrieve me and stood at the rail next to Herr Richter. I spied the men as I peeked around the horses and made sure the two noticed the relationship I had established with the skittish Arabians. Nenad said aloud, "Would you look at that!"

Herr Richter pointed toward me and asked Nenad in the Slavic tongue, "Do you know the boy?"

"Yes, I am his guardian on this trip. His parents left him in my charge."

"Tell me a little about him."

I strained to listen to their conversation without being noticed. I could make out Nenad's voice. "He is the eldest of six children of a very poor farm family in Bosnia, and he is legendary in the village for his way with horses and farm animals. He treats them as well as any adult groomer or veterinarian."

The other man was difficult to understand but I picked up, "How does he behave? Does he argue?"

Nenad answered, "Oh no. He is very well behaved. Smart too. He would adjust easily in any setting."

"Hmmmmm," was the other man's only response.

I began to wonder what they were talking about. But my attention returned to the Arabians. Still, something just seemed a little off about the two and their conversation.

I heard Nenad say, "His family is very poor and would welcome the income if he could find work."

"Umm-hmm," was the mystery man's only response.

The two men continued to watch me and spoke to each other using a pidgen mixture of Serbian, Bosnian, and German that was very difficult to understand. Eventually the man said, "I will pay the boy to tend my horses during the length of the fair. Tell him I will give him one Austrian krone per day to feed, water, and brush each horse daily and keep the stalls clean."

By this time the horses had my full attention. The other man had walked away and Nenad whistled and called, "Boy, come over here." I walked to edge of the makeshift corral and he said, "Okay, Pero, you have a job," and explained my duties and the payment for those tasks.

I could not believe my good fortune and became as excited ever. I had been worried for nothing. The man was offering me a job, not planning something bad with Nenad. "Tell the German he made a fool's bargain. I would have done those things for free just to be around the beautiful animals."

"You just do a good job, Little Peasant," Nenad growled, "I have other plans for you."

Ignoring Nenad, I chased after my new employer until I caught up with him. Breathlessly I said, "Thank you, Sir. I will take better care of your horses than anybody has ever done."

The gentleman smiled and said, in halting Bosnian, "I'm sure you will, young man."

Although I understood the man's comment, his manner of speaking was odd. He didn't sound like people from the village. Of course, he didn't dress like anybody from the village either. He wore high riding boots and more clothes than people in our village. I had seen men dressed like him in Mijo's father's beer garden and they all seemed uppity to me. I hoped my new boss was not uppity. I couldn't wait tell Mijo about this adventure.

The man returned and tapped me on the shoulder. "My name is Herr Richter and I plan to sell these horses. Watch me. This is how you groom them. Long, even strokes from the mane to the tail."

It took Herr Richter only one lesson to show me the art of brushing Arabian horses. When he finished his demonstration I barely heard him say to Nenad, "Tell me the name of the village and the family name of the boy."

I continued brushing and fawning over the horses until dusk approached, then walked to the area where the wagon was parked. I searched until I found several pebbles just the right size, put them in my pocket, and set out into the forest with my slingshot and the nosebag borrowed from the mule. I was again in my comfort zone, hunting for food, especially rabbits. I waited until dusk because rabbits are most active early and late in the day, especially along the fringes of fields, forests, and roadside cover. There, briars and thickets provide hiding places near feeding areas. I'd learned that the trick to successful rabbit hunting is to see them before they see me.

Sitting patiently next to a tree, not making a sound, I heard leaves rustle and saw movement on a nearby tree trunk. It was a squirrel racing up the tree. I had my slingshot ready, pulled back on the rubber, and let go, aiming where I anticipated the squirrel would run. I guessed right and the stone struck it square. A second squirrel perked up its ears and I hit it square as well. I tucked the two dead squirrels into the nosebag, then sat back and waited. Fifteen minutes later I saw movement in nearby leaves as a rabbit eased out and looked directly at me. I let go of the stone and made another direct hit. Gathering my bounty, I returned to the wagon, skinned the animals with one of Nenad's knives, and roasted them on a spit over an open fire.

Nenad arrived while I was cooking. "So, the great hunter has returned." He smiled and added potatoes, cabbage, and wine to our meal. "You brought the meat, I the potatoes and cabbage. Tonight we will dine like royalty."

Each day I tended the Arabians and in the evening we followed the same routine. I left at dusk and returned to camp with a bag full of game. Nenad added vegetables and wine. After dinner each night I returned to the horses, cleared an area in the stall for my bed, carefully packing it with straw, and soon became a member of the Herr Richter Arabian horse family.

In my youth I not only had a love for animals, but a relationship with them. I sang to the horses, "You are tall, I am small. I will brush you one and all. Don't feel bad if I'm busy, I will brush you twice each day."

The regal Arabs accepted and nuzzled me as though I were one of their colts. I felt sure they understood me when I talked to them. "Okay, my Arabs. I am your new brother, and I will sleep with you tonight. Does that suit you, friends?" They nickered back at me.

The second morning of the market, while I was cleaning the stalls, Herr Richter saddled one of the Arabians and left the fair. I was now in full charge of the other horses. I fed and watered them, brushed them, talked and sang to them, cleaned their stalls within an inch of perfection, and brought in fresh straw twice each day. When men came by to examine the Arabians for possible purchase, they often spoke in languages I did not understand but I was still able to point out how good the horse's teeth and hooves were and how well the steeds were defined. I desperately wanted to show the German that he had made the right decision when he hired me to care for his horses. But Herr Friedrich Richter already knew of my capabilities and, as I soon learned, he had other, more long-term plans for me.

Herr Richter returned to the fair and told me that, thanks to my care of them, he's sold all but one of the Arabians to a Spaniard who raced horses.

Nenad's wagon was fully laden, and he made a handsome profit buying and selling. I had enjoyed the best time of my life.

As we squeezed the last few items onto the wagon, Herr Richter approached us, called the huckster aside and spoke to him. I strained to hear the conversation, but no matter, the market was over and I'd lived the life of dreams. I was beginning to miss my family and was ready to return to them, show them the money I'd earned, and tell Mijo of my adventure.

Herr Richter showed Nenad some papers. After he looked them over, the German handed him some money. "This is a fee for you.

Since I am taking your best employee you will need to find another." He asked if there were any questions on the basic points of the contract. Nenad didn't even bother to read the contract. He took the money and smiled with his handsome finder's fee in hand.

My boss motioned to me and I slid off the wagon. "Herr Richter needs your help a little longer. He has other horses that need looked after. You can return home after your job is finished," he lied. "But for now you go with him. I will let your parents know."

I was confused and not sure what to do. I loved working with Herr Richter's horses, but I feared that if I did not return home with Nenad my parents would worry. Of course, if I could make more money to take home when the job was finished, I could help my family. Something didn't feel right about the whole thing but I had to trust somebody. Nenad knew my parents and the German seemed like an honest man. My thoughts were interrupted when Nenad raised his voice, "Move, Boy. I've got to get back to your village before dark. Go with Herr Richter."

I asked him to translate my response to Herr Richter. "I will take the job only if the deal includes board and if you hold my salary until the job is finished, so my parents can have it."

I reasoned that I would have no expenses if the deal included meals. I did not consider the need for clothing and personal items. After all, I might have been wise and perceptive, but I was only eight-years-old.

Herr Richter smiled. He must have been surprised that I had the audacity to negotiate with him. "Okay, young man, I agree to your terms."

We shook hands to unofficially confirm the agreement. I was not sure if I should spit in my hand first like Mijo and I did when clinching a bargain, but since the German man did not spit in his hand, I didn't either.

The mule bellowed and the heavy wagon creaked as it began to move. Herr Richter took me by the arm and led me to his coach that had been parked near his horses. Together we attached the reins of the one Arabian that did not sell to the back of the coach and harnessed the other horse to pull the coach.

At age eight, I believed I was wise and perceptive beyond my years. I knew that my father and stepmother would worry about me but was sure Nenad would explain my temporary absence. I hoped they wouldn't be upset with me for not returning to the farm right away. I reasoned that they were barely able to feed six children, and I knew that as the eldest growing boy, I often ate as much as my father did. A little more time away would ease their burden. Besides, this would be an extended adventure for me. I'll be with them soon enough.

Instead of riding back to Stabandža on Nenad Mikulic's rickety old wagon, I traveled to the city of Velika Kladuša aboard Herr Richter's plush coach. I rode in style all the way to the train depot and then took my first train ride to Germany.

The story I have related on this tape is my own. Private conversations of my time with Herr Richter were told to me from his own lips. I will rest now and share more of my life tomorrow.

(tape ends)

Not a word had been spoken during the playing of the tape as the family members listened spellbound. "Wow! Can you believe this?" asked Francie, "I had no idea Diedo was so versatile! He just seemed like the sweetest grandpa ever!"

Maryann nodded. "You're right, Francie. But I'm still confused about him speaking German on the tape. I never heard him speak a word in German, or much English for that matter. Only Serbian."

"You're the oldest, Sonny, did you know any of this?"

Milan, whose family called him Sonny, had been listening intently. He was quiet by nature and family members said he took after Diedo. "My father told me Diedo's mother died, but I didn't know she died in childbirth. I also heard stories that he worked in Germany as a boy."

"Let's grab something to eat and listen to the next tape," interjected Francie. "I can't wait to hear what happens to him."

Once the cousins were seated, the second tape was set and started. After some hissing and a brief silence the now familiar German accented voice of the professor began.

"This is Franz Friedrich Volk, Professor Emeritus in the German Language Studies Department at the University of Pittsburgh and a native speaker of the German language. What continues is a verbatim translation of the second tape of Peter Novak, unknown American hero."

SECOND LIFE—GERMANY

7

THE METAMORPHOSIS BEGINS

I brought few material goods with me; torn and tattered clothing, ill-fitting pants, and my only possession, the slingshot. I had become a crack shot with the device and carried it with me everywhere.

As the excitement of my new work wore down, I had time to think and wonder about the job that was offered. Exactly where was I going and how long would I be gone from home? The German didn't speak my language very well and I did not understand his at all. But if he needed me to tend his horses for a while, I guess it was alright.

The coach and horses were loaded onto the first train I'd ever seen. We boarded and traveled beyond the border of Bosnia through the Austro-Hungarian Empire to Germany. The sheer geographical size of the setting for this part of my life overwhelmed me. My world had been one thin thread in a tapestry that I could not have imagined. But the further I traveled from my home, the more anxious I became. I decided I would try to talk to my employer, but I was very tired and needed to sleep a little first.

My sleeping room on the train was not much bigger than the one I had at home, but that's where the bedtime similarities ended. The muslin sheets were soft against my bare skin and smelled of flowers. Blankets were so plentiful that I did not use most of them. The swaying motion of the train seduced me into dreamland, and any surprises that might lie ahead faded into the down filling of my pillow.

The next morning awoke from the soundest sleep ever. It took a while to get my bearings. Herr Richter was not in the bunk across from mine, but as I stretched I saw through the window in the door that separated the cars, he was already dressed in a suit, and sitting in the parlor car, reading a newspaper. The porter must have seen me stir and whispered to him. He put down the paper and walked to the sleeper car. "Ready for some breakfast, young man?"

Herr Richter motioned for me to follow. He nodded to the porter who left, then returned several minutes later with a covered platter. "Your breakfast, young sir."

The parlor car seemed like a palace to me. We sat on plush chairs thick pillows. Dark wood tables with hand carved, highly polished legs, and covered with spotless white linens. The tables set with sparkling glasses, a small plate with no chips or cracks, and shiny metal spoons. The porter removed the platter cover to reveal a hearty breakfast of eggs, potatoes, bacon, steak, fruit, and milk—all of which I promptly devoured. I had never seen so much food for one person and gulped it down in a hurry.

The silverware looked pretty but was difficult for me to use. I managed to get the steak down by ripping it apart with my fork and fingers, oblivious to the fact that my manners made me the center of attention. After stuffing my mouth, I started to wipe my greasy hands on the linen tablecloth but paused when Herr Richter cleared his throat. My master held a white cloth with one hand and pointing to it, then my mouth with the other. "Napkin," he said, and demonstrated how to wipe hands and lips on the cloth. I dropped the corner of the tablecloth, and used the napkin, following his cue.

After breakfast the porter brought a shirt, pants, socks, undershirt, shorts and shoes. "You will wear these today," he said matter-of-factly as he handed me my first new, store-bought set of clothing. "Go into the sleeper car and change."

Herr Richter picked up the newspaper and continued reading. The two cars were next to each other so I quickly pulled off my soiled ragged clothing, and in no time returned to the parlor car wearing the new wardrobe.

"How do your new clothes feel?"

"Rough." I tugged at the collar and at the seat of my pants. "These pants are going to rub me raw." I massaged my behind through the material. Like most peasant boys from the villages, I donned only ragged outerwear clothing that had been washed so often that the material felt both soft against my skin, and worn threadbare. My normal attire did not include underwear.

As my master turned his attention to me he chuckled to himself. He walked me back to the sleeper car and pointed to the underwear still sitting on the edge of my bed. "Put these on first, under your clothing."

Since I had never worn or even seen underclothes, I was confused as to why it was necessary to wear two layers when it was not even winter yet. The temperature on the train was pleasant. I didn't need an extra layer of clothing. But I did as told, undressed, pulled on the undergarments, which I found to be pleasant and soft against my body, then redressed and returned to the parlor car. Though still timid in the presence of this great man with fine horses, I ventured to ask him exactly what he expected of me.

"Sir, I am not sure what my duties will be once we arrive at our destination. Are we going to another flea market? Will you buy more horses there? How long will we be? My parents will be worried about me."

"Peter…" he hesitated, gathering his thoughts.

"You can call me Pero."

"Sit, boy. Let me explain."

I strained to understand this German who spoke my language poorly.

"At the flea market, I watched you tend the horses, and said to myself, this lad is a sight. I was fascinated as I watched you, a shoeless country farm boy, handle my Arabians as competently as any adult professional horse trainer. I have a son, Hans, about your age, left behind in care of a housekeeper. Hans has never been exposed to life in the mountains of Bosnia, but as I watched you I thought of him. Hans is taller and hardier than you, but there is an air of confidence about you that Hans lacks. Do you understand?"

I shook my head, but the man continued.

"When I left the flea market and placed you in charge of the horses, I rode first rode to the county seat. Do you understand what I am saying? It is important that you understand what I am about to tell you."

Puzzled, I answered. "I don't think I understand most of what you said. But why isn't your son with you. Is he afraid of horses? My best friend, Mijo, doesn't like horses."

"I'll get to that later. I went to the clerk's office and had papers drawn up. Then I withdrew a sum of money from the bank, and rode to your village."

"You went to Stabandža?" If I understood him correctly, I was surprised at this revelation.

"Yes. It was midday when I arrived at the your parent's house. Your father came from the fields and we spoke."

I sat still, too stunned to speak. Herr Richter continued.

"I introduced myself to your parents and told them what a fine lad and first-rate worker you are and how good you were with my Arabians. They are very proud of you.

"I told them that I wanted to take you with me to my farm in Germany, to hire you for ten years. I paid them in advance for your labor."

At first I was too stunned to speak. This man had gone to my parent's house and bought me? They agreed to send me away to work for ten years?

As the scenario sunk in, I interrupted, "You bought me? Like a horse? I do not believe you. NO! What you are saying... it cannot be true. You are lying to me. My parents love me. They would not sell me."

"Be calm, young Peter. Let me finish telling you what your parents and I expect of you."

"No! You are making this up. I won't go with you. I have to get back to Stabandža."

The parlor car had been taken for Herr Richter's party only, but other passengers sat in the train's second and third class passenger cars.

I bolted from the table and ran through the sleeper car. The porter that had just served me breakfast raced in hot pursuit.

The train's passenger cars were about half occupied. As the porter called for me to stop I raced through the cars and into the arms of a conductor. The surprised man instinctively grabbed and held me as I cried in Bosnian, "Let me go. I have to get back to my home!"

The burly porter wrapped his huge arm around my waist and carried me, kicking and screaming, back to the parlor car.

Herr Richter, who had been so gentle up to this point spoke to me in a harsh tone. "You will sit and listen to what I have to say. We will restrain you if we must, but at this moment, and for the next ten years, I am in charge of your life. So sit and listen."

Wiping the tears from my eyes on the back of my new shirtsleeve, I sat deep into the chair, crushed and defeated.

Clearing his throat, the German continued. "Your parents agreed and signed a contract that indentures you to me until you reach your eighteenth birthday.

He showed me the paper contract, which, of course, I was unable to read. "Your father and mother accepted my cash and placed their X on the line above their names printed on the contract. You will be my indentured employee for the next ten years of your life."

I sat and sulked. The deal was done. Call it a job or indentured servitude, or even child labor; I would be doing the thing I loved most—taking care of animals—and getting paid to do it. But the thought of not seeing my family for the next ten years left me very sad. My family's life would improve with added income and one less mouth to feed. These thoughts helped ease the pain in my heart.

Once I stopped crying and became calm, Herr Richter again spoke. "You will like life on my estate. My Croatian housekeeper speaks your language. That should help you feel less lonely. My son, Hans is about your age. Perhaps the two of you can keep each other company."

I sat, dazed and confused, wondering what possible kind life faced me. The train was posh and offered more food than I'd ever seen at a single sitting. But I already was beginning to miss my parents, my brothers and sisters, and I missed Mijo and all the fun we had. I would never be happy in this strange new place this German was taking me. During my depths of despair I leaned back onto the soft cushioned chair, jutted out my bottom lip, continued to sulk, and cried myself to sleep.

Herr Richter placed me under as little strain as possible during the rest of the trip, and did not require me to follow the rules that I'd face on the estate. He must have figured he'd go one step at a time to educate this peasant lad.

I surely was a sight, hair disheveled, like unkempt straw, thin as a wafer, and several layers of dirt attached to my body, but since I was sporting new clothes, Herr Richter did not press the issue of my cleanliness and allowed me to keep the dirt until we reached the manor.

When the train reached the German station, we disembarked and watched the carriage and horses offloaded from the train. The thought of running away when he wasn't looking crossed my mind but I had no idea where I was or how to get to Bosnia. So I stayed put for the moment. He attached the carriage pulled by one horse, and we climbed into it. The Arabian that had not sold trotted behind; its reins tied to the rear of the coach.

The steed that pulled the wagon clopped along for hours. We passed through country much more lush than the hills of Bosnia that reminded me of some of the places described by men in Mijo's father's beer garden.

I wasn't sure how far we'd come from the train depot before the German guided the horse through open iron gates that marked the edge of the Richter property. We continued for some time as it became more evident that the size of the estate and the richness of the farmland were far beyond anything I had imagined. The place is bigger than all of Stabandža. Arabian horses roamed free on one side of the property and cows eyed us in a pasture from the other.

The estate seemed to go forever; flat land, green rolling hills, pristine air, and a river at the bottom of the valley. From the lush green surroundings I could see that this soil was far better than the rocky farmland of my father's. This must be like heaven.

Eyes wide and mouth agape, I became a little less homesick as we approached a manor, the grandest sight I had ever seen. I peered at a real castle. Herr Richter must be a king or something, and this strange country is surely more beautiful than anything in the world. This must be America or France. I wonder if I'll see rubber trees or wagons that travel without horses, or any of the things Vasie talked about.

Herr Richter's Bosnian language was not very good, but I understood most of what he said. By this time I had resigned myself to the fact that I would labor away from my home and family. I was certain that one day we would be reunited, but for the time being I must make the best of what I had here so the money I earn will be sent to my family. Maybe Herr Richter's son could be my pal instead of Mijo.

I shrugged and nodded, figuring, new job, new life, new name. I replied to him in Bosnian, letting him know I would comply, *"Da, nema problema."*

Herr Richter instructed, "We will now go to the house where our housekeeper Marija will bathe you and clean your clothes. After you've bathed, you will dress in fresh, clean clothes."

I must have misunderstood my new master. Between his pidgin Bosnian, a few words of German, and hand gestures, I figured most of it out. But a bath? In the middle of the week and the middle of the day? I'd never had a bath in my life during the week, at least not one I remember. I was not so sure I would appreciate a woman bathing me as though I were a baby. It wasn't that I was modest, but… well… if I *must* have a bath, I was certain I could do it myself.

We continued toward the house. Around a bend, more residential buildings came into view, and some sort of cathedral appeared before me, larger than any church I'd ever seen. It was painted, and the timbers were smooth and flat like those used to build churches, not raw and rustic like the sticks that built my parent's house and other buildings in Stabandža. This is surely as grand a church as anyone anywhere.

Motioning toward the fine building, which as it turned out was not a cathedral at all, Herr Richter said, "That barn is your new home. You will sleep there with the horses. Also, we will call you by your Christian name, Peter. That is how it is pronounced in German. 'Pay-tear,' not Pee-tar, and not Pero. *Rezume ti?* Do you understand?"

That grand cathedral of a barn that would be my home. The barn? The magnificent structure was a barn? Where horses were stabled? I was awed... no, overwhelmed. If this was the barn, that castle in the distance must be..... no, it couldn't be Herr Richter's house. It was too big to be a house. But that building turned out to be his dwelling.

We stopped next to the barn. "Okay, Peter, climb down. We have a little work to do before going into the house. Unhitch the horses and stable them. Horse stalls are inside the barn. I'll tend to the carriage."

We climbed out of the coach. My amazement continued while we did the chores at hand. With the horses stabled, I followed my new master toward the main castle of a house.

We passed workers and gardeners that maintained the property but lived in the nearby village. They came daily to grounds. He called each by name: "Adi, Ludwig, Oskar, Franz, this is Peter, our new stable boy. He will be living on site with us."

Each man shook my hand and nodded or spoke a greeting. I returned the nods and wondered how I would ever learn to communicate with people whose language seemed so strange to me.

Inside the house Herr Richter's housekeeper, Marija, greeted me in Bosnia's native language. *"Zdravo i dobrodošli."*

"How do you happen to be here, Madam?" I asked her.

She chuckled, "No Madam, just Marija. Like you, I was indentured into service for this household when I was a girl. I was first brought from Croatia to be a temporary guest worker but the lady of the house decided she wanted to have her own maid, so I stayed on."

"Are you still the Lady's maid?"

"No, she died during the cholera epidemic ten years ago when her son Hans was just an infant. She made the master promise to keep me if she died so I became the kitchen maid and nanny to Hans. I've served the Richter family for more than twenty years."

"Do you miss your parents and family?"

"I did at first, but after a while Herr Richter and his wife became my family. I could not have hurt more deeply when Lady Richter died, than if she had been my own mother."

"Do you have any children?"

"No." She blushed. "I'm not married. I have given my life to service."

"I don't know if I will ever stop missing my family. I hate Herr Richter for taking me from my home."

"Hate is such a worthless emotion, dear boy. Put it out of your mind. You will find love and caring on this estate. Now let's get some of that grime off you."

I followed Marija upstairs to a large room where she explained what was about to happen. "The dining room table is set for dinner. But first you must have a bath. Herr Richter has gone upstairs to bathe and his son, Hans, who you will meet later, has already bathed. It is your turn now."

Everything about these new surroundings sounded good and exciting except the mandatory bath.

Marija escorted me into a large bathroom. A long white bathtub with claws for feet sat partially filled with water, in the center of the room. Behind the tub, two large kettles heated atop an iron stove. Towels and another set of clothing—underclothing as well as outer-wear adorned a tabletop.

Marija poured steaming water into the large tub. "I will cover my eyes while you undress."

"Don't peek," I said as I disrobed and climbed gingerly into the vat. "Ouch! That's hot," I wailed as I sat full force in the tub.

"Oh, don't be such a baby. You'll get used to the warm water."

"I feel like tea leaves being dunked into a cup."

Marija smiled. It was the first light moment she'd enjoyed in a long time.

Though at first I grimaced in the hot water, I soon found pleasure lying back against the sloped end of the tub as the water cooled. The housekeeper added more hot water, then picked up a brush, lathered it with soap, and rubbed and scrubbed until I cried out, "Are you sure you're not trying to remove my Bosnian skin and replace it with German skin?"

She chuckled. "That is not Bosnian skin coming off you. It's Bosnian dirt and filth. You will feel much better when you're clean and in fresh clothes. You are a little smaller than Hans. A set of his clothing awaits you.

"I use a special formula in the laundry so your underwear will be soft next to that clean Bosnian skin."

The torment of the bath finally drew to a close and the water had cooled. I was amazed at how black the liquid in the tub had become.

Marija left the room. She had at least given me the self-pride of climbing out of the tub without her being present. I wrapped myself in a large Turkish towel and shivered as I dried, then pulled on the new white undergarments and added fresh clothes. I stared for a moment at the socks laid out next to a pair of shoes. "These people wear way too many clothes." I shook my head and pulled the socks over my well-calloused feet, slipped my feet into the nearly new shoes and walked unsteadily into the next room where Marija waited. I hobbled and teetered, tottered and wobbled like a fat man going through a rat hole in the shoes that squeezed my feet.

My fine clothes hung on me as loose as a clown's pocket.

When Marija saw me she smiled. "Very nice, my Bosnian prince. Very nice. Of course, I will have to alter the clothes to fit you."

"They fit fine."

But Marija stood fast. "We'll see. Also, you will take lessons with Hans in the German language. Herr Richter says one day you will speak like a German native."

"Ha! I'll never learn that language. It sounds like *frfljanje*, gibberish to me.

Hans Richter sauntered into the room. Two years my senior and a head taller, he saw me as an interloper. From that moment he had no interest in a friendship, particularly not with a peasant servant. He made no effort to learn to speak the Bosnian tongue. He called me 'Yak' or 'Boskur,' both ethnic slurs describing Bosnian people. Whenever Marija and I spoke in what he considered our "stupid foreign language," he mocked us and said it sounded like we were talking with a mouthful of food.

He looked over me and sneered, "I see the old man picked up some gutter trash on his trip."

I did not understand his comment at the moment, but his surly manner made his disdain for me evident.

For the most part Hans was condescending or ambivalent toward me, frequently using ethnic slurs when speaking of me. As far as Hans was concerned, I was beneath him. Like all the hired help, we were not of his own high social standing. Despite his father's wishes, the divide remained between us throughout the ten-year term of my servitude.

Aside from my visits with Marija I learned to fend for myself on the estate. My daily routine included keeping the barn clean and the horses groomed and ready for Herr Richter or Hans to ride. I maintained the barn and horses in immaculate condition, and even before my formal language tutoring began, acquired enough rudimentary German language to make myself understood and to understand the gist of conversations between Herr Richter and others on the estate.

Hans and I kept our distance from one another as much as possible. Our paths crossed only when he needed a to have a horse prepared to ride or if he wanted to irritate or shock me as he did one day when he came into the barn with an injured rabbit. "Watch this."

I looked away as he stabbed and cut the animal for a few minutes then said. "What do you think about that?" I picked up a shovel and put the poor thing out of its misery.

"Aww, you ruined the fun. Dumb animals. They squirm so easy. You should try."

I wanted to say, "Hans, you have such privileged life. Why do you do such cowardly things? Just to get attention?" But my language skills had not yet developed to allow me to convey the thought, so I shook my head and walked to the stalls. I didn't want him to see the tears in my eyes for the poor rabbit.

"Stupid Yak." He laughed and stomped out of the barn.

I witnessed other examples of Hans torturing animals and sometimes I was able to intervene and protect them. Eventually, I hoped, he will grow out of this twisted phase of his life.

Several weeks after my arrival on Richter land, Hans came into the barn. "Hey, Boskur, my father is away, but before he left he said I have to show you around the property. Saddle up a couple of horses and I'll take you on a tour."

I stood still, listened, and tried to process what Hans wanted. My German language skills were still very limited. Hans raised his voice; "Hey, Yak! Are you deaf or stupid? Saddle two horses." He held up two fingers and pointed to the horses.

I obeyed. Though I tended and cared for horses, I had not had much experience riding them. The one I chose for myself seemed to sense my limited experience and remained gentle. Hans selected a more spirited horse for himself and we set off into the woods.

The estate was one of the largest in this part of Germany. Within its boundaries, sights included pastures, farmland, streams and a large forest. The only part of the estate I had seen prior to this ride was the entry road and the living area, a small farm, a pond and a stream. The woods, in contrast, were more like a forest, thick and dense, with little light inside. We two pre-teen boys rode silently across the grasslands until we reached the edge of a forest. Inside the heavily wooded area, except for the clip-clop of the horses' hooves and occasional bird calls, an eerie silence prevailed.

Hans noticed my timidness with the horse and decided to show off. He urged his mount faster through the dense thicket of trees. I tried to keep up but the gap between us widened.

My horse took up a trot in an effort to catch Hans, as I bounced in the saddle, hanging desperately to the reins and mane. Terrified, I dropped the reins and clung tightly to the horse's mane, hoping I would not fall. The beast soon was in full gallop. I opened my mouth desperately trying to scream for Hans, but no sound crossed my lips.

Suddenly everything went black.

A low-hanging branch had knocked me from my horse and rendered me unconscious. I awakened to the slobber of horse tongue and spit across my face and hair. My filly was nuzzling me.

"Oh, my head."

I must have been unconscious only a few moments, but lost track of time. I wasn't sure where I was or where Hans might be. At first frightened, I gathered my wits about me and slowly, with the help of the stirrups and saddle, pulled myself to a standing position. I was not ready to mount the beast quite yet, but reasoned that if I led it and walked in one direction, we would eventually walk out of the forest, and from that point, the animal would know its way home. I held onto the reins, more as a security blanket than a tool to lead the horse. It would have followed me regardless.

After walking some distance, my head cleared and except for a bump on my forehead I felt no worse for the wear. I walked the horse to the edge of a clearing, then stopped at the sound of voices. Peeking out into the clearing I witnessed a frightening scene.

Stepping back into the cover of the trees, I wrapped the reins around a tree to keep the horse from giving me away, then crept back to the edge of the clearing. Peering around a large tree trunk, I could see two men who looked to be in their teens or early twenties. One restrained Hans and the other, waving a large hunting knife, stood before him. Had I known the German language at the time, I would have understood what the men were saying, but their gestures told me Hans was in deep trouble.

I heard Hans sobbing and stuttering, "H-H-H-Hans Hans Richter," as tears ran down his cheeks.

Although I was unable to make out their language I heard the names Wolfgang and Alric. Wolfgang ridiculed Hans and slapped his face several times while Alric giggled and egged his partner on..

Alric, who appeared to be the older of the two, waved the hunting knife in the air, then nicked Hans' cheek with it.

Hans sobbed. Blood ran from his cheek wound and mixed with his snot. He cried, "N-n-nien." as they continued their taunting.

Alric undid his pants and pulled out his penis. Hans tried to pull away but Alric punched him hard, splitting his nose and spurting more blood across his face.

I was not sure what was about to happen to Hans but could see my master's son was in danger. Without taking my eyes off the men I reached down and dug around in the soft earth, searching until my fingers gripped two smooth stones. Quietly I picked them up and removed the slingshot from inside my tunic.

One man held Hans firmly by his long flaxen hair as the other tugged at his britches.

Still hidden by the trees, I remained calm, though sweat broke out across my brow. I mentally measured the distance between the bullies, Hans, and myself. Squinting, I focused on the target. The fatter of the two, Wolfgang, still clumsily trying to remove Hans's trousers, while Alric, the thinner, more muscular one, stood before him, cradling Hans' head in his hands, his penis just inches from Hans' face.

I put the first pebble to my lips to wet it, placed it into the center of the rubber strip, then inhaled and held my breath, pulling the rubber back as far as it would stretch. I blinked away a rivulet of perspiration that trickled down my forehead, took careful aim at the eye of the more muscular poacher, and let the missile fly. The rubber portion of the slingshot snapped like a horse stung by a wasp. The projectile tore silently through the afternoon sky.

The hard, round stone struck Alric in the temple with such force that his entire body came off the ground before he shuddered, went down hard, and fell in a heap.

Wolfgang froze. I did not.

My second pellet followed the path of its twin, tearing through the atmosphere and finding its mark, between Wolfgang's eyes. He too crumpled to the ground.

Replacing the slingshot inside my tunic, I unwrapped the reins from the tree and led my horse to the quivering Hans. His face, spattered with snot, dirt, tears, and blood, stared at me blankly. Next to him the two bodies lay unconscious and motionless; one on his back with his exposed penis limp across his thigh, the other face down. Hans pulled up his trousers and wiped his face on his shirt. He did not make eye contact with me but sobbed quietly for a few moments. Then he began a transformation that shook me to my bones.

Hans voice became detached. To this day it is difficult for me to describe what I saw and heard. He related the conversation to me months later as my understanding of the German language began to improve. He said he clearly remembered his exact words.

Hans began talking to the two immobile bodies at his feet as though they were able to hear him. "So now the tide has turned, you pig. You wanted to hurt me, now I might have to kill you. You are a bit depraved, you know."

Hans loomed over Alric. His face twisted, he stomped the unconscious man's genitalia into a bloody mess.

He moved to Wolfgang and spoke calmly. "You were rude. Very rude. I hate rude people." Then, using the heel of his stiff riding boot, kicked and stomped the teen's face until it looked like freshly ground beef.

He picked up Alric's knife and bent over Wolfgang, "You tried to hurt me and now I must hurt you."

With one swipe, he sliced off half of Wolfgang's penis, and stuffed it in the man's mouth. The unconscious Wolfgang gurgled and groaned. Hans wiped the bloody knife on the teen's clothing and tossed it to the ground.

He turned to me, looked directly into my eyes and with a flat, monotone voice said, "You will never speak of what happened here today."

His message needed no translation.

Barely able to believe what I'd just seen, and unable to respond, I backed away, shaking at the scene and the eerie calm that surrounded Hans.

What I witnessed that morning was a thief that stole my innocence. That was the moment I put away childish things and left my childhood kingdom, where nobody is harmed or dies. My heart tightened and a feeling of loss grew within me.

We mounted and silently rode back to the barn.

Hans did his best to clean his face and hands using water from the horse trough. His nose, misshapen from the blow he took, sat askew. He pointed to the house and mimed the shape of a woman. "You distract the housekeeper. I'm going upstairs to clean up and change clothes."

I went into the kitchen and talked to Marija, telling her we had been riding, but offering little more detail. We were still chatting small talk when Hans entered the kitchen. "My cheek is cut and I think I broke my nose. That stupid Boskur gave me a fast horse that galloped full speed into a low hanging branch. Don't tell my father."

Marija stitched his cheek, reset, and placed a poultice on his nose. Hans wore the scar from the knife wound and the misshapen nose the rest of his life, and though he didn't thank me, I believed he was grateful as he no longer referred to me as Yak or Boskur, but could not bring himself to use my given name.

We never discussed what might have happened to the poachers but a few days afterward, as I stood near the barn, I overheard one of the Croatian day laborers talking to our housekeeper. "Did you hear? Two gypsies were found at the edge of the forest, one dead. Somebody cut off his pecker and stuffed it in his mouth. The other one had his head stomped in."

"Do they know who did this?"

"No. The one that lived got his brain kicked in so bad he can't talk. He's a babbling idiot. He doesn't make any sense. Just sits and drools. They think it might have been a rival band of gypsies passing through."

Within weeks after the incident in the woods, I settled into a regular routine, coming to the house every Tuesday, Thursday, and Saturday to bathe, dress, and meet with a tutor to teach me to speak proper German, read and write a little. Since I was illiterate in my native tongue, the task of writing German at first seemed overwhelming, but I was driven to please my master and prepared to work hard. I could not imagine at the time that his interest in my education would become the greatest gift Herr Richter could have given me.

My studies took place nearly a century ago, but I remember my first lesson as though it were yesterday. I wandered toward the house, kicking at dirt clods, unsure of what to expect. My anxiety calmed a little while soaking in the tub of warm water and I actually felt a sense of empowerment as I dressed in my "house clothes." I even learned to walk comfortably in shoes.

After bathing and dressing, I took my time going down the stairs, examining every inch of the handrail for splinters or other imperfections, wanting to make the walk last, and delay the studies as long as possible.

Eventually I made my way into the kitchen and saw not the young tutor I'd expected, but an old man with shriveled skin and thin, gray hair. He had a long, pointed nose like my elderly godfather Goran's. Leaning on a burled walking stick, he hunched over the table, his back so stooped that at first I could not tell if he was standing or sitting.

"Peter," Marija said in my native tongue, "This is Professor Klaus Braun. He will be your professor."

I stared at the old man before me, unaware that it was impolite to do so.

The professor spoke to Marija in German and she translated the message into Bosnian for me.

"From this moment onward you will speak only German to the professor. If you do not understand something, ask, but ask using the German language. You will be ignored if you speak in Bosnian. Do you understand?"

I nodded, thinking the elderly professor must be very poor, as he could afford only one side of his eyeglasses. When I later asked Marija how a man so learned could be so poor she laughed until tears came. "The glass circle over one eye is called *das monokel* and is often worn by scholars."

The professor again spoke to Marija who translated. "He says you are to speak when asked a question. Do not simply nod. The first two words you must learn are, *'ja,'* which means 'yes,' and *'nein,'* which means 'no.' Tell the professor if you understand what I just told you."

I began to nod, but caught myself and said, "Ja."

After another prompt from Marija, I added, *"Ja, mein professor."*

The following day Herr Richter came to the barn. "Professor Klaus Braun is a noted scholar and retired German Language Professor Emeritus. It is a great honor to have him teach you. He is a tough taskmaster, and will insist that you learn not just common German, but properly spoken German. You will also learn some of the written language. You will speak the language as it is spoken at the tables and desks of Boards of Directors."

Between my master's Bosnian language efforts and hand signals, I still did not understand most of what he said, but he smiled when I answered, *"Ja, mein Herr."*

I accepted the language lessons just as I did my other chores at the estate—without complaint. Lessons were difficult, but I studied hard often by kerosene lantern and late into the night. The professor seemed like an ogre at first, scolding me when I made a mistake and never smiling. Little by little I began to feel comfortable with the spoken language of the land and in my new surroundings. The professor's harsh veneer slowly melted and I found myself looking forward to my encounters with him.

My lessons went well but Hans, also tutored by Professor Braun, did not take an interest in studying, nor did he take his lessons seriously. He often disappeared at lesson time.

Herr Richter instructed Hans, the staff, and of course Marija, to speak to me in German only, and required I answer accordingly in proper German. Though it was a difficult task at first, I eventually learned to speak the language well.

As my language mastery increased, Hans and I took some lessons together. Otherwise, he managed to avoid me. When Herr Richter traveled, Marija and I spent much time together. She spoke fluent German and helped me with my lessons. After each recitation she praised me. "Soon your German will become better than mine."

Professor Braun showed patience and I became skilled enough to read and write 'survival German,' sign my name, and catch the gist of contents of written documents. The tutoring helped me speak the German language like an upper class college-educated aristocrat but my Bosnian language remained that of an illiterate peasant.

Marija also taught me proper dining habits and table manners. She showed me which utensils to use and when. I had only seen silver utensils once before, on the train from Bosnia to Germany. But I had never seen most of the items in the Richter kitchen. She reviewed how dishes, glasses, and flatware were arranged in particular fashion, and proper purpose and use of each piece of silver and china on a properly set table. She drew the placement on a paper that I took with me to the barn and memorized, just as I did my other lessons.

After I told her I knew where every item should be placed, Marija tested me. "Are you sure you know where each utensil and plate belongs now?"

I nodded, and she sent me to the barn to fetch something. When I returned, she had stacked all the dishes, glasses, and flatware on a serving tray.

"Now you do it, Peter. Set a proper table for me."

I took my time, but placed every item exactly as she had instructed.

"Bravo! Now we work on manners. This is how you use a knife to cut and take your food on a fork, and you must always chew properly, mouth closed and silently."

I practiced often, not only because I wanted to please my master and Marija, but also because of the benefits of the food consumed at each demonstration. I mastered the correct use of each utensil, plate and glass, and slowly began the transition from peasant to gentleman.

One morning Marija came to the barn. "Peter, you are needed in the house."

"What new challenge has Herr Richter found for me?"

"You'll soon see."

A tailor stood in the front room. Material, pins and needles, and tape measures were strewn about the kitchen table. "I am here to measure and fit you for a formal suit, shirt, and tie."

The ensemble, to be worn whenever I came to the house to dine and meet with guests, stayed in the house. I wore it only after first sprucing up, which always meant a refreshing bath and often a haircut.

Marija treated me like the son she never had, and that helped stave off my occasional waves of loneliness for my family. She also helped me remember what I knew; that both my family and I were better off with me working at the estate.

The Arabians and other horses kept me company. I knew their language without studying or needing a tutor, and when I spoke to them they understood.

Though I occasionally dressed and dined as a gentleman, my duties still included brushing and feeding horses and cleaning stalls.

Once I mastered the routine of the job, even after study assignments and time spent learning proper dinner etiquette, I still had free time. I approached Herr Richter with a plan. "Do you think I could plant a garden alongside the barn? I tended the garden in Bosnia and the soil here is much better. We can grow vegetables for the household. It won't take away from my current duties. What do you think?"

"My boy, you are always figuring ways to improve this place. I appreciate that. Of course you can have your garden. I am anxious to see it."

Once he agreed, I cleared a plot, planted and tended it, in addition to my other duties. I decided to press my luck and asked for permission to grow grapes as well. Request granted.

Herr Richter directed one of his day laborers to bring seedlings for the garden, but he personally selected and purchased the grape shoots. By my third year on the estate I had a fine garden growing alongside the barn. The family ate most of the vegetables, and Herr Richter boasted to his friends that his *zweite sohn*—he referred to me as his second son—grew the finest vegetables in the area.

My master's pride and joy were the grapes that I carefully tended on vines laced through a trellis built from sticks scavenged in the forest. Herr Richter selected grape shoots from area vintners for planting. The grapes were not planted next to the barn or near the vegetable garden, but rather on a part of the estate near the river. The result was that the vines were grown on steep slopes that ensured as much light and heat as possible when the sun was low in the sky. By the third season wine became an unexpected additional revenue stream that flowed to the estate.

When Hans turned fifteen, he left the estate and the Professor's tutoring, and enrolled in an expensive Swiss boarding school. My language lessons continued. Professor Braun came to the house once a week to help me maintain my studies.

Herr Richter did not often come to the barn so I was a bit surprised when he showed up one day. "Peter, I've been talking with Marija. The house is so quiet with Hans away at school. How would you like to move into one of the guest rooms? You will join us at dinnertime and keep Marija company when I am away. I am considering hiring an orphan boy from the village to help tend the horses and the barn. You will train him to take over those duties and to help with the garden if you like. That will free you to supervise the day workers and give you more time to tend the vineyard."

"Thank you, Sir. I will do whatever is best for the estate. I am grateful for being treated like a member of the family."

"You are a member of the family, my boy."

Of course, I agreed to the changes and immediately moved into the house. The village orphan boy's name was also Hans so we called him, "Little Hans" and Hans Richter became "Big Hans."

My life followed a routine for the rest of the decade. As I grew I was given additional responsibilities including supervising the estate's day laborers. Some spoke my native language; others spoke German, Polish, Hungarian, and other languages. Somehow we all communicated. I still spoke the Bosnian-Serbian language in the manner of a peasant, but my German was crisp and clear and though just a teen, it helped give me the aura of an adult supervisor.

8

SADISM RISING

Paradise for a boy is life on an estate. By my teen years, my trepidations about leaving home were long behind me. Although I still missed my family, I'd become a proficient horseman and lived in the lap of luxury. My grapes, the pride of the region, and the green garden, nearly the size of my father's entire farm, both won awards. Conversations in German rolled off my tongue more easily than in my native language.

Herr Richter sent my salary to my parents as promised, and occasionally gave me small bonuses when I traveled to nearby towns for supplies. I did my job as best I could, but Herr Richter's comments such as, "Well done," brought resentment from Hans even before he left for boarding school. He became surly whenever I received attention from his father. "Ha!" he would say, "peasant work. Anybody could do that. It is nothing."

During a visit home from school, Hans's first point of order was to show his ability to exercise control over me. "Let's go to the woods. I want to hunt for fowl and rabbits."

Despite my protests, I saddled two horses and we rode off to the forest. There he reined up and took aim.

"I can hit a rabbit from fifty yards. Can you?"

"Hans, I know you're a better shot than me with a rifle. Why do you always have to prove it?"

"Because I don't want you to forget your place. You're an outsider, a foreigner. You're just one of the hired help. Whenever my father praises you or moves your quarters to the house, it is nothing more than an effort to get you to work harder. I'm the only son. You're nothing more than a peasant dressed up to make the place look nice. Don't ever forget that, Boskur."

He had not used that slur for years. I figured something else must be bothering him and I just happened to be the nearest target to bear the brunt of his ire. I shrugged my shoulders, turned to ignore him, and walked away. He fired a shot that sailed past my head and embedded itself into a nearby tree. I jumped and turned to stare at him.

"Heed what I say, Bosnian boy."

For the most part Hans was away at school, but even on his visits home we did not communicate with one another beyond our forages into the woodland.

I'm a poor shot with a pistol and an average marksman with a rifle, but my weapon of choice has always been my prized sling shot. My greater love to this day, however, is tending horses and growing food, not shooting guns.

With Hans away, I settled into a routine with my work on the estate. Herr Richter came by often just to visit. Too frequently he fretted about Hans. On one visit I could see that he was stressed, so I tried to cheer him up.

"It looks like another good crop, and three mares have given birth. It is a happy time, yes master?"

"Ah Peter, I have concerns about Hans. Does he talk much during his visits home when you boys are together?"

"I'm not sure what you mean. We speak very little. Perhaps Hans is going through a stage that many boys go through. I think. Sometimes he seems angry."

Herr Richter paused for a moment, "I know what you mean. On a recent visit to my old friend, the headmaster at Hans's school, told me things that trouble me. The boy was nearly expelled from that school. The headmaster and I had a long talk and he told me Hans has threatened other boys. He held a knife to a boy's throat for no other reason than the boy is Jewish. I am concerned for him and hope a new school will give him a fresh start. You know him as well as anybody, what do you think, Peter?"

My master had never spoken to me about such matters before. I didn't know what to say. I couldn't tell him about what I'd seen Hans do with the poachers. I answered slowly. "I think... you will do what is best."

It was clear he wanted more from me but I didn't know what to say that might help. I'd seen the ugly side of Hans but still hoped he would grow out of it. "Maybe a fresh start at a new school is what he needs."

I could see that he was bothered by Hans's behavior and embarrassed to be discussing it with me.

"You're right, Son. The headmaster suggested as much. I will find another school for Hans. Perhaps a new start with new friends will help."

The new school did not help. For the next few years Hans changed schools regularly.

❧

Once my language lessons were completed, Professor Braun continued to stop by the estate regularly to visit with Herr Richter, give me refresher tests, and praise my skills. We had become very close. If Herr Richter was the father figure in my life, then the Professor was my grandfather figure. He would regale me with folk tales and stories of politics and fancy, then have me repeat them back to him. He told me that the story sessions were to keep my language and memory skills crisp, but I suspected he did it so often because he had grown as fond of me as I had of him.

Before leaving the house he always concluded with, "My boy, you have mastered the language as well as any student I've ever taught. One day, I am sure, you will use it to further your station in life."

"Danke, dass du mein Professor." I thanked him.

Two days after my seventeenth birthday I was tending the garden and expecting Professor Braun to visit. Herr Richter sent Mariija to fetch me. "Peter, I just received word that our dear Professor Braun has died. I thought you would want to know."

I was stunned. This was not my first brush with death of somebody close to me. I'd watched Hans visit death upon the Gypsy poachers, but I did not know them. My mother died in childbirth, so I didn't remember her. I missed my parents and siblings, but as far as I knew that they were still alive and I would someday return and see them. But I never thought of the death of a person I knew and loved. The Professor's death left me with an empty feeling, knowing I'd never see my dear friend again.

"It is okay to cry. We both cared deeply for the professor."

When I saw the moistness in my master's eyes my own tears began to flow.

Herr Richter reached for a bottle of cognac and set two glasses on the table. "Let's drink a toast to the professor. "He raised his glass and said, "He was a gentleman of the first order and a dear friend."

I raised my glass and said, "He has given me a skill that will last a lifetime. He was the best teacher any boy could have, and I loved him like a grandfather."

We held our glasses high then drank the toast with one swallow, then I coughed and more tears flowed. My first taste of cognac nearly choked me!

~

During school vacations Hans sometimes came home and we rode together throughout the estate. He often would chide me. "One day, when my old man dies, this will all be mine. I'll probably fire Marija and hire some young thing for my pleasure. I might fire you too. You're nothing more than a dressed up dirty Bosnian peasant. You should be thankful we provide a roof over your head."

Besides insulting me he also seemed to enjoy relating details of his infliction of pain and injury to animals and people. "You should see what I did to a Bosnian boy at my school. Do you want to hear about it? I could do the same thing to you if I wanted."

He was looking for a reaction from me, and though I was forced to listen to his depravity, I refused to outwardly acknowledge or comment on it. My lack of reaction eventually irked him enough that he walked away. But memories of what he did to the two Gypsy boys always left me shaking. I prayed that he would outgrow his sick behavior but feared he would not.

Each time Hans returned to the estate he had more tales to tell. "Well, I got kicked out of another school. Too bad. I was beginning to like this one. I'm studying surgery and learning to use scalpel. That's a sharp knife used to cut people open."

I tried to get him to change the topic. "Tell me about what you do in school since I've never been. Are your classes much like our tutoring sessions with Professor Braun?"

"I don't go to classes very often. Instead, I spend most of my time enjoying the life of a playboy. I have a habit of enrolling in surgery courses because I like cutting things, but my main reason for attending school is partying, meeting girls, drinking, but only occasionally attending classes. I do find my laboratory classes pleasant, though, especially when I get to run my steel-bladed tools through the dead flesh of cadavers. One day I'll practice on live subjects.

"I've been expelled from schools for not going to class. Each time that happens, I travel the countryside to find another. Do you have any idea how many schools there are in Europe? Maybe I'll get expelled from all of them. You might say I'm squandering my inheritance in pursuit of higher party education. You'd be right!"

One snowy November morning I awoke at six and as was my custom, had breakfast and went to the barn. Little Hans, the orphan from the village, had gone to the orphanage for the weekend so I was alone in the barn. A fresh coating of snow covered the area but I discovered Hans's horse and carriage that he's driven to school, standing empty next to the barn. It had been pushed aside and sat askew. The horse that had pulled the carriage stood shivering in the barn, so I tossed a blanket over the animal and rubbed it down.

I didn't see Hans and figured he must've slept late. By midmorning he came to the barn and found I had stabled and brushed his horse and replaced the carriage from the previous night in the carriage house.

"Saddle two fresh horses. We're going to the woods for target practice,"

"Hans, I have work to do here. I'll saddle your horse but I can't go with you."

"Come on, boy. It snowed last night. The day workers won't come to work today. I can see the horses have been fed and you turned the straw. You have nothing else to do."

The two men sat in lounge chairs across from Herr Richter. I went to the kitchen and gave the message to Marija, then returned living room. "Will that be all, Sir?"

"No, Peter. Be seated. Since Hans is not here, you have might information that could help. Now, officer, tell me about the missing boy."

"The boy's name is Emil Heller. He attends the university in Konitz. Do you know the town?"

"Yes, I know it well. I have done business there and my son is also a student there."

A shudder passed through me. Could Hans have been telling me the truth?"

"Yes, that is why we want to question him. Emil Heller's family is from Strasburg. That is our jurisdiction. His father is the town goldsmith and reports that he has not heard from the boy for weeks."

"Did you check the school?"

"Yes, we spoke to several of the students, and are still following up. We missed your son and thought he might be here. We had hoped that the two boys might be together. Perhaps the Heller boy had gone home with one of his schoolmates."

"Hans is on the property, actually. Went riding this morning and should return soon. You are welcome to stay and wait for him. Tell me more about the missing boy and what you know of his disappearance."

The police officer glanced at his notes and began, "It seems there was a beer drinking contest between your son and the Heller boy. The tavern owner's daughter," he flipped a few pages, "one Mitzi Fritz, said she thinks she remembers the boys leaving together, arm-in-arm and singing a drinking song together. That is the last reported sighting we have of him and were hoping your son could provide information that might help us."

As the officer spoke, Hans entered the house. "Oh father, I see you have company."

"Come in, Hans, these men are police from Strasburg and are looking for a friend of yours who seems to be missing."

"Hello, Herr Richter, I'm Polizist Netzke and this is Polizist Hopp. We wish to ask you questions about your friend Emil Heller."

"Oh, he is not my friend. I barely know him. I've seen him at the local tavern a few times, but I can't say I really know him. Did he commit a crime?"

"He seems to have disappeared. His parents are very worried. Has he ever come home with you, or visited here?"

"I don't think so. Do you remember seeing him, Peter?"

The focus was now on me. I was torn. I could destroy Hans by telling what I knew, but if I did tell, would it injure Hans, or would he do what he threatened, and incriminate me? It seemed like hours that I sat and considered. If I did not tell, surely that was a sin. If I spoke, Hans was condemned. If I stayed silent, I was damned.

Herr Richter spoke, breaking the silence. "Peter, do you remember a schoolmate that Hans brought to the estate?"

"No, I do not." I looked at Hans. He had a smirk on his face. He knew he had successfully bullied me again.

Polizist Netzke spoke, "Well, thank you for your time, and thank you Herr Richter for your hospitality. We will leave now. If you hear of anything regarding the missing boy, please get in touch with us in Strasburg."

The two officers bowed and left and I went on about my business on the estate, but not without feeling that part of my heart had turned to stone.

Hans followed me to the barn after the police left, and said, "You were wise to not say anything. They think the Jew is missing, but he is scattered throughout the village."

I ignored him. He sometimes talked in riddles. I tried to put the incident out of my mind, but it haunted me and caused many nightmares for years.

Hans stayed at the school and away from the estate for the next several weeks, but eventually came home for a weekend visit. He rode into the barn and sought me out.

"Remember the boy the police were looking for?"

I ignored him but he continued to speak, "Look at these newspaper articles. Oh, that's right. You don't read well. Ok, I'll read them to you. 'Missing boy gone for weeks. Family concerned.' The article goes on to say that he often ice-skated alone and the police thought he might have fallen through the ice and drowned. I was part of the search team, but of course he was not found. Want to know more?"

"No, Hans, you've already told me more than I want to know."

He ignored me and continued reading from another newspaper article.

"'The body of an elderly widow, Gisela Schmidt, was taken to the cemetery for burial yesterday. The deceased destitute woman was not given a funeral ceremony. A grave had been dug and the caretaker wheeled the body to the site in a wheelbarrow. The caretaker spotted a sack near the open grave and upon closer examination, made a gruesome discovery. The sack contained a dismembered arm, and had apparently been tossed over the cemetery fence and lay near the open grave. The arm, belonging to missing student Emil Heller, was identified by a misshapen finger that he had since birth.'"

"Oh Hans, you have done a terrible thing. And by telling me about it, you have implicated me. How many more lives do you intend to ruin? How many others will be affected by this ghastly thing you've done?"

Hans was neither sad nor jubilant as he prattled on. He spoke in even, unemotional tones.

"They found most of the body parts where I'd tossed them. Suspicion fell to local butchers, particularly the one that served our apartment building, Dieter Glock, a Christian butcher. He's a council member and his daughter had been seeing Emil Heller. It was common knowledge in the community that Glock threatened to kill Heller. He disciplined the girl for chasing with a non-Christian. He and several fellow city council members are known anti-Semites."

I became concerned for the poor butcher, and asked, "What happened to him?"

"He was arrested but not charged. The arrest was more like a party. Jailers told me they laughed, joked, and drank beer with their prisoner. I was there when he was released and given a cordial reception by the city council. When the Council finished applauding, Dieter Glock said, 'Whoever killed the bastard deserves a medal.'"

Hans enjoyed telling me of his sadistic exploits. He was in no danger of getting caught by my telling anybody. Even if I told, it would be easy for him to discredit me. He made sure I knew the authorities would take his word over mine.

I became tired of listening to him, and returned to cleaning the horse stalls. With my back to him, I continued to rotate the straw in the horse stalls. I heard a noise behind me. It happened so quickly I barely had time to think and instead just reacted. The noise sounded like an animal in pain, starting low and increasing in intensity until it became a wailing cry. I turned to see Hans racing toward me, a pitchfork in hand, attempting to run me through.

I dropped my pitchfork and twisted out of the way just in time, as he drove the sharp tines into a wooden beam between the stalls. He grunted as the tool stuck fast in the wood, then picked up my pitchfork and made another lunge at me. I gathered an armful of straw, rife with horse manure, and used it to deflect the blow. The prongs flipped upward and the manure-laced straw struck him full in the face and chest.

"What is the matter with you, Hans?"

He let loose with a drunken peal of laughter. "I was just playing about with you. If I wanted to inflict pain, I've had plenty of opportunities. Just remember, barn-boy, I can hurt you anytime I want to."

"Stay clear of me, Hans. I have no intention of telling anybody anything, especially whatever you told me while you were drunk. Just keep your distance from me."

Hans Richter never officially became a suspect in the murder and dismemberment of Emil Heller, but rumors began to swirl about the time lapse between the drinking contest and the murder. The two Prussian police revisited the house and questioned Hans but he was never charged and the case was never solved. It did, however, reveal the ugly anti-Semitic feeling brewing in Europe at the time, as well as Hans's fondness for inflicting pain and worse.

When a government official quietly told Herr Richter that his son might be a suspect because of his knowledge of surgery and proximity to the victim, Hans was immediately shipped off to a school in England.

9

A Narrow Escape, 1907

Ten years is a lifetime for a boy. During the term of my indentured servitude, I grew in many ways from an innocent lad
to a responsible young man. My hair, which had been thin
and grey from malnutrition when I first arrived at the estate, became
thick and black as my diet improved. I grew into a strapping young
man whose physical appearance was lean, muscular, strong and robust. I was not sure of the exact date of my birth so I counted myself
one year older each time the calendar turned to a new year. By that
calculation I was in my eighteenth year. I was a decent horseman,
groom, farmer, and supervisor of peons. Manhood was nearly upon
me. Traces of whiskers began to sprout and my voice was deep and
strong. My term of service contract was coming to an end.

Problems with Hans were no longer much of an issue. He was
mostly in England, supposedly studying at a university. This particular week he enjoyed a late summer holiday trip home from his
new British school, his first such visit in months. We chatted in the
garden while I weeded.

Herr Richter approached us in the garden to discuss my future.
"Peter, your contracted obligation will be completed soon. Have you
given thought to what you will do once you are free to leave?"

Hans found the conversation boring and of no interest so he wandered away, out of earshot.

"I would like to visit my family. I cannot imagine how they will look after ten years."

Herr Richter nodded. "You should do that first," then he added, "I have earned money in the wine industry using grapes from your arbors. I've banked a portion for you. Consider it a commission or bonus for your ten years of loyalty and hard work. You could buy a farm near your family, and live there if you wish. Or if you do not find your old village to your liking, I'll hold a position for you here. You can always come back.

"One thing in your favor is your command of the language. You speak better German than I do. Many opportunities await you. If you choose to return to Germany but live away from the estate, I will help you find work, or finance a farm, or whatever you choose."

The tutorial sessions with the professor taught me to read and write a little of the German language. My spoken German was exemplary, and Marija's lessons in the dining room gave me skills to act the gentleman in social settings.

"You can always come back here, but once your contract expires, you need to strike out and see the world before making a decision. You are fortunate to have so many choices."

As much as Herr Richter would have liked to keep me in his employ, he knew that young men need to grow socially. The first eight years of my life had been spent in the village, and the past ten on the estate. Aside from the fair in Bosnia and occasional forays into the city with Herr Richter or Marija, my social experiences had been limited to supervising day workers on the estate.

Two days after our conversation, Hans was in the open barn telling me of his latest conquests among English girls. "There's this one girl, Christina. You should hear how she squeals when I…"

I stopped listening to him mid-sentence and took notice of a soldier riding onto the property. I walked outside to the corral for a better look and Hans followed. The officer wore a colorful uniform that included epaulets on his shoulder and a helmet with a plume. He sat astride a large steed, bigger than a Percheron. A long knife in a sheath dangled at his side.

"Why does he have a bird's feather on his head and a long knife at his side?" I asked Hans.

"The plume is traditional and the knife is called a *säbel*. It is used in battle."

Once Hans named it I immediately knew of the weapon from my language lessons, but had never seen one. Hans knew about such things. "It is curved with a single edge that is very sharp, to be used in battle. Oh, what I could do with that säbel."

I ignored Hans and instead focused instead on the soldier, wondering what business he might have on the Richter estate. The horseman did not smile, nod, or even acknowledge the two of us as we walked out of the barn, but spoke directly to Herr Richter.

Not wanting to be obvious, I returned to the corral and walked one of the horses around the enclosure. Hans went into the house but I remained in the corral and overheard much of the conversation. At times the soldier's voice became loud. I listened even though I knew their conversation was probably none of my business.

The soldier did not dismount, but remained on his horse as he spoke, "Good afternoon, Herr Richter. I am Sergeant Major Altenburg. My charge is to identify local men for conscription into the armed forces. Our records show that you have a son who is of age to serve in the military. Is that accurate?"

"Yes, my son is nearly twenty-one years of age. Why do you ask?"

"The government has established a program to induct young men of draftable age in order to bring the army up to standards. Is your son physically healthy and mentally stable?"

"Yes, of course. He studies medicine at an English university."

"If he is of age, he must serve his military obligation, unless he qualifies for an exemption."

"Can I review your documents so I can see if he qualifies for an exemption?"

The soldier swung his leg and the *säbel* over the leather saddle and landed the ground. The two men were now on the other side of the soldier's horse. I could only see the plume and helmet above the saddle, but was still able to hear the conversation. I watched the soldier remove a leather-bound book from the saddlebag, opened and reviewed it. After a few minutes he spoke.

"Here he is. Richter, Hans. Age twenty. Draft status, eligible. Does this answer your question?"

"Partly. Does your book list exemptions? Look, Sergeant Major, my son is a valuable asset to our country. He is in medical school now and will be able to treat many soldiers and civilians once he completes his course of study. Surely there is a way that he could finish his studies first."

The soldier appeared to turn several pages of the book. "Hmmm, yes, here it is. If he is actively enrolled in a medical school, he qualifies. But upon the completion of the program he would be required to serve. Until that time it would be necessary to have another serve in his place. There might be some poor families who would benefit from sending a younger son to serve."

"Good, Wait here. I'll be right back. I am a patriotic man and would be willing to pay for the service of one who would take his position."

Herr Richter sprinted to the house and soon returned.

"Here is the money for the replacement, and something for his family to show our gratitude. Here is a like amount for your trouble, having to ride all the way out here on such a hot day. I bid you farewell and thank you for your service to our country."

Herr Richter was talking fast, as though he wanted to get rid of the soldier as quickly as possible. But the soldier did not mount his horse. Instead he continued his conversation.

"Now, about the other boy. The one in your service." He scanned the leather-bound manifest. "The peasant boy, Pero Novachek. Age eighteen. We must make arrangements to enlist him into military service as well. Maybe he could serve in place of your son?"

I was shocked to hear the name spoken, though he used my nickname and mispronounced my surname, but that quirk would prove to be my good fortune, though neither my master nor I realized it at the time.

Several moments passed before the gist of the conversation sunk in. It had never occurred to me that I might be drafted into military service. Why me? How did the Sergeant Major even know I existed? Maybe it wasn't me whose name was mentioned. But who else could it be? I was the only one in service on the estate. Surely there must be a mistake. I snapped out of my fog when I heard Herr Richter raise his voice.

"Peter? You must be kidding! He's not even German. He's a Bosnian Serb. How can the German army claim to hold dominion over him?"

"Our records are very thorough. The Austro-Hungarian Empire includes Bosnia. We can take him because he falls under our jurisdiction. He does not meet the same standards as a German citizen, but we can still draft him."

"That's absurd. He is just a boy. I don't even think he's old enough to be eligible for the draft."

"My records show him as eighteen. That's all I need. We will round up all draftees one week from today and take them to the induction center. See that Pero Novachek is available for pickup."

"Wait. The boy is a member of my family. I was planning to adopt him. Let me pay to have another lad take his place. He'd make a terrible soldier and you will be doing a poor family a great service by giving them this money. Here is another bonus for your trouble."

"I am tempted, but the documents show he is a peasant that you have indentured. If I accepted your money and listed him as another exemption, I could lose my career. It's not worth the risk for me. Keep your money. Have him ready to go one week from today. I wish I could help, but there is just no way. I'm already bending the rules for your son Hans. I cannot do it for both."

He replaced the big book into his saddlebag, mounted his war horse, and rode off. Herr Richter stood, watching the dust from the big horse until the soldier was out of sight, then walked slowly to the house. Later that evening he sent for me.

"Peter, we have a problem to deal with. Do you know the meaning of the word 'conscription'?"

I thought for a few moments and said, "Yes. Conscription is compulsory enlistment for state service, usually into the armed forces."

"Right. That is what the word means. Now let me explain how it affects us and what it means for you and Hans.

I listened intently as my master explained. "The Balkan countries, including Bosnia and Serbia are threatening war. Germany is pressing Austria to increase spending for arms and increase the size of her army.

"Germany has agreed to help by drafting eligible young men and placing them on loan to the Austrian army. To accomplish this, military attachés have been sent to all corners of the Austro-Hungarian

Empire, Germany, and Prussia to identify young men for conscription into the army. The man on the horse came to draft you and Hans into military service.

"Hans is exempt. Tomorrow he will return to school in England and tend to his studies. He will be out of harm's way and out of the reach of the army. I tried to make the same deal for you, telling the attaché that you were my son also. But the soldier's papers show that you are not my son, but my employee, and your place of birth was the within the Austro-Hungarian Empire. There is no exemption for you. Soldiers will return in one week to gather you and draft you into the army.

"There are many things you do well, my son. You are a horse groomer, a farmer, grower of grapes, and have served as an excellent overseer to the day workers. But you would not make a good soldier. You do not have the killer instinct.

"Your strength is more toward finding a negotiated solution to a problem rather than to fight for an issue. Those are outstanding qualities for a diplomat, but not for a soldier. Besides, I could not stand to lose you in battle."

When he stopped talking I said, "I agree with you, Sir. Other than following orders, I do not have the makings of a good soldier. But I am confident that you could figure a plan that is in my best interest.

The following day, the three of us went to town to see Hans off to England. Herr Richter left Hans and me in a pub while he went to visit a close friend of his.

"I can't wait to get back and see all my little British maids. Do you have any idea how easy English girls are to seduce? They're more proper than German girls but behind closed doors, wow!" He railed on as he belted down one drink after another.

I nursed my first mug of ale while Hans downed several and told me of his conquests in England. An hour later, Herr Richter returned and we walked Hans to the train. The father and son hugged and Hans boarded, and was off to the university..

On our way back to the estate, Herr Richter of a conversation with his friend, Michael Buechele, a printer. "As you know, Peter, I am concerned over the possibility of your being drafted."

I nodded as he slapped the horse's flank with a whip and continued talking.

"The recruiter has your name wrong and that might allow us to say that no such person exists. I thought we might try to bluff our way out of your conscription by passing you off as a visiting relative. But he has already seen you and I don't want to take the chance of you're being taken away on the spot. So while you and Hans sat, I went to see a friend of mine.

"I asked him if he could make a duplicate set of Hans's passport documents but change the description to resemble you. I described you and showed him the tintype photo taken last Christmas. Instead of listing you as a student I had him print the documents of a diplomat.

"My friend examined the documents and agreed to do me the favor. He told me they would be ready in an hour. No questions asked. I had lunch in a local tavern, then returned and picked up the travel documents."

I sat quietly until Herr Richter had finished the story. "I don't understand. How will the travel documents help me? I'm not a diplomat."

"I'm still thinking that one through. I have an idea but will wait until we get home to tell you my plan. I want Marija there to be sure you understand perfectly."

We rode the rest of the way in silence, both of us deep in thought.

Upon our arrival home, Herr Richter, Marija, and I sat in the kitchen as he nervously outlined his strategy. "Plans for your future have changed, Peter. You will leave our home sooner than expected for your own safety. The soldiers will come to gather you for military induction next week, but I will tell them you've run away, probably back to Bosnia, although I'm not exactly sure where in Bosnia. They might try to find you in your village, so you cannot go there. I will pay a small fine for not presenting you, and the soldiers will leave my property. Your name will be listed as a deserter."

As my master spoke, I realized that for the second time in my young life I was about to leave a home and family I loved. This time I was not as anxious to leave as the first. It wasn't the thought of consequences of getting caught that made me pine to remain. I had fallen in love with my master, Marija, the estate and its workers, the horses, and even the unpredictable Hans. Well, maybe not Hans, but I wanted to stay here forever.

"Once we put this plan in motion, Peter, you may not stay in Germany or Austria, as the charge of desertion can be punishable by imprisonment or death. Neither can you return to Bosnia. The Austro-Hungarian army has authority there, or more likely the Serbian army would draft you because of your Serbian heritage. Either way, if you stay on the continent you will be drafted into an army.

"If you're discovered hiding on the estate you will be immediately arrested and I would be charged with aiding and abetting a criminal. It is too dangerous to send you to England since Hans used his original set of documents to travel there. America is your best option.

Herr Richter took a breath. "So you will not go to Bosnia and you will not stay here. The plan I have devised is dangerous. I can help you escape to America, but I will not be able to help you once you arrive on Freedom's shores."

He showed me the fake passport documents. "You will use this duplicate set of Hans's documents to board a ship and sail to America. It shows that you are a low level diplomat. If asked the purpose of your trip, tell the officials that you will be studying law and government at the American university, Harvard. If you are challenged in English, just smile and say you are embarrassed by your own English and prefer to speak German until you reach the university.

You speak the German language well enough that you should not arouse suspicion, and you are close enough in age and size to pass as Hans. Marjia will cut and lighten your hair to resemble Hans's receding hairline as closely as possible."

I listened closely. My mind raced. I didn't know what to think, but America did have a nice ring to it, and I trusted my master.

"War is coming to Europe. My own wealth and social status will serve to keep me out of the army or at worst commission me as an officer. Hans is safely abroad preparing to enter the University of London. I am determined to see you off safely."

Once I agreed to travel to America, a powerful series of lessons took place.

"Peter, my son, you are about to embark on the most intense schooling of your life. I will be your instructor, and if you think Professor Braun was strict, you'll think me an ogre. Time is short. We have less than one week to prepare, and you must perform as though your life depends on it—because it does.

"The first part of the plan is your transformation from Peter to Hans. Then the two of us will travel as father and son to the port city of Bremen, where you will embark on your journey to America. The countries we will pass through, France, Holland and Belgium, are not yet at war, and as long as we do not stand out, I am confidant the masquerade will be carried off successfully. Now, let's all get some rest and begin your transformation tomorrow"

Early the following morning I sat on a chair in the kitchen and Marija worked on my hair. When I squirmed, she said, "You must sit still, my dear, and let me perform my magic."

The process took the entire day. First she trimmed and thinned my hair to give it the look of a receding hairline, then she lightened it. I donned a set of Hans's clothing Marija altered to fit. She also rubbed something she called makeup on my exposed dark skin to lighten it closer to Hans' skin tone. Herr Richter paced the entire time.

With the cosmetic changes complete, I could probably pass for Hans at a glance from a galloping horse. But I would not be on a galloping horse. I would be on the deck of a passenger liner, and Herr Richter feared my gait and posture would give me away as a peasant. For all I had learned during my decade on the Richter Estate, I was still a country peon who preferred a horse and barn to any event that required a starched shirt, cravat, and suit.

With the plan firmly in place, I began the rehearsal for my command acting performance. Herr Richter was determined to teach me how to walk, talk, act, and look the part of an upper-class gentleman diplomat about to pursue a university education.

The positive; my excellent command of the language and the dining etiquette lessons Marija had taught me. Those lessons would prove essential in this masquerade. The down side; my self-perception and mannerisms were those of a rough-hewn rube.

"Okay, boy, let me see you walk like this." Herr Richter stood erect and walked stiffly from the kitchen to the dining room table, turned on his heel, and seated himself on a chair that Marija had pulled out for him.

I tried to mimic what I had just seen, taking several long steps into the dining room and gripping the chair.

"No, no, no," wailed Herr Richter. "You are not a horse clomping across a barn! You're a gentleman! Walk like you own the place!" He demonstrated again.

I stood up straight, walked to the chair, pulled it out, and sat. It felt silly to walk as though a board braced my back.

"Better. But not quite there yet. Keep your back ramrod straight and shoulders back. Try again."

I held myself upright, walked to the chair, pulled it out, and sat, proud of my performance.

"Son, you are not a servant. You are in command! Never pull your own chair from the table. Wait for a steward or other person to pull it out for you. Today Marija will play the role of a steward, but onboard the ship it will be a uniformed crew-member, and you must never look the steward in the eye nor acknowledge him in any way. His job is to be invisible while making you comfortable."

We practiced all morning, took a lunch break, and practiced again throughout the afternoon, day after day. They dressed me in gentleman's attire, complete with starched shirts, neckwear, and shined boots, including my best-tailored suit that had been kept in the main house for special occasions. During rest periods I tried on other clothing from Hans's wardrobe that Marija altered to fit. They gave me an overcoat, umbrella, and hat. I stood erect to walk while wearing the hat, and positioned the umbrella. By the third day I had the hang of it, but my walk was still suspect for that of a gentleman.

"Your walk could easily give you away. You do better when carrying the umbrella, but let's try something else. Marija, go to my bedroom closet and retrieve one my walking sticks."

She did as instructed while the faux father and son rested. When she returned Marija had an ebony wooden walking cane with an engraved "R" on a silver knob at the top. The cane was about waist high.

"Take the cane and try to walk as I instructed you but this time lean on the stick as though you have an injured leg."

I tried limping but that didn't work. Herr Richter demonstrated a proper walk, depending on the stick for support. I had to balance my weight differently, but in doing so my peasant way of walking disappeared in favor of that of a statesman.

"That's it!" he cried. "Now let me see you do the same walk ten times in succession."

I tried to do as he had shown, but my first try was so full of overconfidence that I allowed the cane to slip on the floor and went down in a heap on top of it. A sharp pain shot through my hip and down my leg and I used leverage from the cane to stand and give it another try.

"Perfect!" he cried, "Do it again. See if you can mimic that walk five times in a row without falling. If you do we'll take a break."

After performing my fifth consecutive perfect rehearsal, Herr Richter clapped. "Bravo, my second son. Now we will review the rest of plan."

The pain in my hip and leg subsided but the swagger using the cane remained. It was at that moment I began to feel confident enough to pull off the act.

Herr Richter had me repeat the plan several times to Marija; in Bosnian, then in German to both of them in order to make absolutely certain I understood every nuance.

"You will be traveling across the Atlantic Ocean as a junior diplomat with a second-class ticket. With first-class ticket you'd less likely be challenged, but I am not sure we have time to teach you all the things you need to know to pull off a first class masquerade on such short notice.

"First-class passengers are expected to maintain certain social activities, such as taking tea, gambling, and socializing in the men's smoking room, responding to questions of a business and political nature and so forth."

"My head hurts just thinking about it."

"Also in first class you would be expected to play card games for money in the smoker. Have you ever played cards?"

"Cards?" I asked quizzically.

"My point exactly. Should you arouse suspicion or be considered a fraud, you could be subject to ship security and possibly be handed over to the authorities upon docking in America or worse, be returned to Europe to face trial as a deserter. No, first class would be far too dangerous. Second class travel is the logical choice.

"Let me tell you a little about second-class accommodations. While not first class, second is hardly shabby. Fellow passengers will be professionals, professors, authors, clergymen, and government officials as well as tourists."

"You mean professors like Herr Professor Braun?"

"Exactly. If any passenger begins to pry about your work or background, smile and do not answer the question. The passenger will become embarrassed and not engage you in further conversation. I have already purchased your ticket. The ship you will travel on is called SS Oldenburg. It is not one of the newer ships but your quarters will be very nice. You will be in a single cabin."

"Ships have names? Like people? That sounds silly. Your wagon doesn't have a name, does it? I've never heard you call it by name. Do trains have names?"

"Forget about wagons and trains," said the exasperated mentor. "Yes. Every ship has her own name."

"If a fellow passenger strikes up a conversation, be cordial, but reveal as little information about yourself, or Hans, as possible."

"Will there be many passengers?"

"Your ship has four decks and can accommodate nearly forty second-class passengers and about fifty in First, but I don't think there will be that many. Most or all upper deck passengers will be men. Below decks in third class, the company may pack in up to two thousand or more. That's where they make their money.

Ships traveling from Europe to America are usually near capacity, but those returning are nearly empty, so you will likely have plenty of company."

Herr Richter gave instructions for my arrival in America. "Your port of call will be Baltimore, Maryland. Once the ship docks in the harbor, you will disembark. You must find a place out of sight, and destroy all travel documents, as they could incriminate us both. This you must do as soon as possible after setting foot on American soil. From that point onward you are on your own. Once the documents are destroyed you will no longer be Hans Richter, so you can use your own name or choose a new one, but you must have no contact with anybody that could connect you to my estate in Germany or to your family in Bosnia. This is for your safety as well as ours."

As the impact of Herr Richter's words took hold, I gritted my teeth. Marija pinched the bridge of her nose to keep her tears in check but a single tear rolled down her cheek in spite of herself. I knew she would miss me most.

Herr Richter had more to offer. "Onboard the ship you will be out of danger. As long as you are successful with your charade, your only risk will be exiting the ship."

We set up an impromptu gangplank that ran from the outside door to the bottom step and I practiced walking down as though I were an upper class German or Austrian. It took several tries, as Herr Richter often reminded me that by nature I was a humble man and had been a peon my entire life. I tended to slouch when I walked. But with the help of the walking cane I learned to assume the air of a second-class passenger for just this one occasion, to protect Herr Richter and Hans, and certainly myself, and not letting my true identity be discovered.

"I can assure you that if you successfully play the part for just those few minutes, you will soon be breathing free American air."

"How can I ever repay you?"

Herr Richter's became glassy. He hugged me, his voice breaking. "By being happy and successful in America. That would be more than adequate payment."

I turned away so neither he nor Marija could see my own tears.

Early Sunday morning we set out for Bremen but did not travel directly.

"We could take a train from Ulm directly to Bremen in less than two days, but I've planned our route to go through France, Belgium and Holland, then back into Germany to the docks. It will take us longer, but I want to cross as many borders as possible."

"I don't understand. Wouldn't it make more sense to go directly to the ship?"

"Normally, yes, but I want you to become comfortable showing your documents and playing the part of Hans Richter. Another reason is that by the time you board the ship, your documents will appear used rather than freshly printed, and less likely to arouse suspicion. The third reason is to give you as much experience as a traveler as possible. The more comfortable you are, the less likely that your anxiety will give you away.

"At each border crossing, if the authorities ask, we're on our way to consult with government officials. From the Netherlands, we will travel directly to Bremen."

⌒

Our first leg of the trip found me riding in the same carriage that brought me to the estate a decade earlier. Two fine German business-men, father and son, a young diplomat, or so we appeared, traveling on a business trip. At Ulm, we loaded the carriage aboard the train and placed the horse in a separate car.

The train halted at a small border town and we offloaded the carriage and prepared to cross into France at a small sleepy village. "I'm guessing the border crossing in a buggy will be easier at these out-of-the way crossings than on board a train. We don't want your fresh, new passport to be too closely scrutinized."

We approached the border crossing manned by a single guard. Herr Richter paid an entry tax and we passed through without in-cident.

The crossing into Belgium nearly took a different turn. The bor-der guard examined my papers very thoroughly, then asked us to get down from the carriage. "These papers do not look quite right to me. You will wait here, please, until I can reach my superior."

Herr Richter reacted with bluster, "What are you trying to pull? You know those are valid German papers. You are trying to hold us up for more money. I won't stand for it! Give me your name. Herr Janssens will hear of this. You know of course that he is the Director of Diplomatic Travel. I hope you value your position!"

The young man was clearly shaken. "I'm sorry, Sir, I'm just trying to do my job."

"I appreciate that, but my son has diplomatic status in your coun-try and the Director is a personal friend. Challenging his documents is a slap in the face to our country. Now, do you want to make an international issue of this? Or will you let us pass?"

The guard, who appeared to be about my age wore an ill-fitting uniform. He handed the passports back to us and said meekly. "Please pass, Sir. I am sorry for any inconvenience."

Herr Richter flicked the reins and the horse and buggy moved quickly through the checkpoint.

"He didn't even look at your passport! I didn't know you knew the Belgian Director of Diplomatic Travel. Has he ever been to your house?"

"Oh, Peter, I have no diplomatic status in Belgium, and no idea who their Director of Diplomatic Travel might be. Janssens is the first Belgian name that came to my mind. I banked that the guard would not know either."

"But…but, what if he had taken our passports to his superior and…"

"He didn't. Just remember, a little bluster, well placed, can sometimes be more effective than stumbling while jumping through hoops. You are traveling as a diplomat. Heed your lessons. Always walk and act as though you require respect."

"Yes, Sir."

Crossing into The Netherlands posed no problem and we arrived in the university town of Maastricht in late afternoon. The town was abuzz over an event called the Anarchist Congress, taking place in Amsterdam. There were protests and general unrest in the streets. The town was overrun with factory workers and students from all over Europe. It was chaos. Herr Richter did a quick assessment. "We'll be lucky to get a meal here, let alone a room. Let's go directly to Bremen."

We loaded the buggy and horse on the train and rode the five-hour trip to Bremen. There we holed up in a hotel and spent the next few days practicing my "Diplomat" lessons.

Bremen was the largest, most vibrant place I had ever seen. Construction seemed to be taking place everywhere. Wide boulevards passed by the elegant structures. A courthouse and several other grand buildings greeted us, including a new three story Town Hall with a parapet on top. A park with a large gazebo in the center made me stare in awe. We had dinner at a formal restaurant, and I had the opportunity to show off the dining skills Marija had taught me. We then spent the night in a grand hotel and we just relaxed.

The following morning we took a horse-drawn tram to the docks. The tram had upholstered seats but still was not as fine as the Richter carriage.

"There she is," said Herr Richter pointing to a large ship in the harbor. To this day I remember my first view of SS Oldenburg as though it were yesterday. I can see the large red funnel painted black at the top, rising above the steel hull. Two huge masts, one on either side of the funnel reached for the sky. I can still see the ship's flag flying atop the masts, red with a reclining dark blue cross.

"The flag is of Norway. She is of the *Nordeutscher Lloyd* line."

That muggy Friday, first day of March morning, beads of sweat appeared on Herr Richter's forehead as we climbed down from the tram. Once on the ground he handed me my suitcase, ticket, and the forged travel documents as well as the silver-handled ebony walking stick. He also gave me a new overcoat. "My son, do not to lose this coat. Marija has sewn something into the lining that will help you in the new world. Also, here are some additional American dollars. Use them for tips and pocket expenses."

As I later discovered, sewn inside the lining of the coat's lining were envelopes containing the cash that Herr Richter determined was my share of the increased revenue to the estate. He had exchanged the

German Marks for American dollars on the black market without arousing suspicion.

Our boots became muddy as we walked along the pier to the gangplank. "Be sure to leave your muddy boots outside your cabin door tonight. The steward will clean them overnight."

We embraced one final time. "Peter, you are like a son to me. I could not love you more if you had come from my dear wife's womb. God bless you, travel safely, and have a good life in America. Perhaps one day we'll meet again."

I choked back my own emotions, stood tall and walked aboard the ship, just as my master had taught me, using the walking stick. I moved with an air of superiority, flashed my documents to the official, who barely glanced at them, and continued up the gangplank unmolested. Once aboard I waved to my mentor, then was escorted to my cabin by a steward who said, "If you leave your boots outside the door tonight, Sir, I will have them cleaned and polished."

I smiled knowing I had just passed my first test.

10

A New World Journey

The SS Oldenburg left the port of Bremen March 1, 1907, beginning the long journey by sailing up the Weser River to the Atlantic Ocean, I relaxed in my second class cabin, one of a million-and-a-half emigrants to travel to the United States that year.

A steward showed me to my comfortable second-class stateroom that faced the deck and had a porthole giving me a view of the ocean. A faint smell of disinfectant tickled my nostrils. I scanned the suite, two beds and two overstuffed chairs, a vanity mirror, and several drawers and closets providing more than I needed.

The steward, a young, tall youth wore a crisp new uniform with a high collar, starched and buttoned to the neck. He carefully unpacked my suitcase and hung and folded my clothes, placing them in one of two matching wardrobes, then smoothed the blankets on the matching mahogany bed.

Speaking German, he pointed to one of the sofas and said, "This comfortable sofa sir, can also be converted into a bed if you find your bunk bed uncomfortable. And see how the washbasin cabinet also serves as a dresser. If you need anything further, please push this call button, and I will be at your beck and call. Would you be needing anything else at this time?"

I shook my head.

He then straightened the curtains and demonstrated how to operate the toilet, and every other item in the suite. Then again asked, "Will you be needing any other service, Sir?"

I shook my head. "Nein."

"You can rest assured, Sir, that I will take care of your every need during the journey. Leave your boots outside the door when you retire and I will have them polished and shined before you awaken."

At that instant I recognized that my responses could have shown me to be a peasant rather than a professional. I remembered something my master told me about tipping the crew. *"Danke."* I thanked him and handed him a coin.

The steward smiled. *"Bitte,"* and left the room. I made a mental note to be sure to dismiss the help verbally in the future with a tip.

As Herr Richter had predicted, I had access to the entire ship. My walks during the voyage included visiting every nook and cranny from first class to steerage. At first my tentative nature kept me in my cabin. I did not join fellow passengers for dinner, but ate the bread and cheeses Marija packed for me. The meal made me feel comfortable and closer to her.

Eventually, I ventured from my cabin and by the second day, walked the entire ship. By virtue of holding a second-class ticket and wearing the clothes of a gentleman, I soon took advantage of access to all first and second class passenger locations. The ship's promenade shared areas for both first and second-class passengers. Side-by-side they walked, sat, sunned, chatted, and marveled at the ocean view.

Before venturing into the third class abyss I practiced in my cabin, walking like a wealthy gentleman, using my walking stick while taking daily strolls throughout the ship.

As I explored the ship, I came upon a locked gate and steep stairway that led to the bowels of the vessel and third class accommodations. A seaman guarded the entry. Third-class passengers literally traveled as freight in the cargo hold. To reach the steerage level in the depths of the ship required caution and permission. The narrow, steep passageway could present a dangerous challenge.

I said to the guarding seaman in German, "I would like to see the rest of the ship."

The young man, about my age, was probably Italian or Spanish. He spoke street-German as he blocked my path, "Sir, you are free to walk any part of the ship, but I don't think you want to go down there. It's hot, and it stinks, and the people down there are dirty. It could be dangerous."

I thought quickly, remembering what Herr Richter taught me about a little well-placed bluster. "Are you telling me that the *Nordeutscher Lloyd Line's* ship has conditions that endanger its passengers? If so, I must report that to the authorities when we dock. What is your name."

"I-I-I'm sorry, Sir. That is not what I meant. I uh, just meant the ladder might be slippery. You, uh, must be careful. Please pass, and let me know it you have any other needs. Call out if you need assistance."

The young seaman sweated as he inserted the key into the lock and opened the folding gate for me to pass.

Outside of my encounters with the gate guard and my room steward, I rarely spoke, offering instead a friendly smile and nod, to passengers and crew. Wearing a fine suit, sporting a fresh haircut, holding a diplomat's passport, and with my second-cabin ticket readily available, I was never challenged.

I've been told by immigrants who traveled on other ships, that conditions in steerage could be unsanitary, unclean, often indecent, and unworthy of humane travel. Those restricted to the belly of the beast had little opportunity for a breath of fresh air during the entire trip. Many ships provided no third class dining room and required passengers to wash their own tin dishes in a barrel of cold seawater. Steerage passengers on Oldenburg fared much better. Third class amenities offered tables and chairs in the cargo hold, allowing them to sit while dining, and they did not have to wash their own dishes.

My third day out I walked the deck. As the teal-blue sky became tar black, I hurried toward my cabin. The first wind-driven splatter of rain slapped my face, and droplets of water fell from the overhangs. I stood, feet frozen to the deck as the ship was tossed by the sea, letting the rain wash away the salt spray that had gathered on my cheeks and forehead. The rainfall became more intense. Large drops pounded against the canopies that covered the lifeboats.

The wind-driven rain continued. I grabbed the railings as the entire ship pitched fore and aft. The severe storm tossed Oldenburg like a toy. I crawled hand-over-hand along the railing until reaching my cabin, where I stayed, seasick, for two days. The rough seas extended the trip by a day. Effects of the bad weather were difficult for me, but must have been more so for residents of the lower decks. I only went below after the sun shone and seas calmed.

During the crossing, weather permitting, I walked the first and second-class decks even in the rain. Below deck I observed my fellow emigrants, third-class travelers, and listened to their comments; why they tolerated such grim conditions. The most frequent reply was, "Tickets are more affordable."

Most were away from farms or villages for the first time. They followed the orders of any person who appeared in charge or wore a uniform. By virtue of their station in life, third-class passengers were accustomed to tolerating poor conditions.

The state of living status on board the ship did not seem so outrageous to the less sophisticated steerage passengers. They tolerated their plight because they felt helpless to change it. In contrast, first- and second-class passengers often spoke English or the language of the particular shipping line. They felt confident, and not shy about grumbling or taking crew members to task for any issue not up to their expectations. It may seem strange to you as you listen to my story, but times were different then.

Millions of immigrants traveled the Atlantic, but few investigated the vessel from stem to stern, fore and aft, first to third class and top to bottom as I did. My first-hand observations of the contrast between the benefits of upper classes and frustrations of those below remain with me to this day.

During my treks below deck I discovered other problems that plagued third-class passengers besides unsanitary conditions. Gamblers and card sharps attempted to separate the poor from what little cash they carried, and scoundrels preyed on women and girls, whether single and traveling alone, or married and traveling with their families.

Rogues who preyed on the poorest of passengers, often crew members, spent time in steerage spreading tales of their connections in America. Those connections, as the stories were told, ranged from the promise of jobs, to land investment schemes, to living accommodations and ploys suggesting they could allow third-class passengers to bypass the humiliation of exit lines and health checks upon arrival. The scam artists often targeted girls and young women with tales of their ability to make things easier for them and their families "…if only they would be friendly."

Card sharps and swindlers also preyed on first-class passengers. They were not crew members, but well-dressed men who appeared to be wealthy, and mingled with other first-class passengers, availed themselves of the libraries, card rooms, deck games, smoking rooms, and other entertainment, all while fleecing their shipmates. But the far more heinous crimes took place below deck against passengers taken advantage of by the very employees hired to serve and protect them.

By this time I had become so confident that I rarely used my walking stick. When not exploring the ship I spent time in the smoking room where cigars, tobacco and cigarette rolling paper were complimentary. First and second-class male passengers enjoyed a respite from the ship's activities and relaxed in solitude, read magazines, or just snooze if they desired.

Another passenger, also with a second-class ticket, frequented the smoking room. He wore a rumpled suit, smoked a pipe, and nodded to me each day as we sat in silence. The man appeared to be in his late twenties, wore thick wire-rim eyeglasses, was short and stout, and had a receding hairline. At first, I thought him to be an agent of the cruise line, and viewed him with suspicion. Eventually I decided he was just a middle-class worker, probably businessman or government employee.

One afternoon, he extended his hand and said, in English, "Karl Blackburn. I thought we should formally meet."

I had no idea what he'd said, so I smiled, nodded, and did not return his comment, for his language was totally foreign to me. The man again spoke, "Do you speak English?" I shrugged and shook my head. Karl tried again, this time in German, *"Sprechen sie Deutsch? Do you speak German?"* I nodded but said nothing, and Karl returned to his newspaper and pipe.

That night I considered the behavior of the stranger in the smoking room. Perhaps we could establish a casual relationship and when the ship docked, exit together. I rehearsed what I would say when I next saw the man.

Sure enough, Karl arrived at the same location the following day and I was prepared. I said, in perfect German, "I am sorry if I seemed rude yesterday. My name is Hans. Hans Richter."

"Karl Blackburn. Very pleased to meet you, Hans Richter," he stuttered in halting, poor German while extending his hand. "Sorry, but my German is a little off. You smoke?" He tapped the ashes out of his pipe and placed it in his pocket. Then he picked up two cigars and offered me one.

"No, thank you, I don't care for cigars, but I see men rolling their own cigarettes. I might try that."

"There is a trick to it. I learned to roll them in college, but not very well. Let me show you. Follow what I do."

Karl picked up a booklet of rolling papers, blew on them to separate the pages, then slid one out with thumb, handed it to me, and took one for himself.

He reached into the humidor and pinched a wad of loose tobacco, placing it in the center of the cigarette paper. He tried to spread it evenly but rolled it into a poor-looking cylinder, fat in the center and thin on each end. I mimicked him, trying to do the same but lost about half the tobacco.

We both laughed and Karl said, "I never did master it, either. That's why I stick to pipes and cigars. Try one."

Still playing the part of Hans, German diplomat, I smiled and took the cigar. I tried to follow his moves, biting off one end, spitting it onto the floor, lighting the other, and inhaling. I ended up in a coughing fit, eyes watering and nose running.

When we both finished laughing and coughing, I pointed to the cigar and said, "My first. Maybe my last."

"I usually don't light them. Just chew them. Keeps my mind occupied." He showed me that one end of his cigar was badly frayed. He kept talking. "I just graduated from college and got my first job with the government in Washington, D.C. They sent me to Europe for training. This is the second half of my first transatlantic crossing."

Karl spoke German rather poorly, apologizing profusely for it. He managed to tell me he had studied the language as a student at the University of Pittsburgh and knew textbook German well, but his pronunciation was poor. I smiled to myself at the irony that a well-educated American with a college education spoke German so poorly while I, a Bosnian peasant, spoke the language well.

As he spoke I studied his face and realized Karl was not much older than me. I guessed he was probably around Hans's age. "Speaking to you is my first opportunity to try German in a social setting."

We made small talk. He spoke freely about himself, but I carefully avoided revealing anything of a personal nature. After that initial meeting we met regularly, and I practiced rolling cigarettes daily until I mastered the art—one that I practiced the rest of my life. By the end of the journey I knew much about the chatty Karl, but had revealed little about myself.

Besides meeting my newfound friend in the smoking room each day, I continued my regular excursions on the ship, passing through first and second class as well as steerage. By this time word must have spread among the crew because each sailor on duty bowed and unlocked the gate for me. I was never again challenged.

While walking in steerage I heard familiar chatter. Several men were smoking, drinking beer and playing cards. I walked to the edge of the group and listened. They spoke in my native language about jobs awaiting them in the steel mills of America. I pretended not to pay attention to the conversation while I observed the card game.

For hours the game and conversation went on. Finally, the group broke up and men scattered. I walked silently past them, nodding and smiling. I heard one Bosnian say to another, "Look at the stupid German in his fine suit. Doesn't understand a word we're saying. Just watches us play." Then he turned to me; "Isn't that right, jackass?" Looking back to his mates he added, "Maybe I'll invite him to play. If we work together we can clean him out."

The men laughed and I smiled, nodded, and walked on, maintaining the charade of not understanding them. The following day, after leaving Karl, I again walked to the area where my countrymen drank, talked, and played cards. I nodded and smiled at them and they nodded back at me. They called me *Magarac Njemacji,* the German jackass.

The central figure of the group, a tall lanky fellow with frizzy hair and a beard, had a misshapen face and a scar that ran from below his eye and disappeared into his beard. In a gravelly voice and using hand gestures, he invited me to play cards with them. I shrugged, and he repeated the invitation. But I knew their scheme and declined, shaking my head. They returned to their card game while sharing their hopes and dreams and plans for work in America.

Frizzy Hair said, "Well if the boss man won't play, I guess I'll miss my payday on this trip." His cohorts laughed.

I listened closely to the plan he and the men repeated daily. Upon leaving the ship they would go to the train station and buy a ticket to 'Peetz-borg.' When the train arrived in 'Peetz-borg' they would buy another ticket to 'Carlee-roy' where relatives and friends would meet them, and plenty of work awaited them in the steel mill. I decided I would do the same. I'd find my way to 'Carlee-roy' then find somebody who spoke Bosnian or German and get directions to the steel mill and find work. By the end of the journey, I was confident that

I could get to the steel mills and be hired. My first choice for work would be a farm with horses, but I would take whatever job I could find to earn a living.

Each day after I took my daily dose of nostalgia, listening to the card players, I returned to the smoking room to visit with Karl, who continued to be forthcoming about his life. "I grew up in a small mill town and studied Political Science at the University of Pittsburgh. I'm currently attending night classes at Georgetown near Washington, D.C. and working toward a law degree."

I nodded as though I understood, but between Karl's poor pronunciation of words and names that were foreign to me, I didn't grasp much of what he said. Some words like Political Science and Georgetown I guessed were places of which I'd never heard. I did recognize the name of the city that I heard during the card games: Peetz-borg, and wondered if Karl might be from Carlee-roy.

I lit a hand rolled cigarette and took a long drag, letting the smoke drift through my nostrils and climb to the ceiling. "Tell me about Pittsburgh."

He needed no further prodding. "Well, Pittsburgh is located about 300 miles from Baltimore, where we will dock. It is the meeting point of three rivers. America's first president, George Washington had a fort built at the point where the three rivers meet. Plenty of steel mills line the rivers for the steel industry, and though the air can be a little smoky, is a beautiful city. You should visit it some day."

I pretended to understand, but the names sounded like made-up words to me, so I smiled. "I will do my best to get to Pittsburgh, my friend. I am certain it is everything you say and more."

The *SS Oldenburg* docked a little after ten, the morning of March 15, 1907, and passengers soon began to disembark. I had the steward pack all but my walking stick, which I used to continue my swagger, inside my suitcase, tipped him, and waited on the promenade un-til I saw Karl. By the time we joined one another many first and second-class passengers had already left the ship. At first I thought I might wait for the steerage passengers, and disembark among them. It might be easier. But I remembered Herr Richter's plan, so I stood and chatted with Karl until nearly all-first and second-class passen-gers disembarked. At the last moment he said, "Shall we go?"

I sidled up next to him, took his arm with one hand and used the walking stick with the other, walked down the ramp in my fine German clothes with my new-found friend and conversed with him. I nodded and smiled at the exit guard just as I had rehearsed. The guard glanced briefly at my documents, and without looking at Karl's documents, must have assumed both were German diplomats. The guard said to us both, *"Willkommen heiben America."*

Karl responded, *"Danke schön,"* then said to me, "I guess our conversations have improved my language skills. Thank you for the company on this trip, Hans, my friend. You made it much more pleasant than the eastbound crossing. I hope one day our paths will again cross."

I nodded. "That is my wish as well. Godspeed."

We shook hands, bowed to one another, and went our separate ways.

(tape ends)

After several seconds the tape tripped the OFF switch. The room-ful of cousins sat rapt until Francie stood up to change cassettes. She was quiet as she approached the machine.

After a moment or two, George, the youngest cousin, broke the spell. "Well, that explains his ability to speak German, but by my accounting he must have been about eighteen at this point in his life. He was ninety when Baba died and ninety-two when he made the tape. He didn't pass away until ten years after that. I think the family can agree none of us ever heard him talk in German. It's amazing that he retained the language that long. I wonder if Baba knew."

Kathy shook her head, "What was even more amazing to me is that after more than eighty years in America he didn't learn to speak English."

John stood and stretched. "Is that the end of the tapes? If so, I need to be going. If not, maybe we should play the rest tomorrow."

Maryann answered. "No, there is one more full tape. Let's take a break, get some more food or another beer and meet back here. I can hardly wait to find out how he got from Baltimore to Pittsburgh, and how he ended up in Clairton then Monaca."

"I'm guessing he just took a train from Baltimore. After all, New York, Philadelphia, and Baltimore were the primary ports of entry in those days. I'm guessing train transportation was pretty common."

"Well, from what we've heard so far, I wouldn't be surprised if he had another adventure," added Kathy.

"I still can't believe it," said Francie. "He was so kind, gentle and quiet. I never heard him raise his voice. Who would have guessed he had a past? Well, at least that evil Hans is out of his life. I wonder what ever happened to that sicko."

Once the cousins were reseated around the large room the last tape was reset and the narrative continued.

The tape hissed. After a brief silence the familiar German accented voice of the professor began:

"This is Franz Friedrich Volk, Professor Emeritus in the German Language Studies Department at the University of Pittsburgh and a native speaker of the German language. What continues is a verbatim translation of the third and last tape of Peter Novak, an unknown American hero."

THIRD LIFE—AMERICA

11

STRANGER IN A STRANGE LAND

My shipboard charade as Hans Richter, low-level diplomat went without a hitch, just as Herr Richter had predicted. Officials took little notice of me during the crossing. First and second-class passengers were presumed to be well to do. Many traveled with staff and therefore did not require the scrutiny that awaited the unwashed masses in steerage.

There was no way my forged documents would have allowed me to successfully navigate the intense scrutiny placed upon the huddled masses of steerage passengers. Too many questions asked. I surely would have been found out. Herr Richter must have known this when he purchased the more expensive second-class passage. The chance meeting of Karl Blackburn was fortunate, as it assured the plan worked.

Once ashore, we collected our luggage, said our goodbyes and Karl disappeared into the crowd to find his way back to Washington, D.C. I stood on the dock admiring the beauty of the gigantic stone port of entry building and Baltimore's vibrant waterfront. Across the harbor, to the north of me construction workers vigorously rebuilt much of the area that had been decimated by fire three years earlier.

At my side on the wooden pier sat my new, expensive suitcase, another gift from Herr Richter. It contained all my earthly belongings—which were not many; one set of work clothes, socks, toiletries, a pair of work shoes, a couple of changes of underwear, and a heavy winter coat with a cache of American dollars sewn into the lining. I now felt a little silly using the walking stick that I no longer needed.

In the pocket of the winter coat my slingshot was hidden next to a Catholic crucifix Marija had insisted I carry so God would watch over me. I did not wear the crucifix since my family was not Roman Catholic, but it worked so far.

First stop was a men's lavatory, where I changed clothes, replacing my fine tailored suit, topcoat, starched white travel shirt, fancy gentleman's shoes, and expensive woolen topcoat with the work clothes, comfortable walking boots, knit cap, and winter coat from the suitcase. I did this for two reasons. First, I felt much more comfortable in the clothes of a common man rather than those of the elite. Second, I did not want to stand out in a crowd. Now in America, I wanted to blend in and find my way to a place that offered work.

I had not undone the lining in the winter coat I now wore, so I didn't know the exact amount of money that Marija had sewn into it, but it certainly must have contained at least a few hundred American dollars. I planned to retrieve cash as needed, but for the moment left it safely hidden. I pulled the heavy winter coat snugly over my work clothes, felt my trusty slingshot inside my breast pocket, and stuffed the forged travel documents in my side pocket. In the other side pocket I crammed tobacco, cigarette papers, and matches, gifts from the ship's smoking room.

As I left the building, a brisk wind slapped my face and chapped my lips, making the forty-degree temperature seem chillier. The overcast sky threatened rain and the air felt heavy with smoke from nearby factories. After traveling several paces from the lavatory, I realized I'd left my walking stick behind. No matter. I no longer needed it to help me be Hans. My new life was about to begin without walking sticks, or bleached hair, or makeup. I pulled the knitted cap down around my forehead and ears and lit out from the docks, suitcase in hand.

It was not long before I heard the familiar strains of my native Bosnian language. The speaker had a Croatian accent.

"Excuse me, sir," I began in my native tongue, "I heard you speaking to that couple in Croatian. Can I ask you a question?"

"Of course. My name is Drago. I work as a translator. How can I help you?"

"What is the best way to travel to Pittsburgh?"

"Pittsburgh is in the state of Pennsylvania, northwest of us. From the Camden Train Station, you want to take the Baltimore and Ohio Rail line, we call it the "B and O," to Cumberland. There you will change trains to Pittsburgh. The train on track number two will leave for Cumberland this evening. From Cumberland you will transfer to another "B and O" train to Pittsburgh. You will follow the setting sun. It is an enjoyable, beautiful ride."

The translator pointed me in the direction of Camden Station and gave easy to follow directions, then he nodded, turned, and walked away. I left the docks, walking along Nicholson Street when I spied a deserted dead-end alley. The alley curved as I stepped deeper into its passage, until I was at a place where I could be seen by neither the crowd that passed nearby, nor prying eyes within.

There, alone among a city full of people, I kept my promise to my benefactor. Using matches from the ship, I struck the one on the brick street, and touched it to the passport documents. As the forged travel papers erupted in flames, all references to Hans Richter in America were extinguished. Watching the paper crackle, I knew my own youth, and my life in the entire old country, burned in the same flame. I could never again cross the ocean or return to Europe. I was now an American, however an undocumented one. No official record showed Peter Novak had ever arrived in the United States. As the flames scorched my hand, I dropped the burning embers to the ground and watched them disappear. I had just become a non-person, a man living in America but a man without a country. Peter Novak no longer existed.

I left the backstreet and continued to make my way to Camden Station to purchase a train ticket. I had not purchased passage beyond Baltimore, of course, because I didn't know my final destination when I boarded the ship. At the ticket counter I requested purchase of a ticket to Pittsburgh using my native Bosnian language. "*Je li ovo gdje sam kupiti kartu?*"

The clerk, a pimply-faced young man appeared to be about my age, and wearing a new, freshly starched white shirt, buttoned to the neck. He seemed to be aggravated at the collar, as he tugged at it in an effort to ease the red irritation that banded his neck. While he was helping the person ahead of me, I noticed the ticket seller fumbled with papers and seemed clumsy and new to the job, repeatedly asking the clerk next to him for help. In response to my question, he shrugged his shoulders and responded in English. I didn't understand what he said but I'm sure it was something like, "I can't understand what you are saying."

I tried again, this time in German. "*Ich brauche ein Ticket für den Zug zu kaufen.*"

The ticket seller again answered, but this time in a louder, more irritated voice. I'm guessing his comment was, "I have no idea what you want. I cannot understand you. Can't you speak English?"

Not wanting to draw attention to myself, I picked up my grip, turned, and walked away frustrated and ticketless, trying to melt back into the crowd. My face reddened. I felt uncomfortable as several patrons, hearing the clerk raise his voice, looked in my direction, and was relieved when a young man approached me and spoke in what I think was Italian. When that did not work, he tried several other languages until he asked the question in German. "Can I help you sir?"

"I need to buy passage to Pittsburgh and beyond to Carlee-roy but the boy at the ticket counter couldn't understand my request."

"My apologies for the behavior of my rude and ignorant countryman, Sir. A man of your standing should not have been treated in such a manner. You are at the wrong station. I will take you to the one you need. Did you just arrive?"

I nodded.

"First time in the U.S.?"

"*Ja.*" I answered.

"The clerk was probably a new hire. There are so many new arrivals that clerks are often not fully trained. If your clerk does not understand, simply say, 'Pittsburgh.' That should work.

"You are at the wrong station. The other station is nearby. Follow me. I will buy the ticket for you—first class for the price of second. My brother works at the ticket counter on Pratt Street."

He picked up my new, expensive suitcase and sailed through the crowd, with me doing my best to keep up. Soon we were away from the station, away from the crowds, away from the railroad tracks, and away from any building that resembled a train depot. The young man shouted to hail somebody.

A second youth came into view. Just as I was about to ask if this was his brother, the boy carrying my bag swung it around and hit me with it, square in the stomach, full force, sending me sprawling to the ground and knocking the breath out of me.

The second boy joined his partner in crime, and sliced at me with a knife, then kicked me in the head, stunning me momentarily, as the two took off with my suitcase.

Dazed, I sat up, reached to the ground and picked up two pebbles, each about the size of a marble, and took off after the thieves. As the gap between us began to narrow, I slid my hand into my coat pocket and pulled out my trusted sling shot. The two thieves continued to run.

I dropped to one knee, pulled back the rubber, took aim, and let a missile fly. In a heartbeat the pebble struck the boy carrying the bag, squarely in the back below his neck. He stumbled forward, letting go of the case, and it skittered across the bricks. He extended both hands to brace his fall as he staggered toward the ground. His cohort turned just as the second missile hit. With a shriek of pain, the second boy dropped his knife, grabbed his shoulder, and took off running, leaving his friend alone on the ground and groaning.

With my head still throbbing from the kick, I walked over to the boy sitting on the pavement, shook my finger at him, and said, *Du bist ein schlechter mensch,* "You are a bad person." I picked up the suitcase, tucked the knife into my belt, and walked back toward Camden Station.

The walk cleared my head, and I took a moment to assess my assets and liabilities. I was a hard worker. I knew how to farm, make wine, tend and groom horses. I could do any number of things that I learned during my years on the Richter estate. I spoke no English and my Bosnian was poor, but my German was crisp and clear, thanks to Professor Braun. I knew I'd survive somehow. My capacity for languages made me a curiosity to be sure.

As I approached the railway station, I thought I recognized a familiar face from the docks. When we locked eyes, I recognized Drago, the Croatian translator who had been so helpful at the pier. I wondered what he was doing here at the station. He was speaking to a policeman and pointing toward me. "There he is! That's him! That's the one! Look at the new suitcase!"

I glanced at the suitcase in my hand and cursed it as a traitor. The fine luggage had given me away as a peasant with a rich man's property. Drago surely thought I'd stolen it.

The looks on their faces spelled danger to me. I took a hesitant step away from the two men, and the police officer's words, "Stop! Thief," needed no translation.

Drago commanded me, in my Bosnian language, to halt. Confused, I complied. The officer grabbed the case from my hand. The clasp came undone and it opened, spilling contents onto the platform—all items that would be in the possession of a wealthy German businessman.

I stood in dismay, unable to understand commands of the Irish officer but I clearly understood Drago as he yelled at me, "You're going to prison, you dirty Bosnian thief."

I'd just burned the passage ticket and documents that might have cleared or convicted me. In an effort to save myself, I turned on my heel and sprinted away, running for my life. The distance between us increased.

The policeman stopped chasing me, lifted a whistle to his lips, and with a hearty toot, summoned other officers. Hearing the whistle caused me to panic, turn back toward my pursuers, and grab a stone. I loosed the slingshot from my coat pocket, took aim, and let fly a missile, hitting the sergeant in the chest with enough force to knock the wind out of him and silence the shrieking alarm.

The Croatian raced toward me. I let a second stone soar that struck him on the kneecap. He stumbled. I turned and fled as fast and far as I could go. Turning onto Howard Street toward Pratt, where the two thieves had led me, I continued running until my lungs were about to burst. Then, after looking back and seeing nobody following me, I slowed to a brisk walk as I gasped for breath, continuing to move as quickly as I could, turning right, then left, then right again, in a serpentine way, hoping to lose my pursuers..

By the time I felt safe enough to stop, I had crossed a bridge and was well away from the docks and railway station. I must have come several miles and reached the outskirts of the city. The urban setting gave way to woods and the paved streets deteriorated to little more than a poorly maintained wagon path.

I sprinted off the wagon path several hundred yards, and into the cover of trees and undergrowth, where I sat on a log and cried. Fear gripped tightly at my throat as paranoia erased the happy thoughts I'd had earlier. I couldn't remember the last time I'd wept. I felt as helpless as a sparrow with a broken wing. My tears flowed. I was exhausted. Tension from two weeks playing the role of Hans followed by the events at Camden Station had drained me. Despair loomed over my heart like a dark cloud.

Perhaps it was the release of tension after two weeks playing the part of Hans when I knew I could never really fill his shoes. It might have been because I came so close to getting caught and losing everything, disappointing Herr Richter, failing and being deported as a criminal.

I loved my master dearly, but knew I could never be the gentleman he hoped I'd become. I came so close to getting caught and losing everything, disappointing Herr Richter, and putting him and myself at risk of being arrested. I felt like such a bungler, unable to cope with this overwhelming life.

I wondered, how many policemen had seen my face? Were they combing the streets and woods, looking for me at this very moment?

What a clever boy I was, managing to avoid all the risks of second-class travel and the humiliations and dangers of steerage, only to be scammed by thugs. What an idiot. Hairy Face and his friends were right to call me Jackass. I was a complete failure!

My life was overwhelming. I wanted my daily routine back. I wanted the smell of the barn and the garden tingling in my nostrils, and the touch of Marija's hand on my shoulder. I feel unsafe, and especially fearful of being seen near the train depot or the docks.

I'm not sure how long I wallowed in my self-pity, but eventually must have fallen asleep. I opened my eyes to a clear, starry night sky. I regained my composure and considered my circumstances. Were the authorities still combing the docks, railway station, streets and woods looking for me? Had they posted my description among the constabulary to be on the lookout? I dared not board any trains leaving Baltimore or I'd surely be recognized and immediately arrested. I'm not even sure I could find the train station. Forget the train. I'd walk to Pittsburgh, or somewhere. Anywhere, just to get away from this place, or at least far enough away from Baltimore that nobody could identify me.

A full moon smiled down, easing my feelings of gloom. I realized I'd had nothing to eat or drink since this morning. I was thirsty down to my toenails, and my stomach felt like it was shaking hands with my backbone.

An owl hooted above my head. Aha, could this be a sign my life was beginning to improve? Carefully, I slid the slingshot from my pocket, placed a pebble in the center and shot. Missed. I was so hungry my hand shook as I aimed. Tried and missed again as the "Whoo" of the owl mocked me. I steadied myself, held my shaking hand against my knee and let loose a third shot. This time I heard a screech and the bird fell next to me. Dinner.

I had never seen an owl up close. The talons and hooked beak made me realize this bird is was a raptor. The contents off its stomach, decomposing mice, confirmed it was a bird of prey. Had there had been any doubt, the contents proved it.

I didn't start a campfire for fear of being seen, so I tried eating the bird raw, but the taste was terrible. The bird was all sinew and feathers. The few bites I managed to get down, came back up. Marija would have fainted had she watched me tear the bloody carcass apart with my fingers and the dull knife, courtesy of the two hooligans.

The skimpy, tasteless meal was something I'd hoped would tide me over until morning. It did not, so I looked and listened for other animals but my only companion that night was a growling stomach.

I curled up under my lumpy winter coat, and awoke a few minutes before sunrise. Though it was mid-march, a light frost had set during the night. The birds announced daybreak.

As I stood and stretched, working out the kinks that had accumulated from sleeping on the unforgiving ground, a noise caused me to pique my ears. What sounded like dogs lapping up their drink turned out to be a crystal clear, running spring. After dining on wild berries, washed down with fresh, clear water, my trek away from Baltimore carried on. My shoes were old enough to be comfortable and not cause blisters, but had plenty of wear left.

Determining my direction from the rising sun, I returned to the poorly-kept road, and walked north until noon, away from the route that the B&O train would be traveling, and following roads that were little more than rutted wagon trails and walking paths.

Late that morning I came upon a kiosk along the roadside, and a gate that blocked passage. A man emerged from the hut and said something to me in English. His tone was not threatening as he held out his hand to me. I extended my hand to shake but he withdrew his, and repeated his words.

I responded, *"Ich nicht Englisch sprechen."*

A feeling of fear began to rise from the pit of my stomach. This must be a border crossing. It looked just like the ones in Europe, and the man demanded my papers, which, of course I did not have. I was puzzled, sure that Herr Richter had told me there would be no border crossings in America. No need to show papers once safely off the ship.

The man then took a coin in one hand, held it up, and placed it in the other, and pointed to a sign, which of course I was unable to read, but I gathered he was trying to collect a bribe or fee before checking my travel documents and lifting the gate to let me pass.

Fearful of being arrested, I turned and raced for the woods, leaving the border guard shaking his fist and shouting after me. I stayed there, avoiding any person that might question my status.

I tarried in the woods, wondering what my plan would be. My stomach again began to wonder if my throat had been cut. With the sun was directly overhead, my noontime meal consisted of eating more berries for lunch. The woods were rife with sustenance.

Having grown up in a one-room shack with five siblings, I'd always coveted my solitude and felt no fear as I meandered through the woodland, walking parallel to the road but far enough away to not be spotted. My trek that day continued for several hours until dusk. I settled in under a large oak tree and sat quietly, watching for movement in the brush. My second dinner in America consisted of a rabbit, thanks to my slingshot, and wild berries for dessert. I was deep enough into the forest that the small fire would not attract attention.

Thinking back to the flea market and Nenad, and remembering the first time I'd killed a rabbit for dinner I recalled what a great time we had! I chewed the rabbit meat, and a chill ran through me as I remembered the rabbit that Hans had tortured, until I put it out of its misery.

My succession of traumas had begun with the visit of the soldier's arrival at the estate. After that, my life became one stressful situation after another. I needed time to unwind and dispel the paranoia that sat like a rock in the middle of my body. In order to heal, decided to spend as much time as I needed alone in the wilds of this great country, living off the land. I built a lean-to near a brook, and spent the next several months resting and repairing, rarely venturing more than a mile or two from my camp unless it was to pull up stakes and wander to another camp. I saw no other people for the next few months as I moved stealthily through the woods. Though I passed several farms, I avoided them. I was not ready to show myself.

I'd lived off the land during much of my early life so my trek was as good an introduction to America as I could have had. I wove a backpack from vines in which I carried my coat and occasional game, fruit, and other food. I learned to feel the plants that grew in the wilderness, smell and touch them to see how they responded. Wild blueberries, one of my favorite treats, grew on low bushes that spread across the ground like a carpet. There is nothing like the smell of a woodland in the summer after a rain.

Besides the fruits and berries, ripe in the summer and autumn sun, and the game so readily available, plenty of unspoiled streams full of fish ran through the rolling hills, expanding my appreciation for this place. This was a land of plenty.

∽

I'm not sure how far I'd come during the summer months, or where exactly I was, but as the surroundings showed signs of summer's ending, my wilderness habitat gave way to farmland. My confidence had returned and I ventured out onto roads. The summer sun warmed my back as I walked.

During my time in the forest and along the farmlands, I realized America did not seem much different than Bosnia, or even Germany. This country is more rustic than the manicured estate property, but more bountiful.

I awoke at the crack of dawn each morning and sucked the fresh air deep into my lungs, then made myself tea, using local leaves. I'd created several different kinds of tea from local tree and bush leaves.

After tea, my custom was to take a walk. Early one morning I walked along a road, feeling so positive that I nodded and waved to a few buggies and an occasional auto that passed. By now I had seen plenty of automobiles and didn't care for them. They were noisy, frightened horses, and I felt certain the noisy, smoking, stinking machines wouldn't be around for long.

On my third day walking in civilization, a horse and buggy driven by a bearded man dressed in black called to me as he passed. *"Guten morgen,"* a German greeting.

I called back, also in German, "And a good morning to you, Sir."

The buggy driver, caught off guard at hearing another person speak his language, pulled the reins tightly on the horse. He held up and waited for me then asked, "Where are you going and how do you come to speak my language?"

His language was coarse. Not like Karl's but more like that of a German farmer. "I recently arrived from Germany and am walking from Baltimore. How is it you speak the language, my friend?"

He wrapped the reins around the whip holder and grinned a

toothy grin. "We are farmers. My father came to this country to escape religious persecution and he purchased a farm just outside York. Americans call us plain people. We are many."

The boy, about my age, or perhaps a bit younger, chubby with rosy cheeks had a smile that did not leave his face. "My name is Herman, Herman Lutz. Will thee please ride with me? I would very much like the company."

"Thank you for your kindness, Herman Lutz. My name is Peter."

I climbed into the buggy and we rode together to Herman's parent's farm. He appeared different from the farmers I'd seen in Bosnia and Germany. He wore a dark-colored suit, a straight-cut coat without lapels, broadfall trousers, and suspenders. His shirt seemed to be from hand spun muslin. The black socks and shoes were similar to my own. On his head was a broad-brimmed straw hat.

I noticed his shirt fastened with buttons, but his suit coats and vests fastened with hooks and eyes. It was an outfit that I had not seen before.

As we rode he asked, "How doest thou like America so far?"

"It is almost like being back in Germany, except the soil here seems to be richer and land is made up of long rolling hills rather than mountains."

Herman added, "And we can worship as we please. Our families and farms are our top priorities, second only to God."

He continued, "What think thee of out toll road? Have you ever seen one before?"

"Toll road? I do not understand."

"York Road, part of the Baltimore and Yorktown Turnpike. It is a privately owned, poorly maintained, toll road. It is the primary highway from here to Baltimore and requires one to pay a fee to use it. Collectors are posted in tollhouses to collect for use of the road. The fees are to be used for maintenance, but the road is poorly maintained while the owners get rich from the tolls." He laughed a hearty belly laugh. "I assumed that was the way you traveled."

I thought of my fears that the toll house was a border crossing that required papers, and joined him in the belly laugh.

"No I came through the woods. I've been camping for months. I plan to walk to Pittsburgh to find work."

He stared at my knapsack. "Did thee make this thyself? It is beautifully crafted."

"I did, thank you Herman."

"I wish thee luck in thy quest, Peter, but tonight thee must dine with my family."

Time went by quickly as we chatted until we arrived at his farm.

Herman introduced me to his parents, *"Mutter, Vater, Dies ist Peter,"* then to his five brothers and two sisters, all farmers. The girls giggled.

"They want to know if thee are married since thee has a beard."

I blushed and said nothing, just shook my head..

Herman's mother intervened. "Thee shall be our guest tonight. Dine with us on the bounty the Lord has provided."

We enjoyed a delicious dinner, then went to bed early. I slept in the barn, and felt much more at home here than I had while crossing the ocean in my luxurious cabin.

I awoke again at the crack of dawn to discover the family already working in the fields, harvesting their fall crops. I joined them and helped them reap their harvest, working hard and having fun. That evening after a considerable amount of praying over supper, I said, " You have been most gracious, but I must leave in the morning."

The following morning I found Herman, his father and brothers had gone to the field, and his mother and sisters working in the house. "Take this knapsack. It is packed with food and items thee will need as thee travels."

"Thank you Mrs. Lutz. You have a wonderful family and a fine son."

I left my hand woven vine-knapsack as a memento for Herman.

The bite of autumn air was a mere nibble that year. With the morning sun at my back, my journey westward began on a beautiful Indian summer day. I trod walking paths and roads that would one day become part of the Lincoln Highway, while stopping often to admire my surroundings. Autumn in the forest came alive. A choir of birds announced my presence and welcomed me to their home. Slivers of blue sky peeked at me through the canopy above, like reflections through shards of glass. The surrounding air, rich with the aromas of fresh soil, rotting leaves, and trees taller than the longest mast on a ship, provided a cool breeze.

Leaves of fall colors crackled underfoot. Stalks of Indian corn grew wild along the road. I watched a family of squirrels scamper up an oak tree and store acorns for the coming winter. Another squirrel scampered halfway up a tree trunk then leapt to the ground. Birds of many colors flew from limb to limb high in the canopy, chirping and chasing one another. Their flapping wings caused berries to fall, providing food for rabbits and other animals on the ground. Twigs crackled under the hooves of deer that ran throughout. Outside the forests, miles of farmlands dotted the edges of the area. Occasionally a wild turkey would cross my path and after killing it I always shared the meat with fellow travelers or farmers along the way.

I climbed mountains, and occasionally walked along railroad tracks toward the setting sun. Some days I dined alone, other times with hobos, some of whom spoke my native language. Many hobos spoke various German dialects and languages of Eastern and Central

Europe. Though certainly not a Biblical scholar, the chatter sounded at times like the description of the Tower of Babel. Somehow the languages blended and with the help of hand gestures, communication was achieved.

Along the way I sometimes stopped at farms and offered my labor, chopping wood or helping with chores in exchange for coffee and essentials. At one house I knocked and a woman answered. She spoke neither Bosnian nor German, but with a combination of pidgin and mime I asked, "Do you need help on your farm?

A man came to the door, his arm in a sling. He spoke no German and I spoke little American, but I understood that he had been injured and needed help tending his animals. I stayed at the farm for two weeks, doing chores that required two strong hands, chopping wood, and doing odd jobs. When he was able to get back to work, he rewarded me with a canteen, lard, and a frypan, all of which I used in my travels. Some farmers gave me small amounts of cash in exchange for my labor.

Plentiful game ran throughout in the rolling hills of Pennsylvania, which suited my living off the land. I thought of the poachers whose biggest crime was the taking of food from the Richter estate. Their sins mirrored my style of living, except the estate of Pennsylvania seemed to have no laws against poaching.

Fellow travelers and residents gave me directions in Bosnian, German, and pantomime to confirm my route to Pittsburgh. The weather changed as late summer became autumn and autumn, winter. Had one walked briskly each day, stopping only to eat and sleep, a person could have made the trip in about a month. But my pace was easy as I was in no hurry, and became just another hobo easing my way westward.

Mild temperatures that winter were pleasant, and I took shelter in barns, under trees, and occasionally in parked railcars with fellow hobos. On one such occasion, heavy rain drove me into an abandoned barn that was occupied by a group of hobos. A small fire smoldered on the dirt floor. I nodded a greeting and offered meat from a wild turkey taken earlier that day. Several men playing cards glanced up at me. I immediately recognized one. The tramp that sat nearest the fire had a misshapen face and scar that ran from below his eye, disappearing into his beard. Frizzy Hair, the Bosnian who tried to goad me into gambling aboard the ship held the floor, telling of card games and other high sea adventures.

Interrupting his story and speaking in the Bosnian language I said, "Good morning. Can a traveler get a cup of coffee? It goes well with this turkey I have to share."

It was clear that an irritated Frizzy Hair didn't recognize me, for I'd been walking the woods for months and had become disheveled, bearded and of course, without my proper travel attire.

"Sit down hobo," he said, handing me a steaming cup. "Welcome, stranger. We're about to start a card game. We will cook your turkey while we play cards. You're Bosnian?"

I nodded, making eye contact with Frizzy Hair, "You're quite the card player. What happened to your pals? Did they ever find work in the place you were seeking?"

He stared at me blankly. "Do you know me?"

"Of course I do. You were the best card player on the ship. You and your friends planned to find work in a place near "Peetz-borg." But here you are by yourself. What happened? Didn't like the work?"

I enjoyed the teasing him and watching his bewilderment.

He studied my face suspiciously. "I have not seen my fellow Bosnians since shortly after I left the ship. I don't know you. Who are you and how do you know me?"

"We crossed the ocean together on the Oldenburg." I smiled and sipped my coffee without saying more.

Frizzy Hair studied me for several more moments. "I don't remember you. How do you know so much about me and my friends? After spending two weeks in that hell hole of the ship I'm sure I knew the face of every man down there. Maybe I would recognize you without the beard."

"Perhaps. But you might also recognize me if I wore a fine tailored suit and stood for hours without a word, watching you take money from the other players."

He paused, giving the matter serious thought, "The German Jackass? It cannot be. I had no idea you were Bosnian. How could it be that a man of means ended up penniless and a hobo?"

"You assume many things, my friend, about my so-called wealth then and now. I cannot say why I traveled as I did but you can surely tell from my speech that I am from the earth – I was a Bosnian farmer same as you. Peter Novak from Šišljavić."

I extended my hand and after a moment's hesitation we first shook hands, then embraced like old friends.

"My name is Tahir Virkkula. I come from Nahorevo, a small village near Sarajevo, traveled with four friends. Two were my cousins. We received letters that told of work in Carlee-roi, a town near Peetzborg that needed workers, so we planned to travel there and find work together. But the plan didn't work out. My cousin, Ismet, was detained for an arrest record he had in the old country. He was sent back on the same ship. I think he is going to try again, maybe this time through Canada or Argentina."

"And the others?"

"Hadži, lost all his money gambling and lacked the fee to exit the ship until I paid it. We went to a local tavern, got drunk and fought with a group of Italians. Tore up the place pretty good. We all went to jail, sobered up and became friends. By then working in the city no longer interested me. I'm a farm boy, and decided to take to the woods. I've been wandering around ever since, mostly just living off the land. None of us made it to our original destination. Don't know what happened to the jobs that awaiting us."

He grinned. "How is it possible you're the German Jackass? I will wonder about this for a long time.But for now I'll probably live off the land until springtime then look for work. How about you?"

"I have not given my future much thought. But like you, I will probably live off the land and pick up occasional work from farmlands. At some point I'll look for steady work."

As I did on the ship, I watched the card game, then pulled a skillet from my pack and cooked turkey for the group. One of the men had a flask of whiskey that he passed around to top off the meal. I spent the night in the ramshackle building with my newfound friends. By morning the rain had let up, I bid my them goodbye and packed my gear.

As I bid them goodbye, I was certain Tahir was concealing something about his past. Perhaps he too had a police record in Bosnia. Maybe he too was in this country to avoid military service. But regardless of his reasons, his secrets were his to keep, just as mine were mine to keep.

                                              ~

By springtime I sported a substantial set of whiskers and shoulder-length hair. I had walked nearly the entire three hundred miles from Baltimore to the greater Pittsburgh area. Rivers became wider and signs of civilization appeared. I thought this must be the general vicinity of Pittsburgh.

I'd picked up a few words of American English to go with my strong German and native Bosnian languages, and decided to begin the plan I had developed during the transoceanic trip. The long arm of Baltimore law enforcement surely could not reach me here. I was sure they'd long forgotten about me. By this time, however, I could not remember the name of the town the men had spoken of on board the ship as they gambled. I remembered Pittsburgh, but that was all my memory would allow me to grasp. I probably should have asked Tahir when I had the chance.

As I walked a set of railroad tracks along the riverbank, I came upon a group of hobos cooking lunch. They invited me to join them for coffee, although none were Slavic or German. I think they spoke Italian. I decided to try to find the town that I had been searching for since the card games.

After spending a few hours with my newfound hobo friends, I thanked them but still could not remember the name of the town. In halting English I asked, "For work, which way for Carlee...?" I stuttered and stammered, trying desperately to remember the name of the nearby town of Charleroi.

Finally one of the hobos smiled and asked, "Meaning you for Clar-tone?" I nodded and smiled. It sounded similar to the name of the town I'd heard on the ship.

They pantomimed and spoke in pidgin and broken English, "Stay tracks fifteen kilometro. See big mill. Lots work for Clar-tone."

I thanked them in three languages and set off on my accidental journey to Clairton, twelve miles south of Pittsburgh on the Monongahela River, and teeming with jobs in the steel mill.

12

THE BOXCAR BOARDING HOUSE

Bidding goodbye to the hobo camp, I walked along the railroad tracks for a few hours, past villages and toward "Clar-tone." My mind focused on my life up to that point, not the work I might seek. I thought of the family I'd left behind as a child, and my second family I recently left in Germany.

It had been nearly a year since I landed in America. I'd met so many fine people along the way; the Amish and Mennonite families, the farmers, the hobos, all part of the rainbow of new Americans who had crossed my path. Approaching civilization and the mills, I thought of my arrival and difficulties at the docks and began to realize that I really was a stranger in a strange land. I had no contacts, no family, and once again spoke a language few people here understood. For an instant a shiver of panic ran through my body, but soon the rhythm of walking along the track and stepping from tie to tie calmed me. I tried to imagine what my next venture would be. My days as a recluse, hermit, hobo and wanderer had been healing and fun, but it was time to settle down and find work. I had arrived at my destination.

By the time I made it to Western Pennsylvania, the greater

Pittsburgh area teemed with opportunity. More than thirty-thousand immigrant workers helped increase annual steel production from three-hundred eighty tons in 1875 to more than fifty million tons three decades later. Little available housing for workers existed, but that did not concern me at the moment, as I'd been doing odd jobs and living off the land for the past year.

My greatest strengths, farming and horse grooming, could not help me in the huge factories that lined the rivers. What would I do and how would I even be able to make myself understood to even ask for work?

I continued my stroll, oblivious to how far I had strayed from the hobos that had shared their coffee with me that morning. The walk from their lair to Clairton took fewer than three hours. As I approached the area the hobos called Clar-tone, I saw a stationary boxcar on a side rail. Smoke rose from a chimney built into the roof of the car. Outside the boxcar a man and woman hung laundry. The man rested one hand on a cane as he passed damp laundry items to the woman, who then tossed them over a rope to dry.

After having wandered the rolling hills of Pennsylvania for a year I must have looked a sight, a bewhiskered tramp in tattered clothing. I approached the couple with a smile, and nodded to them, and was stunned when they nodded back and cried out, greeting in my native tongue, but with a Croatian accent, *"Dobro Jutro."*

"Are you Croatian?"

The woman nodded and answered, *"Da."*

I was surprised to hear the language of my youth. Bosnia is a small country but its inhabitants are a diverse lot. Croatian Catholics, Serbian Orthodox, Muslims, Albanians, Jews, and others occupied the country and spoke a variety of languages and dialects, but the most common were Serbian, Croatian, and Bosnian. The three languages are all spoken similarly, but with different dialects.

The couple beckoned me nearer. The wife then asked my nationality, *"Hrvat? Bošnjački? Srbski?..."*

"I am Bosnian." The Croatian couple welcomed me with a smile.

The woman gave me a lighthearted scolding, "What is a nice Bosnian boy doing looking like a bum? Why aren't you working?"

The man was a little more gentle with his approach, "Might you be looking for work and housing, son?"

They must have thought me a tramp. With remnants of forest vines dangling from the pack strapped to my back, dirty hair, wild and disheveled, a beard, chest-length and straggled, work clothes and my once respectable-looking coat and now tattered rags whose lining had been sewn and resewn. I looked like any other bum, hobo or tramp that populated the area.

I had taken care to stuff leaves inside my boots to lessen the sticking of thorns through the holes in my soles, and had repaired my coat as needed to keep the packets of cash hidden.

The man called me "son," in a way that reminded me of Herr Richter and I was immediately taken with him.

"I have taken my time to cross this country. Now I am ready to earn a living. Friends told me there is work in Clar-tone, but I am surprised to find my people here."

The man smiled. My boy, there are more Slavs in this area than in all of the old county."

The woman spoke over him, "Oh Papa, don't tease this nice young man." Then, turning to me she added, "We have a bed that just became vacant, if you are interested. You can pay once you begin work."

"I am interested, and though I don't have a job yet, I have money. I can pay."

I agreed to their offer immediately, hoping that family bonds might develop as they had on the Richter estate.

"My name is Stela Radić, and this is my husband, Ante. This humble boxcar is our boarding house. Now, let's get some of that dirt and hair off you. I can alter some clothes to fit, from tenants who are gone."

Stela went into the boxcar and retrieved a set of used but clean underwear, work clothes, boots, soap, and a towel, and handed them to me. "Bathe in the river, then I will tailor the clothes to fit you."

I crossed the tracks and went down an embankment to bathe in the frigid river, a far cry from the steaming tub on the estate. When I returned in my new garb, I gave Stela all my old clothes to burn —except for my coat. "I would like to keep this. It was a gift from a very dear friend and it means very much to me."

Stela tossed the rags into a burn barrel and sat me on a chair near the hanging clothes. She cut my whiskers, shaved my cheeks and neck, and with the addition of my new wardrobe, transformed me from tramp to teen.

Before long the residents of the boxcar awakened, ate, and scurried off to work. I watched as the men ate and left. Shortly another crew arrived. They introduced me to each tenant. The newly arrived workers ate, then some smoked, a few played cards or lounged until all were asleep.

When it was quiet again, I spoke once more, "I have money to pay for my room and board. Money I've earned doing odd jobs along the way from Baltimore." I didn't mention the funds sewn into the lining of my tattered coat. We moved from inside the boxcar to the benches outside and continued to talk.

I'm normally a quiet person, rarely taking part in discussions, other than to listen. But after my bath and shave I felt so good that

I talked for hours. For the first time in ten years I had a meaning-ful conversation in my native tongue with somebody other than Herr Richter's Croatian housekeeper Marija. I told them about my mother's death during childbirth, the abject poverty of my village, and my leaving home at age eight to work for Herr Richter, who became not only my employer but a benevolent friend. I told the entire story of my life except for the part about traveling to the U.S. with forged papers and my run-in with the Baltimore police sergeant, firmly believing those secrets would remain with me until my death. I told my new friends of my skills: farming, which I learned at my father's side, the grooming and care of horses, gardening, as well my other responsibilities on the estate. I told of my fear of not being able to find work in this new land since I knew little of the language or modern machinery.

Ante and Stela listened intently. My need to unburden myself with my life story made for the most conversation they would hear from me for the next several years.

"It is good you offered to pay, but I have a better idea," smiled Stela. "Since you are a farmer, you can live rent-free for your first month in exchange for putting in a garden. Now, let's get some food into you."

"Dear Lady, you have just captured my heart." I agreed to her terms, and that night after we struck the deal for room and board, I was asleep almost before my head hit the cot's pillow.

The following morning Ante took me to a Serbian foreman at the main mill gate. "Slobodan Vuković, this Bosnian Serb farmer is looking for work. Do you think he can survive in the mill?"

The foreman, who routinely hired men from the Serbian, Bosnian, and Croatian regions hired me on the spot as a laborer. The long, hard, dangerous and dirty work became one more thread of my life's brocade.

I soon became one their favorite boarders. My quiet personality, frugal handling of money, paying of my rent on time, and not drinking, fighting or carousing, made me fit in almost as a family member. During my days off and free time, I often chatted with Ante and Stela on the benches outside, or took Ante on walks to exercise his leg. I did not ask how he came to be injured, but on one of our walks he told me the story.

"I was a freight hauler on the Kupa River in Croatia," he began. "Times were hard. My business slowed and many customers were unable to pay on time. Some went out of business and did not pay at all. When we decided to come to America, it was to be a temporary move, only until I could make enough money to return to restart the business. I still hope to one day return home.

"I arranged for the government to rent part of my house for office space. That provided a small income for Stela's mother, Mara, who remained behind to take care of our five-year old daughter."

"Did you find work immediately?"

"Yes. My cousin, Stevo worked in a nearby coal mine and his boss hired me the day after I arrived."

"That was good fortune."

"Yes and no. I remember as though it were yesterday. Stela was brewing a strong pot of coffee, blacker than the coal we mined, to get me ready for the day. I asked if she thought we made the right move coming here. The work was hard and filthy and the pay was less than we hoped, but my Stela, ever the optimist, reassured me that we will survive."

As we walked he continued to talk, as though the story had been pent up inside him, and was fighting to get out.

"Trying to be as optimistic as she, I told her that digging coal from the rich soil was a good fit for me. I was used to hard work and the pay was enough to live on with a little left to put away for our return home.

"By then it had been two years since we had seen little Kata and Grandma Mara. Stela and her mother wrote regularly, and like Stela, Mara gave all good reports. She did not want us to worry about Kata and Stela did not want to share her concerns for safety concerns in the mine.

"You know about our mill's steam whistle. Every mill and mine has one that is loud enough to be heard throughout each community. Once you've been here long enough you will learn each whistle's sound and be able to tell the difference between ours, the whistle in Glassport and the one in Elizabeth. That high-pitched, piercing scream of steam reverberates throughout the area's hills and valleys, and you can hear it regardless of where you are. Children at school, merchants tending their shops, wives and mothers, whether out shopping or working in their homes, all hear the whistle announcing many different happenings."

"I didn't know that. I thought it was just to announce shift changes."

"You're lucky." He kicked a pebble with his shoe, took a deep breath and continued. "There has not been a serious accident since you've been at the mill. Otherwise you would have heard it from the whistle messenger. When it blows at an unscheduled time, the scream usually means disaster. Families and co-workers, alerted by the death whistle to explosions, slate falls, accidents, or other catastrophes, rush to the entrance of the mine to learn of the problem.

"The very morning that Stela and I had the conversation, my cousin, Stevo Čolić and I went deep into the mine. You cannot believe the blackness inside a coalmine. Our only light was the red-yellow glow of a lantern. We worked, side by side, digging a rich vein.

"We barely strained to get the load. I remember saying to Stevo that the coal comes too easy as we chipped away at the fertile seam, and he agreed.

"I remember his exact words, 'Yes, cousin. This must be our lucky day. The black lady is seeking us out instead of hiding and making us find her.'"

Ante's voice cracked and he shuddered. I led him to a tree stump. He sat and cried for several moments, then wiped his swollen eyes with a large red and white work handkerchief, took a deep breath, and continued the story.

"There was no warning! The mine trembled and shook, and then an explosion tossed everything into disarray. Lanterns hurtled through the air. Dust came in waves, making it impossible to see. We were both thrown like ragdolls, I think in opposite directions. I lost sight of Stevo and the other miners as the disaster turned our workplace into a tomb, burying our entire crew.

"Several pieces of slate fell from the ceiling onto the mine floor, covering all of us and our equipment. A large slab struck me in the neck, and the concussion sent a whirlwind of soot up the tunnel and out the mine's opening.

"I passed out for I don't know how long, but as soon as I was able I cried out for Stevo."

Ante's face was flushed as memories raced back to him. "Do you want to take a rest for a while?" I asked.

"No, I have not been able to talk about it since the accident. I want to get it out of my gut. Then maybe I will stop having those awful nightmares.

"I called out for Stevo again, but there was no response from him, only groaning, but in the dark I could not to tell who made the noise.

"Once I finally spat enough choking dust from my mouth and

lungs, I yelled again for my cousin, 'Stevo, Stevo, can you hear me?' Still no response.

"My head began to clear but my ears were still ringing. My thoughts went to Stela. She must have heard the dreaded death whistle and it's ear-splitting squeal."

He clutched the handkerchief and dabbed his cheeks as he went on.

"I knew a rescue crew would find us quickly, and my fellow off-duty miners and rescue crews would rush to the site. The area would soon fill with family members and neighbors. I heard emergency crews struggling to remove the slate and debris from the tunnel in an attempt to get to us that were crushed and buried alive.

"Rescue crews worked without stopping. As miners pulled me from the mine and carried me out on a stretcher, only two thoughts rattled in my brain, that my back and leg hurt worse than ever, and that Stela would not recognize me with thick black soot completely covering me from head to toe. Each of us rescued miners looked identical to the other.

"I choked out a few words as the stretcher bearers who carried me passed her. 'I'm okay Stela.

"Stela found me among the many rescued miners rushed to the field hospital for treatment and emergency surgery. That was all I remembered at the moment.

"She told me later that a surgeon informed her that I was severely injured, but would live.

"The surgeon posted a list of those rescued and injured. The names of Stevo Čolić and a twenty-seven other miners did not appear on the survivor list."

Ante leaned forward on his cane, buried his face in his hands and sobbed. I placed my arm around his shoulders and tried to comfort him.

Ante told me that the weight of the fallen slate had fractured his femur and broken an ankle, and a jagged edge had pierced his neck, injuring his spinal cord, rendering one arm nearly useless.

He took another deep breath and said, "Emergency doctors saved my life but from that time forward I will need the use this damn cane. The accident ended my career as a miner and the injury assured that I had no chance for a steel mill job. I'm a cripple, Peter. There is no work for cripples in industry.

"Within weeks, I was able to hobble with the help of this cane. The company took care of my medical bills and paid a small financial settlement."

He lifted his chin and rose from the stump that had supported him while relating his story, and squeezed my arm. "Thank you Pete, for listening. I had to get the story out. I did not want to discuss it with Stela again and give her another reason to hurt. I couldn't tell the other men in the boarding house. They are tenants. We think of you family."

His spirit brightened. "We will have to take another long walk another day and I'll tell you how the boarding house came to be."

12

Building a Dream Home

Over time and with regular walks, Ante not only exercised his body, but regaled me with many stories of the old country, the journey to a new land, and his life in America. My favorite story told of events that led up to their lives as operators of the boxcar boarding house. I knew how to get him to tell it.

"I have seen a few boarding houses in my travels, Kum Ante, and have ridden a train or two during my travels, but I must tell you I've never seen a railcar and a boardinghouse. How is it that this one came to be?"

Without missing a stride, as we walked he took my arm and told the tale. "Let me tell you, Pete, my boy, that is quite a story. Here we were; an ocean away from the poverty of the old country, and after the slate fall in the coalmine, my disability prevented me from getting a job and earning a living.

"Stela refused to be cowed by a little thing like a tragedy," he chuckled. "She told me how fortunate we were to be together and reminded me that many coal mine widows were not so lucky. They faced a life of poverty in the states, with no means of support. Some turned to prostitution to survive. Others returned home to live with relatives. Those with children were even worse off.

"We could no longer afford to live in the apartment that had been our home for years, and once our savings and settlement were gone, we would surely face poverty. But we were both confident that as long as we have each other, we would survive.

"We needed to make our money last as long as possible so we agreed to live outdoors. The weather was nice, a peaceful summer, with all plants in full bloom. They would provide shelter if we found the right spot. We walked the railroad tracks looking for a temporary place to call home. Stela walked slowly and I shuffled, one hand gripping the cane and the other arm entwined with Stela's.

"We examined the area between the tracks and the street until coming upon a seldom-used spur track. Stela saw it first and pointed out how the overgrowth hid the entrance to the spur. We peeked behind it, hoping to get lucky. She climbed through the low hanging branches and vines, then motioned me to follow. I was surprised at how big the place was, and protected from the elements. This place suited us nicely.'"

When Ante paused, I spoke up, "After owning your own home and business in Croatia, did you feel bad not having a home?"

"If you do not already know this, my boy, pride is poison. Humility is grace. The Bible says, 'When pride comes, then comes disgrace, but with humility comes wisdom.' My Stela was both humble and wise. She did not pity me, but led me to our temporary home.

"The place was not exactly ready for immediate residence. The rich soil produced an abundance of foliage, though the coating of soot that hung in the air discouraged it. Grime lit on the leaves of brush that grew along the street and riverbank, as it still does. The black, grit-coated plants thrived outside, but the interior of the dug-out, where the residue did not reach, was clean.

"I gave the interior a long look, then suggested that if we hollow out the interior area a bit more, it could serve as a cave."

He paused, reflecting. I thought for a moment, and then asked, "Did you have belongings to store? Surely they did not fit in your manmade cave."

Ante was now in full storytelling mode. He stood and waved his cane as he spoke, as though conducting an orchestra.

"Oh yes! Stela returned to our former residence and retrieved those belongings. All our earthly goods were packed in one large trunk that we'd brought from Croatia.

"I remained at the site to put finishing touches on the new dwelling, weaving vines and actually making our bed.

"A water spring flowed underground from the hillside, and emptied into the river. Much as you did on your journey, I figured we would live off berries and wild fruit that grew abundantly in the rich riverbank soil, and small game that I trapped. The natural spring provided fresh water. All the comforts of home!

"By the time Stela returned, I had cleared the area and picked berries for snacks. I greeted her with a kiss and a handful of blackberries."

He was on a roll. I wanted him to continue. I had not seen him this animated in a while. "Were you able to cook? Did you use a campfire?"

"Stela set up a makeshift stove just outside the natural cave, to heat water for coffee. She built it from rocks and a discarded grate. Our castle had an outdoor kitchen.

"Once word circulated of our plight throughout our church and community, we were invited to dinner at the homes of many of our co-workers. The priest was also helpful, asking the congregation to take us into their hearts. We made a list and planned to dine with one or two different friends each week until we got things sorted out. I'll tell you, Pete, we were certain this was the low point of our lives. It seemed that just as we were about to break the cycle, another blow knocked us down. But we each managed to help the other stay positive.

"Stela reminded me that the church guild offered food to the destitute. I was not too proud to ask them for help. We had our savings and my settlement, but I didn't want to dip into that just yet, as I didn't know how long it would take me to figure out how to earn a living.

"I recuperated in the hollowed-out, overgrown thicket near the railroad tracks that was home. But we were not alone. Others lived in similar temporary housing nearby. Immigrants passing through the area and jobless men frequently chose to live in natural accommodations in the spring, summer, and into the fall seasons. But winter weather cleared the area of most squatting residents, and we understood our temporary home would disappear at some point."

By this time we had walked all the way to the railway station as Ante regaled me with his story, and I could see that he was tiring. "Let's sit for a while in the station and have a smoke," I suggested. Then I winked and added, "I can barely match your pace."

We sat on the stiff wooden benches. Ante pulled out his Cutty Pipe tobacco pouch, took a pinch, and wrapped it in a Zig-Zag rolling paper, using the technique I'd shown him. He had become a master cigarette roller.

We sat for an hour or so as the sun smiled on us. Ante dozed as he repaired for the trek home and the rest of the tale.

Walking along the tracks in the other direction, he continued his story. "We sat in our new surroundings on chairs scavenged from a dump site. Opportunities abounded in America for healthy, strong immigrants, but what could a man do to earn a living cursed with a physical disability like mine? I had no formal training, though I operated my own transport business in Croatia. Even if I had the training to seek an office job, my English was too poor."

"Stela wondered aloud if perhaps we could use the rest of our savings and my settlement as a down payment on a boarding house. She could cook and clean and I could manage the business end and do repairs.

"The following morning we gathered all our cash and placed it into a shoulder bag, drank tepid, weak coffee, bathed, and dressed in clothes laundered in the fresh spring water.

"With tree limbs pulled around the entrance of our nature home to disguise it, we hoped it would not be discovered and scavenged. We took the trolley up the St. Clair Avenue hill, got off at Fifth Street and walked into the bank, full of hope. The bank was then, as it is now, the grandest building in the city..

"Inside, we waited patiently, sitting on plush chairs, until an officer beckoned to us. He sat behind a rich wooden desk decorated with hand carvings. He wore a stiff white shirt and perfectly knotted tie under his pressed suit.

"Using a combination of limited English skills I'd learned in the coal mines, and sign language, I tried explaining our vision and plan to the gentleman. 'Ve vant for buy house for stay work men,' I stumbled, 'for eat, and *spava*... uh, sleepink.'

"I mimed the state of sleeping by placing my head on clasped hands and closing my eyes, then lifted my hand to my mouth in an eating motion.

"I tried to describe my plan to get a bank loan. 'Ve vant fine house by mill gate for sell. Bank geef moneys. I haf leela bit moneys here.' I showed the banker the cash in the bag. "Bank make me loan moneys for more.

"The banker sat stiffly behind a gold embossed name placard that read 'Mr. J. W. Walters.' He yawned as he listened, eyes glazed, and seemingly barely caring or trying to understand what I said.

"I know that look. What Mr. J. W. Walters saw before him was not a pair of successful businesspeople from Croatia, but two unkempt foreigners with little command of the English language.

"He held up his hand, interrupting me in mid-sentence. Clearly irritated, Mr. J. W. Walters began, 'You people come here with your grand ideas, with visions of streets paved with gold. You are dirty, bring diseases, do not speak our language, and are not familiar with our customs. Sometimes you get a loan, then discover that you cannot make payments, then just disappear—go back to wherever it is you came from, or move on to another town. You are what we in banking call a bad risk. I simply am not able to make the loan you are requesting. I'm sorry.' With that he showed us to the heavy plate glass door.

"I was humiliated and embarrassed, and hoped Stela did not understand his words, but she recognized the inflections in the banker's voice. Neither of us were ready to give up on our idea. Despite my physical limitations, I was a hard worker and an entrepreneur at heart.

"I led Stela to a bench in the park across the street from the bank, and we brainstormed, trying to figure what other possibilities might exist. She suggested we try another bank, but it was clear from what Mr. Walters said, no banks will loan to foreigners. They do not trust us because we don't speak their language or worship in their church or understand their customs. We had to figure another way to reach our goal."

"We sat on the bench for more than an hour discussing options, most of which were not viable. In Šišljavić there was a need to move cargo and we filled that need. When we first arrived here, there was a need to dig coal from the ground and I filled that need. Many people in the area are in need of housing, but Mr. Walters said he is afraid we will be unsuccessful to fill that need. Anglos do not eat our food, speak our language, or understand our customs, so they will neither patronize us nor help us.

"Stela agreed that trainloads of men from the Balkans arrive each day. Croatians, Serbians, Bosnians, Austrians all speak our language, eat our foods, and understand our culture because it is the same as theirs. Our boarding house will serve men from the Balkans. Let's walk the places where our people stay. Perhaps we can get some ideas and find a building that we can somehow buy without the help of a bank loan.

"We walked across the freshly-trimmed lawn to the trolley. This time we decided to save the nickel trolley fare, and instead, walk down the hill. Although I needed the help of a cane, I walked with an extra spring in my step.

"Confidence was brimming as knocked on doors along State Street until our knuckles were raw, looking for any building that might be for sale, but found none. As afternoon turned to dusk we walked the railroad tracks, returning to the dugout shelter and temporary home.

"Nearing the spur line and Stela spotted it first. The answer to our prayers had been in front of our eyes the entire time. On the abandoned spur of railroad track near the dugout stood an equally abandoned and ignored boxcar. We had passed it dozens of times but paid it no mind. Judging from the undergrowth wrapped around much of the car and the rusted wheels, the boxcar had been there for some time; the railroad must have discarded or forgotten about it.

"If we cut the vines around it, replaced the rotted wood, cleaned it up, and built steps for an entry, the boxcar had some possibilities.

Add a table and chairs outside where tenants can eat during good weather and this could be the answer to our prayers.

"The following morning we began the transformation. The steamer trunk held hand tools carefully packed before leaving Croatia. We went to work hacking away at the vines and brush that grew around the railcar. By ten o'clock we had removed most of the foliage, and retraced our steps from the previous day. Again we knocked on many of the same doors, but this time in search of beds, stoves, and other items to equip the Boxcar Boarding House.

"It took a few weeks to purchase all the necessary items. I scavenged lumber and made stairs to the entry. Several gallons of paint found its way from the mill to the boxcar and a we added a fresh coat of paint inside and out.

"We sanded and cleaned twelve rusted cots, purchased along with used bedding from a brothel that had been closed by the authorities, and positioned two stoves against the far end of the car.

"As the place began to take shape, I asked Stela, 'What do you think, my dear?' My arm encircled her waist as we stood in the doorway examining the new house on old rusted wheels.

"Stela answered, 'I think that we are about to become business owners.'"

His story ended as we approached the home on wheels.

During our many walks Ante revealed more of the story. He told me they worked for weeks to bring the boxcar up to standard for use as a boarding house. Several men from Balkan countries helped, partly out of friendship and partly in hopes they would be chosen to rent a spot when the habitat was ready for occupancy.

The first order of business was, as Ante said, was "...to get the baby out of the womb." Men who brought sickles and hatchets cleared the vines wrapped around the coach. Those with sling blades and scythes cut surrounding weeds. The rest followed, picking up the cuttings and stacking them in that clearing to be burned.

Heavy overgrowth between the spur and the main line was left untouched to keep the Boxcar Boarding House barely visible from passing steam locomotives on the main railroad tracks. Underbrush between the car and State Street, except for a crooked path to the street was also left to grow. No prying eyes were welcome.

By sunset of the second day the surrounding area had been cleared, and Ante announced that Stela was burning steaks, and he was about to break out the beer. He encouraged the workers to eat and drink with his blessings.

Ante wrote the names on scraps of paper, of everybody who helped, then placed the paper scraps in a bucket. Before opening for business, the first twenty-four names pulled from the bucket would be the first tenants. Two men shared each cot, one for day shift and one for night turn.

The mills operated twenty-four hours per day. Each man worked a twelve-hour shift, so each bed had two occupants; one who worked days and slept nights and the other who worked nights and slept days.

Each time a man helped, his name was placed in the bucket. The more often he entered the drawing, the better his chance of securing a bed.

Every man whose name had been put in the bucket showed up for the grand opening. Six-foot-six inch Stretch Jakovac had the honor of claiming the first cot in exchange for allowing the bucket to sit on his head while names were drawn.

Cheers rose from the group as the selection began. Each man

hoped his name would be one of the twenty-four to win the lottery and earn a cot. Stela stood atop a wine barrel and reached into the bucket on Stretch's head, drew six names and called them out: "Marinović, Mrozinski, Shevchenko, Berezovsky, Tadić, Grisnik."

A cheer erupted each time she called a name. Stela called out Evan Mrozinski's name three times. He had entered multiple times for luck. Each time his name was pulled, she winked and looked over at the big steelworker and shouted, "Sorry, Ski, you only get one bed."

Stela continued to dip and call until all beds were taken, then she called five more names as alternates in case any winners decided to opt out. None did.

Once the boarding house was officially open, Stela cooked and prepared food for each man's lunch bucket, and provided hearty meals at the boarding house.

From spring to autumn, plants kept the dwelling hidden from the main railroad tracks and river to the east, and State Street to the west. In late fall, surrounding trees and flora shed their leaves, and throughout the winter passersby were able to see the car behind the bare trees, but nobody of consequence seemed to notice.

Many boarding houses took advantage of workers by providing poor food. Some owners stole from their tenants, but the Radić family did neither. Residents paid a premium to live in a boarding house that filled their lunch buckets and stomachs with meals that tasted like the food back home.

Despite his physical limitations, Ante served as the handyman, custodian and all-around superintendent, performing most of the labor on the property. Tenants pitched in to help as well. They brought tools and odds and ends from the mills for maintenance and repairs.

The pieces to the puzzle that shaped my life began to come together one morning as the boarding house's night turn workers returned from their shift in the mill. The whistle awakened Stela during the night and she silently prayed that the problem that initiated the sound did not involve any of her boys.

That morning, four years after the Boxcar Boarding House began operation, Stretch Jakovac returned from the his shift to give them the grave news, that their boarder, Fabijan Tadić was killed during the night shift.

Work in the mill—particularly in the blast furnaces—was not only low paying and dirty, but shifts were long, hard, and dangerous. Twelve hours a day, seven days a week. Men alternated—one month on daylight, one month working night turn.

Fabijan had just switched to the widow maker double shift. No one wanted to work the dangerous transition from days to nights because of the danger. Twenty-four hours with barely a break always led to accidents.

Stretch told Ante the details. Fabijan had to be tired. During the long shift he'd yawned so much he made Stretch yawn. The boss said he must have set the heat regulator wrong. Stretch further said that somebody else made a bad mixture and the furnace blew up. It bubbled, belched, and exploded in a shower of sparks that covered Fabijan. He was hit full force when the molten steel spewed into the worker's area. It got him and two other workers. No bodies remained for burial. They were all burnt to a crisp

Stela and Ante made the sign of the cross in Fabijan's memory, gathered his belongings and packed them in the trunk that sat beneath his bunk. They had become numb because deaths happened so often.

Because Fabijan Tadić had no family in America, the closest to kin were the operators of his lodging facility. He was fortunate. Other victims lived in company-owned housing, less personal and more antiseptic. Their property simply vanished, and notification to next of kin often did not take place.

The couple lugged the trunk along the tracks to the train depot for shipment home to his family, the tenth time they'd made the death trip in the four years of the Boxcar Boarding House's operation.

Upon their return to the boarding house, they continued their routine of preparing food, doing maintenance, washing laundry and generally keeping the property in order.

I could not have known of the tragedy that had just taken place, causing a cot to become available.

The journeys of Fabijan and my own began under much different circumstances, and our paths crossed under equally different circumstances—Fabijan's life in America had just ended, and mine was just beginning.

14

THE GROOMING OF A GROOM

Several months after moving into the boarding house, I approached Stela while the other workers were asleep. She was sitting in an overstuffed chair reading a Croatian newspaper and sipping a beer. She patted the seat next to her and said, "Sit, Pete. Tell me what is on your mind?

"I would like to buy some land."

"Oh, no, my boy," she replied, with a look of shock. "Are you going to marry and leave us already?"

I blushed. "Not now, but maybe one day, if I find a nice lady like you, and marry her, I want to have land to build a house."

"That is an wonderful idea, Pete. I'll tell Ante to begin looking for property for you. But I must warn you, the banks won't lend you money so you will have to save up enough cash."

"I have cash."

I pulled a trunk from beneath my bed, opened the footlocker they had given me, and removed the tattered overcoat, took a knife from the kitchen sink, and sliced open a small section of the lining. Stela's eyes widened as she looked at the packets of American money sewn into the lining.

"Where on earth..." she began, then guided me outside, away from the other sleeping tenants, and motioned Ante to follow.

Once outside I explained. "Herr Richter put away money earned from my ideas and inventions. He called it a commission. Marija sewed the money into the lining of my coat."

Stela exclaimed, "Pete, you must put this money in a bank for safekeeping." Ante nodded in agreement.

Ante spoke up. "Do not take it to the bank on the hill. They don't like foreigners. You lived in Germany for ten years. How well do you speak the language?"

"I speak German much better than Bosnian. My professor saw to that. Why do you ask? Is a German bank nearby?"

"Not exactly. But I hear there is a bank across the river that caters to wealthy Germans and the German-Jewish community. We will take you there as soon as you can arrange to take a day off from the mill."

I replaced the packet of money in the old coat, refolded it and replaced it, and slid the footlocker back under my bed. None of my roommates stirred, and within minutes I was among the group sleeping soundly.

The following Wednesday, payday at the mill, I arrived at the boarding house and had breakfast after working the night shift. It promised to be a big day. I donned a suit that Stela had altered for me, and Ante helped me transfer cash from the old coat's lining to a small suitcase that resembled a briefcase. We crossed the bridge to the village of Elizabeth and found the bank, a frame building on the corner of Second Street and Plum Street, in a newly-constructed building. The bank flourished at the time, paying handsome dividends on its stock, and generous dividends on savings deposits.

Ante, also wearing a suit, and I walked into the bank and in flawless German I said, "My name is Peter Novak and I would like to open a savings deposit account."

The cashier who greeted us walked us to Mr. Frank, the bank manager, who treated me with the utmost respect—a far cry from the treatment Ante received during his only visit to the bank on the hill.

"Please be seated, Mr. Novak, and your friend too."

We sat in plush, overstuffed chairs. "Now, Sir, how can I be of service?"

"I brought this money with me after I left my business in Germany. I hope you will be able to help me."

"We can offer you an excellent interest rate of return on your money, Sir. It will be safe with us. Our bank assets exceed one-half million dollars."

I dug back into my mind, remembering a lesson from Professor Braun. It was a lesson on business transactions. "I am confident that your rates will be competitive. Therefore, I should like to deposit my funds in your bank. I opened the briefcase. The banker's eyes widened as he saw the amount of cash inside. At that moment I became one of the bank's most coveted customers. Banks were loosely regulated at the time, and preferred customers were given considerably higher interest rates than small investors.

"Oh yes, Sir, we will take the utmost care of your deposit. Please let us know if there is any other financial service we can offer you. We can advise on investing, or offer your business a loan if you require it."

"I am also looking for a plot of land to purchase, preferably in or near Clairton. Perhaps you can advise me of an agent who also speaks the German language."

As Mr. Frank completed the paperwork for the deposit, he said,

"The bank owns several properties that might interest you. One in particular is located in Clairton. It is a large corner lot that overlooks the river, and has been surveyed and staked. It would be ideal for a large home and a small farm. Does that pique your interest, Sir?"

"That sounds like it has some possibilities. What is the condition of the property?"

"It is raw. No building on it and it is overgrown and backs into a hillside, but it has tremendous potential. I can give it to you for an excellent price, Herr Novak."

Ante stood silent, as he only understood a few words of the conversation, but watched and we both smiled at my being called 'Herr Novak' for the first time in my life.

"My associate, Mr. Radić, and I will look over the property and I will give you my answer in a few days. Thank you, Mr. Frank. I will keep your offer in mind."

With the my mission complete, we left the bank. Ante suggested, "You should make one more purchase while you are here. Buy a fine suit to wear on special occasions. Someday you will marry. Every man should have a nice wedding and funeral suit. A tailor in this town has an excellent reputation, and I believe he is German."

I thought of my first fine tailored suit. Herr Richter had seen to it that I owned the best. But that suit was long gone, a victim of my venture with the police on the Baltimore pier. I still shuddered at the thought as I entered the premises of a Jewish German-speaking tailor. My measurements taken and I ordered my new wedding and funeral suit.

After returning to the boxcar, we changed clothes, and went to look at the bank's property that Mr. Frank had suggested, located on a corner of Arch Street, one block uphill from State Street. We took our time, walking the parcel from one end to the other. From the steep hill at the west end of the lot, the sight was stunning. It was a clear day and our view took in the mill in the foreground and the Monongahela River behind, with a clear view of Elizabeth on the opposite bank.

"What do you think, Pete?"

I surveyed every inch of the land and could not believe my good fortune, that this might become my own. "It's perfect. If I am ever be fortunate enough to find a wife I will build her a home on this property with my own two hands."

My vision pictured the house sitting in the far corner, at the highest point of the land. Next to it a large garden, and on the far end a pen for animals, a sty for pigs, and still have plenty of room to grow.

Ante advised, "Wait a week or two before you make an offer. Let the bank know that you've seen the property. Don't be too anxious. See what they are asking for it, then tell them that in return for your placing all your money in their bank, you will offer fifty percent of their asking price. They won't come down that much but you won't get a discount if you don't ask."

The following week I took another day off from the mill and returned to the bank. "I looked over the property we discussed. It has some possibilities. What is your asking price?"

"Well, since you are one of our best clients, I can offer you the land well below market value." He gave me a price.

Pretending to lack interest I tried to look pensive as I scanned the interior of the bank's new building. Finally, my eyes returned to his desk. "As I said, it has some possibilities, but is very rough. I don't see how I could justify paying more than half the amount you're asking."

Mr. Frank began to pale. "Would you excuse me a moment, Mr. Novak? I want to present your offer to the bank president so we can give you an answer before you leave."

Ante, showing his years of business experience, whispered to me that the bank wants two things desperately—to get the property off their books, and to keep my money in their bank. From Mr. Frank's initial reaction, he believed their offer to me would be a reasonable one.

Whispering back and shaking my head I said, "I want that land. I'll agree to whatever price he wants. I should have told him that."

"Not in your interest to do that, Pete."

Mr. Frank must have noticed me shaking my head. He scurried to return, with the newly appointed bank president who shook my hand and said in English, "Hello, I am J. W. Walters. I apologize that I do not speak your language, but let me assure you that I have always admired and held sacred the richness and diversity that our recently arrived Americans bring to this land." He obviously didn't recognize Ante from their earlier encounter.

Mr. Frank translated the bank president's words. The bank president smiled and added, "Your offer is accepted without negotiation."

Again Mr. Frank translated and the three of us shook hands. We left the bank, but not before Bank President J. W. Walters gave us each a package of expensive cigars to show his appreciation.

After strolling around the corner from the bank, I let out a whoop. "Hot damn!" I cried in American. It was one of the American expressions I'd learned at the mill. "Let's get a beer and smoke a couple of these babies."

Ante teased, "But I thought you didn't care to drink."

"I don't smoke either Last time I tried a cigar I nearly choked. But today, we're celebrating. I'm an American landowner! My treat."

We ducked into a tavern and had a quaff or two, and Ante showed me how to smoke cigars without choking to death. As we talked and drank and laughed, Ante told me of his and Stela's first encounter with Mr. J. W. Walters. "What a hypocrite. He certainly didn't recognize me from our last meeting. He changed his tune about immigrants when he saw the color of your money. Back then he said all immigrants were dirty and brought diseases to America. Last time I saw him I got thrown out of his bank. This time I got cigars. What a two-faced man! But that's business."

Arm in arm, we left the tavern, then walked to the tailor shop to pick up my suit. It fit perfectly, and I left whistling a tune from my childhood in Bosnia, but not before paying the bill and rewarding the tailor with a fine cigar.

15

A Plan Hatches

A nte and Stela were so happy I'd gotten such a deal on the land. We had become closer than a normal tenant-landlord friendship. Ante and I often continued our regimen of taking walks together to exercise his leg. We had many conversations about life in general and the fate of the loved ones he'd left behind. He mostly talked. I listened.

"I can tell when Stela gets letters from her mother. She hides the letters with bad news, but eventually tells me. The problem is Kata. She dropped out of school because, according to Mara, 'she already knows more than that prissy old hag of a teacher will ever know.' She runs the streets and has a boyfriend. We hope this is just a phase that will pass. Besides, there's not much we can do from America. What do you think, Pete?"

"Ask me about horses or gardens and I'll tell you anything you need to know. I know little of women."

I'd set the foundation of future marriage and family with the purchase of the plot near State Street, but the realization of my dream took ages to develop. I settled into a routine and wondered if I would ever have my own home and family. Of course, I had Ante and Stela as adopted family, but I yearned for more.

During my seven years at the Boxcar Boarding House I'd under-gone a complete transition. Hard, physical, dirty work in the steel mill and clean living at home changed me from a gawky teen into a strapping, quiet bachelor of twenty-five. I caused no trouble at home or work, and regularly sent money to my family in Bosnia. Otherwise I lived frugally and saved most of my paycheck.

I paid taxes on the Arch Street property but made no improve-ments. It continued to languish in heavy overgrowth. My co-workers in the mill teased that I had become quite the eligible bachelor and Stela said I would no doubt be some lucky young damsel's beau.

My life took a turn one morning when I arrived home from work-ing a long night shift. "Hello, Kuma," I said to Stela as I entered the boarding house. I always addressed her affectionately and with respect, as though she were my godmother.

"Sit with me on the bench, Pete." Stela patted the seat outside the boxcar. "Have a coffee. I'll have a shot. Ante is out for his morning constitutional." She handed me a steaming mug and filled her own cup with whiskey.

"We haven't talked in a while. How is everything in your life Pate?"

"One day at a time. Go to work. Come home and sleep. Some days, walk with Ante. How about you?"

"Oh, we're worried about things in the old country. Politics are bad. People are concerned about war. My mother is getting older. Kata is no longer the child we left. I miss her and my mama, espe-cially when we have to send somebody's belongings back. Do you ever get homesick, Pete?"

"I try to keep busy and not think about it, and I have been away for a long time. But yes, there are times I feel lonesome."

Stela bit her lip and brushed a tear from her cheek onto her apron with her free hand. "Sometimes I just think about how much has happened in the years since we left our home. One day we will move back.

"We have been fortunate in America. I love all our boys, especially you, Pete, but I do miss Kata, and wonder how her baby features have changed. She was five when we left. She is now fifteen"

The conversation continued under the peace and tranquility of the murky Clairton sky. We covered many topics until she made an unusual comment, "Pete, you should think about marrying and starting a family."

I blushed but said nothing. Stela sat patiently until I stammered, "I-I-I know, but I never meet anybody. There aren't any girls around here or in the mill, or even in the bars along State Street except the ones who want money to date you." I blushed again, cleared my throat, and continued. "There are a few nice girls who go to church, but the ones who are not bad girls are already spoken for."

Stela comforted me. "I know, dear one. It can be difficult to find the right kind of girl for you in America. You need a nice young, hard-working girl who is smart and will give you many children, a girl from the old country. "

I nodded in agreement, unsure of where the conversation was headed.

"You are like a son to me, Pero, and I think you would make a good husband for my Kata. What do you think?"

I turned beet red with embarrassment but felt a definite thrill from her words. I had become convinced I would remain a bachelor for life. Now this! I wanted to enthusiastically say, "Of course I am interested! It would be my honor. I have enough money saved and own land nearby to build a house; the biggest, grandest house in the neighborhood. I will treat Kata like a queen!" But my shy nature would not let the words flow. Instead, I spoke haltingly.

"I-I-I am, I mean, I-I dream of one day having a wife and family. You know how much I am indebted to you and Ante. I trust you two totally and I'm in full agreement with whatever ideas you have in mind. I will pay for her travel and build her a house on my lot."

Stela grinned, "Are you sure, Pete?" I nodded. "Okay, my dear, we will send for her."

I went into the boxcar to rest. The first part of Stela's plan was in place. Next she must approach Ante with the idea. She did not want to give him too much information, as she was not sure how he would react.

I heard Ante's uneven footfalls as he returned to the boxcar. My cot was the nearest one to the door so I was able to hear their conversation.

"You know that Kata is giving my mother fits. She is fifteen now and as Mama gets older she has more difficulty with Kata. What do you think of bringing her here for a change of scenery and to take the burden off her grandmother?"

I can still picture the two whispering so as not to disturb the tenants.

"Okay, I know you and your mother are cooking up something. How bad is it with Kata, and what are you planning?"

"I have much to tell you. Kata stays out very late. Some nights she doesn't come home at all. You remember your cousin Tomas Grgurić, the constable?"

Ante said nothing.

Stela sighed. "He told my mother that Kata has a boyfriend."

None of what had been said so far concerned me. But Kata has a boyfriend? I strained to listen to more of the conversation.

Ante answered. "That isn't so bad. She's acting like an adolescent. It is a phase that will pass. She is becoming a young woman. One day she'll marry."

"I'm getting to that. But first, listen to the rest of what Constable Grgurić reported. The boy is older than her by about ten years. They suspect he is a political radical. He has had several run-ins with the authorities and is suspected of theft." She paused and took a breath.

"Go on." His voice betrayed him with a sound of concern.

"Kata and this boyfriend go into a store and she distracts the owner while her boyfriend steals cash and cigarettes."

"Is that the worst? Or is there more?"

"They strongly suspect this boy, who is more man than boy, was sent to our village to plan some sort of a political disruption. Grgurić knows who he is and where he holds his meetings, but they have been unable to catch him in the act, or they would arrest him and send him away. They are certain the reason they cannot catch him is because Kata acts as his lookout and tips him off to impending raids. When the authorities arrive, the boy and his confederates appear to be simply playing cards. They look like a cat that just swallowed a mouse."

A smile crossed my face as I thought what a clever girl she must be to outsmart the police and remain aloof. "According to Mama, Kata has become difficult. She is not outright defiant, but she often disregards Mama's attempts to discourage her from putting herself in danger."

"I understand why you did not tell me this earlier. You did not want to worry me. But I read the Zajedničar. Big political trouble is brewing in our homeland. It might not be a safe for her. But if we can't help your mother with our child's behavior, then we must work to get Kata out of harm's way."

"I'm sorry I did not tell you sooner, husband, but you are right. I did not want to worry you. Mama and I have set a plan in motion to bring Kata to America."

Ante paused. "But how? How do we get her to leave her boyfriend? If she comes, where will she stay? We cannot keep her here with the two of us and all these men! Whatever would we do with her?"

"What if she came here and found a husband?"

"But how? Who? You said yourself she is strong-willed and has a boyfriend. It might take months or years to find a husband who suits her. And what would we do with her in the meantime?"

"Think about it, my dear. Who do we know that needs a wife, would make a good husband, and already owns property to build a house?"

"Pete?" he said, puzzled. "But…"

Stela interrupted, "I have already spoken to him. As you might guess, he would be honored to have her as his bride. He has all the good qualities a wife could hope for, and money in the bank. He is gentle and kind and would make an ideal husband and son-in-law."

Ante took Stela's hand. "Once again, my brilliant and beautiful wife, you have found a solution to a bewildering problem, at least a solution to half the problem. How will we get Kata to leave the boyfriend and agree to come to America? And how do we convince her to marry Pete?"

"You leave that to me, dear husband. Some parts of my plan must remain secret until the time is right. We will take one step at a time my love, one step at a time. Mama and I have a plan to get Kata here. Then we must let nature take its course with Kata, perhaps with a little boost from her mother."

"Okay, then, I leave it in your capable hands."

I drifted into dreamland, hoping what I'd just heard was not a dream, but reality.

16

THE PLAN UNFOLDS

May 28, 1914

Dear Mama,

As we have discussed, Kata is a rebellious teen, headstrong and argumentative, but also predictable. I have carefully laid out a strategy for Kata's activities once she arrives. Now you must get things going on your end.

I do not think an army general could make a better battle plan than ours. The first step will be for you to wait for the next argument with the Kata. Once the quarrel begins, you say, "I'd like to send you to America to live with your Mama."

You know what her answer will be, "I cannot wait to get out of this stupid, stinking pig sty of a place. America is the land of opportunity. Branko says everybody there is rich, even the peasants."

When she says that, you can tell her that she can go. I have great hopes that the plan will work. I love you and think of you often. Ante is doing well. He sends his love.

With great affection,

Stela

April 18, 1914

My Dearest Stela,

The scheme is working. The opportunity presented itself when Kata arrived home late last evening. I had warned her that good girls do not stay out until all hours, but of course she ignored my chastisement.

The moment she entered the house we began to argue. The same scene played out as before, and as expected, Kata said she'd love to get out of this hellhole and go to America to see her parents.

I told her, "Fine. I'm fed up with your nonsense. I'll book your passage as soon as I can."

She smiled and said she was happy to get her way, but she thinks her boyfriend Branko will follow her and they will walk streets paved with gold. She said she planned to write you a letter. I'm not sure what she will say.

Give Ante my love. Tell him he is fortunate to be in America. Old Man Horvat had to shutter his business last week. People talk only of war and bad times. You are better off where you are.

Love, Mara

April 20, 1914

My Dearest Mother and Father

Baka Mara told me I could come to America to see you. It has taken a long time to get Granny to let me come. I can hardly wait. I have so much to tell you. But first, let me tell you about my soul mate, Branko Kukić. He is so dreamy. I am so excited. Tomorrow I'll give him the news that soon I'll be on my way to the new world. I'll finish this letter tomorrow. I don't think I'll be able to sleep tonight. Night. KR

Here is the rest of my letter from last night...

This morning I was so excited that I raced from our house to tell

Branko about the trip and that I would be back soon, unless he wanted to go with me now. I even thought I might scout out a place for us to live. Or maybe I'll come back here after I visit you, and Branko and I go to America together. I might bring some American money home, and we could get married here, before we leave for our new life in a new world. Or, once I settle in America, I can send for him and we'll get married in America. There are just so many possibilities. I knew Branko would be equally happy to hear the options for us.

When I arrived at his flat, I pounded on the door and called, "Wake up, lazybones. I have big news for you... for us!"

I couldn't roust him so I climbed through a window expecting to find my love asleep, but instead I found a stripped bed with a rolled up mattress in an empty room. I was confused, so I ran to our secret hiding place and looked in the crack between two bricks. A corner of paper stuck out from between them. I tugged at the paper until a note appeared.

Here is what he said in his note.

"Draga moja mala curica, *My Dear little pumpkin,*

I have been called away to complete a very important and dangerous mission. I do not know how long I will be gone or if I will be alive to return. I am going into a risky situation and it is possible I will give my life for the cause. This must be goodbye. You have been a big part of my life during my days here in Šišljavić and I shall never forget you. You played a huge role in the changes that are coming. We could not have been successful without you. You will always have a special place in my heart.

Zbogom malo sunca, *Goodbye Little Sunshine, Branko.*"

Can you believe this? The love of my life did not have the testisi to face me with the news?"

At first I was in shock, then I got really mad and fumed over Branko's cowardice. How dare he kiss me off... and with a note? After what he *said what we meant to each other? That son of the devil! Who the Hell does he think he is to play with my feelings? If he were here right now I would kick him right where it counts. To hell with that eunuch! I'm glad to be rid of him. I'm coming to America to see you, and when I return I'll track down the bastard and fix him good! I can't wait to see you both.*

Your loving daughter,

Kata.

June 23, 1914

Dear Stela and Ante

By now you have probably gotten Kata's letter. She left it out and I read it before she posted it. Her letter was full of bravado, but I saw tears running down her cheeks, the rantings of a precocious teen that just had her heart broken for the first time. If she says that if she ever sees him again she'll forgive him, but she will make him do lots of penance to make it up to her before she takes him back. Here's hoping that won't be necessary with her in America and him God knows where. Good riddance

Kata believes a trip to America will make her boyfriend realize how much he misses her, but Ante's cousin the constable tells me that the boy is gone for good. I hope this event in her life does not make it harder for you to be a matchmaker. She can be very hard-headed.

I told Kata that a child of fifteen, especially a girl, could not travel across the ocean alone. Fortunately, a couple from our village, Mr. and Mrs. Horvat, have booked passage on the same itinerary. They agreed to list Kata as their eighteen-year-old niece. All documents including the ship's manifest will show her to be eighteen, not fifteen. We dressed her in adult clothes and she easily passed as a young adult. Before she left, I lectured Kata about dangers she might face aboard the ship, and insisted she carry a large kitchen knife. I told her there are bad men on the boat and to be sure to protect herself always."

I rode with the couple and Kata on the train to France and saw them off before returning. They boarded the ship, La Savioe Sunday, June 21, 1914 for a seven-day crossing. They are on their way. The Horvath couple will accompany her as far as Pittsburgh, then make sure she gets on the right train to Clairton. She'll probably arrive the last day of this month or early July.

It will be lonesome without that little scamp running around and driving me crazy. I will surely miss her, but we both know it is for the best. I'll close for now.

Love,

Mara

July 3, 1914

Dear Mr. and Mrs. Radić,

I must begin by telling you that had we known that your Kata had a wild streak, we would have given serious consideration to declining the offer to be her chaperone. I don't mean to be an old hen, but I think it is important that you are told of her behavior. The day before we docked in New York, we were summoned to the Captain's quarters. As we were listed as her escort, the Captain provided us with an account of her behavior during the crossing. We had no idea.

We were barely out to sea when she disappeared from our sight. According to the account, Katherina somehow gained entry to the upper decks of the ship, an area off limits where third class passengers were not permitted. Much of her time above deck was spent walking the forbidden area, but in at least two instances were serious enough that she could have been confined.

On the first occasion she found herself in a compromising position with a married man in a deserted galley walkway. He claims he was assaulted, but a crewmember who had witnessed the scene attested that the passenger attempting to get fresh with her and she bit the man's ear. The injury required stitches but the gentleman declined to press charges.

The second incident took place when Katarina again was able to make her way to the upper decks where she met a crewmember about her own age. The boy invited her to his quarters, also off limits to passengers, but she went anyhow. There were two other young seamen in the room. The boys offered her beer, then attempted have their way with her, but Katarina, apparently armed with a knife, was able to get herself clear of the young men and return to her own station. The three sailors were all put on report and punished for fraternizing with a passenger.

I attempted to talk to her and explain the dangers that were present onboard a ship, but she said that she missed her boyfriend, and had spent the time after the incident on deck, looking up at the starry sky, and wondering where the boyfriend, who had been called up as a soldier, might be.

After the incident, and for the remainder of the journey, she mostly stayed below with us. One Croatian sailor told her that the aggrieved crew members spread the word to their colleagues that the 'cute little dark haired girl was trouble.' She told me that steerage suited her. Life among upper class travelers did not impress her. Besides, she is certain that one day she and her boyfriend would travel as first-class passengers.

I felt it was my obligation to give you a full report.

Sincerely,

Ada Horvat

17

NEW WORLD, NEW ADVENTURE

I accompanied Ante and Stela to the Clairton station and we all waited anxiously as the train blew off steam and several passengers disembarked. I'd spent the morning doing errands, gathering my suit from the cleaner, shining my shoes, and having a professional haircut and shave before meeting my bride-to-be at the railway station.

Kata emerged like an angel through the hissing fog of the noisy train engine that announced her arrival. Though Stela at first did not recognize her daughter, Kata immediately spotted her mother on the platform. It had been a decade since they had last seen one another.

"Oh, Mama, you look exactly the same," cried the girl.

Stela stepped back. "Katarina! Let me look at you. You're all grown up and ready to be a woman!"

Kata hugged her father. He looked haggard and frail as he stood to embrace her. She remembered him as a big, strong man, but he seemed to have shrunk. His crisp black hair had become thin and grey. He wiped the perspiration from his forehead with the back of his hand, revealing wrinkles that had deepened across his brow.

"Hi Papa," she squealed. "I missed you and Mama so much. I am glad to see you."

"You look beautiful, my little princess," Ante said. "So grown up. So pretty."

Kata blushed. "Aw, Papa, you have been around men too long and have not seen a girl."

Ante grabbed my arm, "Kata, this is Peter Novak, our favorite boarder."

She barely noticed me, giving me a weak nod and then turned her attention back to her parents.

The joyous reunion continued with Kata at its center. They hugged and kissed and Stela cried. Kata seemed too grown up to cry, at least when people were watching.

I took Kata's suitcase and trailed behind as we walked from the depot to the Boxcar Boarding House.

Kata took a nap while Stela prepared a feast for dinner. Then she took center stage. All eyes were on her after she awoke and joined her parents and the workers. The men gathered at the outside dinner table. Kata was the center of attention. I sat at the table, wearing my finest freshly pressed wedding and funeral attire, hair combed straight back and slicked down with Pomade. From my cheeks wafted the aroma of an extra-large helping of the barber's after-shave cologne. One would never have known by looking that I was a common laborer in a steel mill.

She gave a shortened version of her shipboard escapades, then told of her train ride. "I ditched my stuffy mentors before the ship docked, and, playing the role of an eighteen-year-old, fearlessly got through Ellis Island with no problem. Wearing my best outfit and best smile, I sailed through the inspection process, then made my way to the railway station by showing my railway ticket to men in uniform.

"At the station I changed my money into American dollars, and struck out across Pennsylvania on my own, free of my 'uncle and aunt' Horvat, who had constantly looked over my shoulder during the crossing. Seated on the same bench inside the train was a couple not much older than me. The long ride to Pittsburgh went quickly once I discovered the young couple came from Karlovac, near our hometown.

"Klaudija Šimundić and her husband, Damir, were en route to McKeesport, just a few miles upriver from here.

"Klaudija asked if I'd heard about Archduke Ferdinand's death in Sarajevo.

'No,' I asked. 'Did another royal die in bed with his mistress?'"

Some of the men laughed at the remark. My face reddened.

She giggled and continued. "Klaudija answered, 'Not this time. It was an assassination. Some radical Serbs shot the archduke during a parade in Sarajevo. They killed his wife, too.'

"I asked if they caught the assassins and Damir said there were several involved. One was caught one for sure. The others were still running. And here is the scary part; some of them might have been living near our village."

When she paused to take a breath, the men sat as silently as church mice.

"I might have known one of them."

She sighed dramatically. This girl knew how to work a crowd.

"We girls were still chatting when the train arrived at the depot in Pittsburgh. I showed my voucher for Clairton at the ticket window and was directed to a local train, and again rode with Klaudija and Damir. After a short ride we stopped in Mckeesport. Before they left we promised to keep in touch. The locomotive rumbled and in no time I'd arrived in Clairton."

I did not talk much during dinner. Kata, on the other hand, held court, barely took a breath between tales of the old country. "Austrian and German soldiers are everywhere. They drink and curse a lot. Of course that doesn't bother me because I'm modern, but some of the younger girls are simply shocked at their wild behavior."

Of her aged grandmother: "Baka Mara is a sweet old lady but everything frightens her. She is afraid of her own shadow. She needs to live a little."

Of the older boys: "The boys are always talking about going to war. I don't think they really want to go. They just talk that way so girls will pay attention to them."

Of her boyfriend: "Branko is such a dreamboat. He says I'm an important part of what he does. I can't talk about it because it is a secret, but he might have been involved in the shootings in Sarajevo. He wants to marry me but I'm not ready yet. Maybe when I get back. He is a big shot in the political movement. He might have already been killed in the war, I'm not sure, but he carries a lock of my hair for good luck wherever he goes, especially on dangerous missions."

My heart was pierced as she spoke of Branko. I thought our marriage had all been arranged. My confidence sagged, but I would not give up hope.

Of the ship: "I met so many people in first and second class. We weren't supposed to go up there but the crewmembers invited me and it was lots of fun, except when a couple of boys tried to get fresh with me. But I showed them. They're probably still hurting. And so many people on the ship. All different, and everybody sounded silly speaking their own funny languages."

She held court for over two hours rarely stopping. The other tenants and I sat in awe, listening carefully to every word she said. Kata loved the attention.

Thankfully the other boarders did not tease me but everybody noticed how dapper I appeared. Everybody, that is, except Kata, who paid me no mind at all. I thought to myself that she would never agree to marry me, especially after tales of Branko.

Dinner finally ended. Stela cleared the table and the men went to nap or play cards or to chat.

Finally, the chores were done and the men asleep. Stela and Kata sat on the benches outside the boxcar. In the quiet of night, as I lie on my cot, unable to sleep, I eavesdropped on their conversation.

Stela spoke, "Our priest is Croatian. He will come by tomorrow in preparation for the ceremony. You must accept your responsibilities."

"The ceremony? What ceremony and what responsibilities are you talking about?"

"Katarina, you are no longer a little girl. You are a woman now, and circumstances of war prevent you from returning home. You must make the best of your life in this country. We are not wealthy and there are few options for a young girl who does not speak the language of this country. You cannot work, so your only option is to marry. That is what Father Drobak is coming to talk to you about tomorrow."

Kata laughed. "Ha! I know you are teasing me. First, if I was going to marry anybody it would be Branko, if he would have me and if he has not been killed in the war."

"Your grandmother told me about this boy and his radical political views, and how he steals and gets into fights. He is trash, and you don't even know if he lives."

"Oh, really? Well, who is there to marry in this pigsty? One of those dirty steelworkers with black grease under his fingernails?"

Stela snapped at her daughter. "How dare you judge the people who live under this roof? They pay rent and that is how we have provided you and your grandmother with extra cash all these years.

Your father and I work our fingers to the bone and so do these men. They are strong, honest men and deserve better than your smart mouth remarks."

Stela regained her composure. "Kata, you are betrothed to that quiet young man who wore fine clothes at the dinner table. You met him at the train station. His name is Peter. Peter Novak."

The girl was dumbfounded for a moment as her mother's words sunk in. "Marriage is not in my plans, and certainly not to that old coot from the dinner table with axle grease in his hair and who stinks like perfume. I want to live, to soak up and enjoy America. This was supposed to be a vacation for me and I'm not about to ruin my vacation with talk of marriage to some old fogey."

I cringed as the words poured from her lips.

"From what I hear you have been doing a lot of living lately. It is time for you to grow up. This trip will not be a vacation for you."

Stela softened her approach. "Peter is such a good man. He is like a son to us. He saved enough money to build a house. He already owns a large plot of land that overlooks the river. He is a gentleman and a kind man. He will treat you well."

Still Kata was not swayed. She crossed her arms and uttered a flat, "No! No, no, no, no, no. I will not marry him or anybody."

Stela stood fast. The priest comes tomorrow."

When Kata realized her mother would not change her tune, she became a dramatic, defiant teen. "That old goat? I cannot stand the stink of his perfume. No way, no how. I'd rather eat broken glass."

I sunk deeper into a depression.

"Think it over and we'll talk about it tomorrow morning after the day shift has gone to work and the night shift is asleep."

"There is nothing to talk about because eight mules pulling four plows could not drag me to the altar. Besides, I already have a boyfriend. Branko is cute and lots of fun and I'm sure he's waiting for me back home. Someday we'll marry and be rich. I'm not ready to be the wife of some old man!"

As I listened to the conversation between mother and daughter through the open window, my heart continued sinking. I wanted to crawl into a hole and never come out.

The night shift left for work. I had taken time off so I remained. I sat on a bench outside as my cot would be occupied. An extra cot had been set up and blankets hung, serving as curtains for Kata's privacy. Stela could not find sleep that night. Ante tried to comfort her but she was too upset at how far the night's events had strayed from her plan. After Ante fell asleep she left the bed and walked outside and sat with me. As the first rays of sunlight peeked through the trees, she said, "I know what I must say and do."

It was well I did not witness what happened next or I'm sure I could not bear it. Years later Stela told me of the events that took place.

The following morning mother and daughter barely exchanged a word. Stela filled the men's lunch buckets and I left with the day crew. The night shift returned to the boarding house after a hard night's work. The men ate, then took their places, and within minutes all slept soundly. Stela directed Kata to join her outside and the two women sat stoically on the bench. I remained awake in my bed and listened.

Stela began, "Kata, you are my only child. I will never have another."

The girl began to say something but Stela shushed her. "There is nothing in the world I would not do for you. Your father and I work day and night in order to send money. We have sacrificed and saved for a better life. Times have been difficult for us. When the men strike they have no money to pay, yet they still expect to eat. We cannot afford to keep you here or hire you as domestic help. There is simply not enough money. Now you have to step up and sacrifice the same as we have done. You are no longer a child. Pete is a good man. He has lived with us for years. He is clean, saves his money, works hard, and is as gentle as a lamb. He does not drink, gamble or chase women and he will make a good husband."

Kata protested. "But Branko...we planned to be together forever. I told him I would only be here for a short time. What about Branko? What about my life with somebody of my own choosing?"

"In time you will forget Branko and he will forget you. Besides, Mara told me all about his drinking, fighting, and problems with the law. Pete is your best choice."

Kata folded her arms and clenched her jaw. "I won't marry that old man. I can either go home or stay here with you until Branko can come for me. But I will not marry him."

Stela took a deep breath. This was not a moment she had hoped for, but she had not been a den mother to two dozen hard-working, often drunken steel mill workers without learning a thing about the art of persuasion.

She focused steely eyes on the teen, and said flatly, "Girl, get a dose of reality! There is a war in the old country. Even if we could afford to send you back, which we can't, you could not go. Ships have already stopped carrying passengers across the ocean and are being refitted for war. Unless you are prepared to swim, you have no way to return. You are stuck in America, at least for however long this war lasts. When it is over you might not even have a home to go back to. If the artillery shells don't destroy our village surely the enemy will loot and pillage it. Your Branko will be called up to fight and could be injured or worse, if he has not already, so there is nothing to go back to. Your future is here."

Still Kata's resolve was not broken. She bit her lip as her mother explained further, "Things are hard here, too. We survive during the good times but word is another strike is about to begin. That means our income will fall. We cannot afford to keep you. That leaves you two options. Marry Pete and have a good life that he will provide for you." Stela paused and took a deep breath. "Or go out to that railroad track, sit between the rails, and wait for the train to come and finish your life. Those are your only choices."

"But I can work. I can sew or keep house for a wealthy family…"

"You cannot. Nobody will hire a spoiled girl who has never done an honest day's work in her life and who does not speak the language. I have given you your choices." And with that Stela dabbed her red eyes with her apron, turned on her heel, and climbed into the boxcar.

Kata sat without moving. For a long moment she was too shaken to realize the impact of what her mother had just told her. Although only fifteen, she had aged at least three years in the past twenty-four hours. Kata was strong, however, and stubborn. She accepted intellectually that the Europe she left would soon be thrust into war, but she was not ready to surrender so quickly. Using the melodramatic logic of a teen, she decided if she could not spend her life with Branko, then life was not worth living, and she would end it now, in front of her mother.

She picked up the hem of her long skirt and raced from the Boxcar patio onto the railroad tracks, prepared to sing her swan song. She sat at an angle on one iron rail, and stretched her legs across the railroad ties toward the other rail, waiting for the train to squash her. At the first sound of the train she would hurl her body across the tracks.

There she sat as she cried, sat and cried, and sat and cried some more, praying silently that the train would come soon and end her miserable life. Branko was probably dead, or worse, he no longer cared for her. She prepared to leave nothing of herself but a spot on the tracks in a foreign land.

As she sat and cried she thought of the boys and girls back home. Of the games she used to play, of swimming in the Kupa River, and of her grandmother. She thought of the clean, fresh air that swept over her beloved village and how different it was from the dank cloyed filthy air that hung over the Monongahela River, and how much she missed all things from home. She looked toward the nearby belching smokestacks that lined the river before her, and thought of the strange people in the train depots who spoke a language she could not understand. She hated this place and she hated the old man her parents wanted her to marry. She wiped the snot from her nose onto the hem of her dress, and then cried some more.

Kata sat and wept. Each ticking second stole one speck of resolve from her unyielding constitution until nearly broken, though her stubbornness still would not let her surrender.

After five hours she was all cried out. She looked skyward and asked aloud, "What shall I do?"

A feeling-voice inside stirred. Your plan has been set. Marry Pete and you will have a life you could not imagine.

She had not heard from the voice inside her for some time but still held it in high esteem. "But Branko. What of my true love?"

The words formed in her mind, His life will change. You may one day see him but you will be disappointed in what he has become. You must embrace your new life.

Nothing could have changed Kata's mind except the voice inside her. She had absolute, unwavering faith in it. With no tears left to cry and little hope of ever seeing Branko again, Kata slowly lifted herself from the track and made her way to the boxcar.

"I will marry the old man," she told her mother, without further emotion.

Stela heaved a huge sigh of relief. What she knew that Kata did not, was that no trains ran that day.

"Good. We will all take the train to Pittsburgh tomorrow—you, me, your father, and Pete—to get the marriage certificate."

By seven o'clock the following morning a fog hung over the Monongahela River valley, having snatched dawn from the lower end of Clairton. The mills along the river screamed and belched smoke, mingling with the fog to produce a dark morning smog along State Street and the railroad tracks. Streetlights up and down the State Street cast an eerie shade of blue. In an hour the whistle would blow for the men who worked the night shift to find their way home, creeping catlike through the smog, just as those who worked the day shift found their way to the mill.

It was a hot, muggy, summer day and the residents of mill towns along the river all the way to Pittsburgh were trapped by the smoke and fog. Kata was certain the foul air was an omen of bad things to come.

The trip to Pittsburgh did not take place that day as had been planned, but not because of the air quality. I needed to arrange to miss work and the process of getting the proper papers for the wedding had to be confirmed.

The week also gave us time to get to know each other a little. "I'm happy to marry you, Katarina. I will be a good husband. You will see. We will be happy together."

215

"Just remember, Old Man, this is not my choice. We are both trapped here; me by the war, and you by fate. I'll do my duty but don't expect me to be happy about it."

Somebody at work had told me that a girl must be twenty-one years of age to marry in Pennsylvania. I didn't know if that was accurate but like many immigrants of the era, government officials frightened me, so just to be on the safe side, I stated that my bride was twenty-one years of age. Poor Kata had aged nearly seven years in two weeks. The friend at work had also told me that I could get into trouble for marrying a girl so much younger than me, so to be safe I dropped a few of my own years, and attested to being age twenty-two.

By the following week plans had been finalized and on Thursday, July 9, 1914, in the Allegheny County courthouse downtown Pittsburgh, my bride, Katarina Radić and I, Peter Novak, placed our signatures on a marriage license. Ante and Stela added theirs as witnesses. Neither my wife nor I, nor our witnesses spoke English. The County Clerk did not speak Serbian, Croatian, Bosnian or German. The official who signed the document, Austin D. Stevens, was an Anglo man who wrote our names as they sounded to him: Catherine instead of Katarina, and Peach instead of Pete.

In addition to the marriage license listing an Anglicized spelling of our names and the names of both of Kata's parents, the license stated that neither applicant is "…an imbecile, epileptic, of unsound mind, under the guardianship of a person of unsound mind, or under the influence of any intoxicating liquor or narcotic drug." Such was the legal procedure for obtaining marriage licenses in Pittsburgh, Pennsylvania in 1914.

Like most ethnic Croatians, Kata's family attended the Roman Catholic church, but not religiously. I'm a Bosnian whose religion is

Serbian Orthodox, but I was not particularly religious either. Kata agreed to follow my religion, and when children came along, they'd be christened in and attend the Serbian Orthodox church.

Kata resigned herself to perform her wifely duties, but her streak of independence did not allow her to warm up to me emotionally or speak my name. From our wedding day onward she addressed me only as, "Old Man."

We returned to Clairton on the train, sitting next to a well-dressed Slavic-looking man reading an English newspaper. Ante ventured, in broken English, "Anyting for Europe?"

The man looked up from his paper and said, "They caught all but three of the men who killed the Archduke. They're still looking for—" he scanned the paper and read three names, two of which meant nothing to any of his fellow passengers. The third name, however, made Kata stiffen with fear "—twenty-four-year-old Branko Kukić."

Stela was asleep and did not hear mention of the name. Kata bit her lip and showed no outward emotion as the train chugged along, and at first I didn't give it a second thought. But as I felt her stiffen next to me, and glanced over at her, my mind began to race. Branko was the name of her boyfriend. What was his last name? Was it Kukić? Could Kata's boyfriend be an assassin? I wanted to ask her but did not think this was the right moment. Maybe it wasn't him. But why did she flinch at the mention of the name? Perhaps one day I will ask her of this, but it would not be today.

18

A Child Has Died; A Woman Has Been Born

Kata and I moved out of the Boxcar and into a lean-to that I built on our property. It served as a temporary residence while we improved the overgrown lot.

"Look at all this land. It is all ours! No mortgage. No bank landlords. Just ours. Yours and mine," I boasted, my chest swelling with pride. "And look at the view. From the higher ground, where our house will sit, you can see the river. This is my dream. I hope it will become yours as well.

"What do you think of our new living quarters, Mrs. Novak?"

"Ask me when it is a home," she replied.

I deeply loved my new country by this time, and knew it would always be my home. I also knew that because I came into the country illegally I'd probably never become a U.S. citizen, but still, I wanted to be as American as possible. The first step in that process meant a name change for each of us. At the urging of Kata's parents and other immigrant friends, we dropped the more formal Peter and Katarina and nickname Kata, began our new lives together as a more American-sounding, Pete and Katie Novak.

Katie showed little outward emotion, but she had to admit that the land belonged to her and that gave her a measure of freedom. Until that time, she didn't appreciate the empowerment that came with property ownership.

The three-acre parcel, unusually large for a city lot, showed promise, but presented several challenges. Rich Western Pennsylvania soil combined with fresh springs throughout the property to produce an overgrowth thick with weeds, vines and trees. Katie and I, with the help of neighbors, friends, and church members, worked daily, chopping trees, weeding, and burning the cuttings. With the help of many hands, the large lot that sat on the corner of Arch Street and Park Avenue, overlooking State Street, began taking shape. With weeds and overgrowth gone, the mill and the Monongahela River offered a spectacular panorama.

Katie and I walked the sloped property together each day. "I think this is the best place for our house. It is the highest point and will offer the best view. What do you think?"

The southern part of the acreage increased sharply in elevation. My location choice for the house was not on level ground.

"How can we build a house on a steep hill, Old Man? We need the floors to be level. I know that much."

I did not change my expression. She was showing interest in our future home. "We'll dig part of the hillside away to make a little nook."

Within the first couple of weeks we had cleared corner of the property of most trees and other vegetation, and cobbled together a shack on the premises to replace the lean-to. The back quarter of the property, hilly and rustic, presented other challenges. The same friends who helped clearing the lot of vegetation became our excavation crew, digging and removing part of the hillside. Wheelbarrows found their way from the mill, and friends brought their own shovels.

I chose the highest point on the property that could accommodate a house. The location allowed for sunlight into the early evening. The rest of the property, including the garden, had full sun all day and well into late afternoon. The hillside also had a spring of fresh clean, cool running water, making the saturated mud and muck difficult to remove.

When the area was nearly completed I took Katie by the hand and led her to the level spot that was the site of our future living quarters. "See, Katie. With the house here, the highest point on the property, look at our view."

She took several moments to survey the scene before her, saying nothing, but I could tell by her smile that she was pleased.

With a smile and the slightest bit of pride and affection in her voice she said, "Ok, Old Man. I'm seeing your vision."

"Keep the picture in your mind, Mrs. Novak. One day you will be the envy of the neighborhood. We will build a house as fine as those up on the hill, where the rich people live."

With the help of church members, co-workers, family, neighbors, and friends, we hacked away at the dense foliage daily, until the entire parcel had been cleared. Then we began to prepare for the foundation and a nearby garden. Serge Dukić, a family friend of Ante and Stela, was a construction worker in the old country. He had drawn an informal set of blueprints for the house.

The mill had prepared me for hard work, but Katie surprised her parents and me. She worked as long and as hard as anybody on the site, including me. She remembered the voice inside her and took ownership of her life and her property. This was the first thing that belonged to her; not her parents, not her grandmother, but to Katie and her husband. She put every ounce of strength and effort into building her own home.

The daily toil of digging away the hillside and clearing the land was not work for me, but a labor of love. I had worked long hours in Bosnia and on the estate in Germany. Long hours were nothing new to me. Although I'd labored in the grime and heat of the steel mill each day for the past several years, my heart still belonged to the earth. My roots ran deep into the soil. I would forever be a farmer and cultivator.

My garden was planted and harvested during construction of the house. "Look at these onions and tomatoes," I proudly told Katie. "Have you ever seen vegetables that looked so good?"

"I give you credit, Old Man, the garden is good enough. Tomorrow I'll pick some lettuce, cabbages, tomatoes, and onions and see if I can sell them to the green grocer."

My essence was the soil, but like her parents, my Katie had the heart of an entrepreneur.

The garden became one of the finest in Clairton. Katie supplemented our income by selling the garden's fruits and vegetables to green grocer merchants as well as neighbors.

My slingshot came in handy when I lived at the Boxcar Boarding House. I'd used it during my life there, to drive away pests and supplement meals with small game. I did the same on the Arch Street property.

My bank account continued to pay generous dividends, and remained a nearly forgotten secret. I didn't tell Katie. My in-laws knew of the account since Ante helped me open it, but they respected my secret as well. I was determined to live frugally off my mill income and Katie's entrepreneurial ventures, and let the bank hold the money.

Katie resigned herself to live the life to which she had committed, but she never forgot Branko. Even decades later, though she never discovered his fate, she confessed to me that thoughts of him remained in her heart. She wondered if the authorities had caught him, but assumed he had been killed in the war or executed for his role in the assassination.

Katie's confessions about Branko made me jealous, of course. I tried as hard as I could to win her heart. "Katie, I wish you could forget Branko. I'm your husband now."

"Old Man, a person only has one first love and no matter what happens after that, they never forget their first love."

"You are my first and only love, Katie. I understand what you say, but I wish things can be different between us."

Unable to pierce her heart of steel, I accepted the one-way love. As we grew together, my hope was that Katie's love and passion would focus on her children and grandchildren.

Once construction began on the house, Katie refocused her life and put all the energy and spunk that had encouraged her to cross an ocean at age fifteen, into building her home and life in America.

Each morning over breakfast I'd tell her, "These are the instructions for the workers today."

She would write them down as a guide for the day's labor. Then I'd leave to work a full shift at the mill.

Katie carried out the instructions, to the letter. She was the best site worker and supervisor ever. When I'd return to our property after my shift ended, the two of us would continue working side by side until dark, sometimes beyond.

Several silver-haired immigrant retirees from the mill would come by each day to serve as 'sidewalk superintendents.' One of the daily 'supervisors' called me aside.

"Young 'a man," he said in his best English with a heavy Slavic accent, "you muss never be slave to house. Let 'a da house be slave for you."

I stared blankly at the old man who said, in his steel-mill Slavic-English pidgin, "You have plenty room here, lots building material. How easy you make house double size?" He pronounced the word "double" as "do-blay," but I understood.

"You mean four stories, not two?" I asked in Bosnian as I held up four fingers on one hand and two on the other.

"No, no, keep a two-story. Doblay 'a size you foundation. You have plenty space."

I nodded, "Okay, but… why would I want to do that? Family comes some day and fits in my house. I don't need two houses."

"Assa right, you doggone betcha," the old man smiled. "Live a one side, rent udda side. Renter you best friend. He 'a gonna pay you house."

I thought for a moment, then smiled at the old man, shook his hand and thanked him, "Hvala, thank you, Mr. Štokić. You'll be our first guest for dinner in the new house."

I raced over to Katie who was talking to Serge Dukić, our construction manager. He had drawn an informal set of blueprints for the house.

"Serge, you've built lots of buildings in Croatia. What if I want to double the size of my house?"

Serge rubbed his chin. "You mean add two more stories on top of what you have?"

"No. That is what I thought at first, but Mr. Štokić suggested we build identical buildings side by side with a common wall."

"Doing it that way would be easy, but you'd lose part of your garden."

"What if we go to the other side of the house and dig away more of the hillside? One wall would be common with the house we're building now, and the opposite wall flush against the hillside, like a wedge. Can we use the same specs for both houses?"

Serge teased, "Are you sure you're not an architect?"

We both burst out laughing at the suggestion.

Our laughter quieted. "Yes, we can use the same set of drawings for both houses by flipping the specs. One house will be a mirror image of the other. The only possible problem I foresee is, by taking out more of the south hillside, that spring is so close it might soak the floor of the second house during heavy rains, but other than that, the idea is solid."

"Okay, friends," I cried out to my workers, "grab a shovel. We have more digging to do."

The men dug the foundation and did other building tasks each morning under Katie's direction. Once work got underway Katie left the site and walked to the lumberyard to select materials and supplies.

Simon Chottiner owned a lumberyard a block from the home site, and supplied lumber for many of the local homes, including ours.

"Simon, how much this lumber?" She would ask the question in Croatian peppered with bits of English and large helpings of panto-mime.

He'd give her a price. If she felt the price was too high, she'd shrug and say, "No understand."

Katie's negotiating skills regularly got the best of Simon over the price of goods. If materials were not exactly the size and cut she wanted, she would argue and haggle until the man finally gave her the best product and best price possible. Some days the exasperated

Simon would shake his head and say, "I'm selling this inventory to you below my cost. I'll include delivery. Just leave so I can attend my other customers."

When I stopped by after work to pay for the materials Katie had purchased, Simon would repeat his daily mantra to me. "Pete, your woman is killing me. I don't know how long I'll be able to stay in business. With her dickering, I'm losing money."

I didn't say much, only shrugged. But his comments always made me smile with pride as I walked back to the home site.

"How did your day go with Simon?"

"I could've done better, but we got a good price."

"Mr. Chottiner says you're going to drive him out of business if you keep beating him up over the cost."

She looked blankly at me. "Do you want me to not argue so hard?"

I put my arm around her waist and kissed her on the cheek, "No Mrs. Novak, I want you to continue exactly as you are, my best foreman and chief negotiator."

"Hrumph." She tried to act aloof, but I'm sure I saw a glisten in her eye.

The double house began to take shape. A large yard occupied the space between the home and rugged unpaved path that was officially named Arch Street. I built a grape arbor that separated the porch from the street, and added a chair swing that took up most of the room on the porch. That swing would become my favorite place to sit and contemplate the world as I smoked my pipe or hand-rolled cigarettes, using only Cutty Pipe brand tobacco.

By the second summer we had completed the kitchen and living room, which we used as a temporary bedroom until the master was finished.

As we stood admiring the house, my arm around Katie's waist,

I said, "What do you think, Mrs. Novak? Shall we move into this mansion?"

"We will move in, but we can't forget those who helped us. I've been thinking of having a housewarming party. Mama likes the idea. It will be a good blessing of our house."

The event was very well attended. Neighbors who helped clear the plot, dig away the hillside, and build the house, provided food and drink. Even the sidewalk superintendents came to the party. Mr. Štokić had a seat of honor for his duplex idea. Stela and a group of neighbors, with help from the Ladies Auxiliary of the new Serbian Orthodox church spent the entire day cooking and serving favorite dishes from the old country.

The wooden porch served as a covered entry to the solid oak front door. A large window pane, which Simon had reluctantly included free of charge, graced the center of the door.

"Come see the kitchen," Katie said proudly to the latest group to walk onto the porch. "My Papa made the kitchen table. It seems large for just two people but it is perfect for entertaining friends. And look, my Old Man bought me a brand new Franklin stove for an anniversary present."

The crowd of guests followed Katie through the kitchen area. "This is our temporary bedroom before the upstairs is finished, but today we moved the bedroom furniture out back so it can serve as a dining room."

"Up these three steps," she opened the door at the top, revealing a manmade cave. "Here I have my own laundry room, so I can wash and even hang clothes in here when the weather is bad. And behind it, deeper into the cave, is a cellar that stays cool for when my Old Man makes wine. "

Back in the kitchen several ladies oohed and aahed over the large front window that provided a stunning view. "Look! You can see the mill and the Mon from here!"

The crowd finally dispersed and we lugged the bedroom furniture back into the living room. That night Katie and I had our best sleep ever.

～

The living side of the house was finally completed and the rental side was still under construction. Katie loved showing off her pride and joy of a house. Her neighbor, Millie Vucanović, was one of the first to take the grand tour of the finished house. Millie gawked with each step as she followed Katie.

As they climbed the stairs, Katie felt a little lightheaded for a moment. It quickly passed when Millie posed a question. "What will you do with all the pears from the sapling Old Man Skokić gave you?"

"Sell some. Give some away. What do you think I should do?"

"I'll show you tomorrow."

The following day Millie returned with a bag full of pears. "These are from a tree in Skokić's yard. Let's skin them, cut them up and put them in a large pan."

The women went to work, removing the skins, stems, seeds, cutting the pears and adding water and sugar. "You stir for a while, Millie, the smell is making me a little noxious."

"Ok," Millie replied as she took the wooden spoon from Katie's hand and continued stirring.

"Now, boil this for three hours. I'll be back with something that I will let you borrow."

Millie returned with copper tubing, a cask, and a few other items. "Watch while I strain off the juice. See? Get out as much pulp as you can until only juice is left. Once the juice cools we'll add brewer's yeast to it."

Katie, always a quick study, memorized each step of the process. "Now we pour this into the cask I brought. You can borrow it for a few weeks, while the concoction ferments. I'll come back and show you how to condense the fermented stuff. We'll be passing it through this copper tubing. The liquid will cool and drip into a jug. That will be the best homemade pear hooch you will ever taste."

"Millie, you just showed me how to make a profit from pears! Thank you."

"We're all in this together, honey. When my man got busted up in the mill and couldn't work, I'd 'a starved if my old Armenian neighbor didn't take me under her wing. She helped me. I help you. You pass it on. Now, show me your upstairs."

We walked up to the second floor using the narrow staircase between the kitchen and against the common duplex wall. "This room above the kitchen is my master bedroom," Katie said as she motioned Millie to follow. A glass panel door led them onto a balcony above the porch. The air was crystal clear that day.

Millie swooned, "Will you look at that beautiful view of the mill, the river, and hillside communities across the Mon!"

Katie added, "During bad weather we don't have to go outside on the balcony. We can see the river through the picture window next to the door. We have two more bedrooms for when children come, and the privy behind the laundry room."

Millie took a long look at Katie. She was about to tell her how lucky she was to have this house, but stopped in mid-sentence and said, "Honey, when did you have your last monthly?"

Katie thought for a moment and answered. "I don't know. I've been too busy to pay attention. Why?"

"Unless I miss my guess, you're pregnant."

"What? No!" answered the shocked teen.

"I've had nine, honey. I know the look. Your color and thick waist don't lie."

Katie wasn't so sure, but in August, one year after our house was completed, she gave birth to a baby girl. We named her Ruža, after my mother. I was anxious during the entire pregnancy, as I thought of the tragedy that surrounded my own birth and the death of my mother. But my fears proved unfounded. Katie had an easy birth and barely broke stride building and taking care of her home.

The decision to build the mirror image second house into the hillside led to problems. As Serge had predicted, the fresh spring that provided the property with crystal clear water, flooded the second house during each heavy downpour. After each flooding, we painstakingly pulled up the floorboards, cleaned the muddy mess, and re-laid the floor. We lived on the dry side and the second home was used at various times as a rental, storage, and gambling establishment—the latter unofficially, of course.

My Katie, with direction from her mother, proved to be a natural at managing our household. She became an excellent cook and baker, and thanks to Millie, a bootlegger. Mladen Ilić, one of the Serbian mill workers who lived at her parents' boarding house, stopped by one day with machine parts from the mill. "Katie, your mum and Ta have been very good to me. They took me in when I had no place to stay. Now I can do something nice for you. See these parts?"

Katie nodded, "Uh-huh."

"I'm going to build you a still so you can return Millie's. Where do you want it? You can't have it in the kitchen. It needs to be in a place with room to bury the mash and where government agents won't see it."

"How about we put it in the woods behind the house toward the back of the property?" She took him to view the area.

"Perfect!" It took Mladen a few hours to construct the device, and soon the lady of the house had her very own still.

Mladen showed Katie how to operate the bootleg firewater machine to make moonshine whiskey from corn that grew abundantly in my garden. Her still was a little different than the one Millie had loaned her, but the end product was the same. She'd already learned how to make booze from pears. My young wife, the entrepreneur, was a quick study. She easily mastered the art of making moonshine and selling the illicit brew to Stela's boarders and other steelworkers.

⁓

Wednesday, the day the eagle screamed at the steel mill, was otherwise known as payday. Katie, the intrepid businesswoman, provided a place for workers to come after work on Wednesdays, drink a little homemade liquor, and gamble. The front room of the duplex had card tables set up. Stela came to help and her tenants followed. Wednesday night became poker night at the duplex. Katie graciously took a percentage of the winnings from the gamblers, but took nothing from those who lost money.

We both worked hard but Katie was also enterprising. She kept chickens and sold fresh eggs to nearby stores as well as neighbors. She learned how to bake the ethnic pogača bread just as my father told me my mother Ruža had baked it. The bread became such a hit that ethnic Slavs came from miles around to purchase it.

By our second year wedding anniversary we had cleared all of the habitable land, completed the duplex, regularly planted and harvested one of the finest gardens in the area, and settled in as a married couple with a child. Katie managed the household with self-assurance, supplementing my mill income with her assortment of enterprising activities.

Katie's change from rebellious, angry teen to mistress of the house took place at breakneck speed. She refashioned herself from a cocky stripling that had run the streets, into a housewife, mother, and businesswoman. With the second half of the duplex completed, Katie occasionally took in boarders. She ran her boarding house much the same as her mother had run the Boxcar. Men slept on cots and took their meals at tables set up in the front room that doubled as a mini-casino on payday nights.

Baby Ruža was asleep in her bassinet in the kitchen as Katie baked *pogača*. She heard a knock at the front door and answered it to face a shabby-looking man.

"Dear Lady, a friend told me it is possible that you might have a room to rent. I have been to dozens of boarding houses but none had a space. I'll sleep anywhere." He spoke in her native language. "Please, Missus, I beg you."

"I'm sorry that you can't find a place, but we are completely full - two men to each cot. I wish I could help."

Something told Katie to turn the man away, but he looked so pathetic that she felt certain the impulse could not be her inner voice speaking, so she ignored the feeling, thinking it must be a false alarm.

"Madam, my name Arben Bizi but most people call me AB. I am from Albania, and speak the Slavic languages. My friends know me as a sober, hard worker with many talents. Perhaps I could offer my services to help in any way, if only I could find a place to put my head at night." He began to sob as he spoke. "Please Madam, I beg you."

She thought for a moment, then said, "I have one room that is not quite finished. There is no bed and the walls are still rough. You can have it for half price."

"I'll sleep on the floor," he implored her. "I can finish the walls, too. I'm very handy. Please, Madam. I will pay in advance."

Certain that she had misread the feeling inside, Katie agreed to rent the unfinished room to the bedraggled AB for half the normal rental fee with the agreement that he would finish plastering the walls. She led him to the unfinished room, which was little more than a closet-sized storage space.

"This is perfect Madam. Here is the rent money in advance as promised." He placed the money in her hand, which he held with both of his, as he kissed the back of her hands.

Almost from that first moment Katie knew she'd made a mistake. AB did not finish the interior of the room as promised, his personal hygiene was filthy, and he bullied other tenants. Katie later told me the man made inappropriate and sexually suggestive comments to her when I was not around. He proved to be a drunk and paid his rent late each month. When Katie told me of this over breakfast one morning as I prepared for work, I decided to tell AB to find another place to live once his month was up. But Katie insisted that it was her responsibility to do it, since she ran the boarding house and it was she who had taken him in.

Later that morning, while cooking, she heard rapping at the screen door. The heavy oak entry door had been propped open for circulation. Katie turned and saw AB, drunk, standing on the other side of the locked screen. He had wrapped some money around his exposed genitals and said, "Hey, baby, here is the rest of your rent money. How about sliding it off, nice and slow."

Katie wore an apron with the edges wrapped around a pail of boiling water she had just taken from the stove. "You filthy pig. You need to clean your dirty money and your smutty mind. Let me help you."

She tossed the boiling water through the screen and onto the tenant's exposed groin. AB howled as the hot water splashed over the cash, his genitals, and his hands. Screaming in pain, he dropped the money onto the porch and turned away, clutching his manhood and spewing expletives toward Katie in Albanian and fractured English. "I'm gonna' kill you, whore!" he cried as he limped off the porch.

"Don't you come back here no more, you no good son of a bitch," Katie yelled after him. She unlocked and opened the screen door, retrieved the soaked money and placed it on the table to dry, then smiled to herself at how she'd fended off the crude Albanian.

Even so, the voice within her offered a warning. It took a moment for Katie to clear her mind and focus on the message. That man is dangerous. Be sure you are able to protect yourself when he returns. Katie did not believe AB would return, but she'd ignored her inner voice once before when it warned her about AB. The voice had never been wrong. She would not ignore it again.

That night after dinner Katie told me about the inner voice that had protected her since childhood. "You know, Old Man, it's hard to describe. It is more like a feeling than a voice, but I can understand exactly what it says. My first memory of the voice came when I was about seven years old. I had a fight with the teacher the previous day and she told me not to return until I was ready to do penance.

"I wasn't ready the following day so I dressed in my school clothes and took my lunch because I didn't want my Baka to know I'd been kicked out of school. Instead of following the other kids, I went swimming alone and in my altogether in the Kupa River. I was having a wonderful time enjoying myself when something stirred inside me. At first I thought it was a shiver from the cold water but it happened again. The feeling was very strong and warned me to get out of the water immediately and run.

"The feeling, or voice, sounded so compelling that I swam as fast as I could to shore, ran up the riverbank, and grabbed my clothes. When I looked back, the river roared wildly. A dam had burst upstream and the river raged, taking several lives and causing much damage. The thing inside my gut saved my life.

"Remember when at first I refused to marry you? My inner voice was the reason I agreed to marry you. The only time I ignored it was when it warned me to not allow AB into the house."

"Why do you tell me this now?" I asked.

"I had a warning that AB would return."

I listened in horror as she told of the times she had been in danger, and was nearly reduced to tears as she told me why she had agreed to marry me. Katie told me the rest of the story in vivid detail what happened that morning. Her pride would not let her show fear, but she did say that she had concerns about being alone in the house while I worked, on the slim chance AB skulked nearby.

"As long as you keep the front door bolted and there are other tenants within earshot that could hear you scream for help, you would probably not be in much danger."

Still, after she told me about her inner voice's warning, I worried that the ex-tenant might try to do something to harm her. What to do?

"Tomorrow when I leave for work I'll tell the two policemen walking the beat to keep an eye out for AB and to watch the house. I'll find out where they get their whistles and buy one for you to blow in case you sense danger. The police on this beat know us. If they hear your whistle they'll come immediately." Meantime I'll get you a gun to keep around the house."

A German co-worker at the mill came to mind. I only knew him as Otto. He was a German immigrant, and we had become friendly, often speaking in his native tongue. After all my years in America I spoke little English, but my German was still impeccable. Otto was always short of cash and frequently tried to sell his possessions at work.

The next day on my way to work I spoke to I saw our neighborhood beat officer. O'Leary, an immigrant, told me he would tell the other policemen as well, and they would keep an eye out. He also said he had an extra whistle we could borrow for a while.

Inside the mill I asked Otto, "I need to buy a pistol for my wife for protection when I'm at work. Do you have any idea where I might get one?"

He paused for a few moments then spoke quietly. "My cousin worked as a gunsmith in the old country. As luck would have it, he brought several pistols with him from the Fatherland. What do you have in mind?"

"Something small for a woman. Easy to load, easy to concealed, but accurate."

"I think I know the pistol that would be ideal for her. The weapon is a side latch Mauser pocket pistol. Might you know of it?"

I shook my head. "No, I don't know about guns."

"My cousin worked in the Mauser gun factory. He sold me a Mauser for my wife's protection. The pocket pistol is a small gun that will fit easily into a purse or an apron pocket, and it is accurate at short range. It is very popular. For you, my friend, I will arrange the sale for a very good price. But I cannot bring the gun into the mill and my cousin will insist on meeting you face-to-face. I will talk to him and make arrangements for the sale."

The next day Otto gave me the details. "My cousin is very nervous about selling his guns in the U.S. He, shall we say, did not exactly purchase them from the factory. I assured him you are my good friend, but he is still a little nervous. He has the pistol you want but insists you meet him alone in the mill parking lot to do the sale."

I agreed and the meeting was set up for the following night between shifts. Rain drizzled that night as I left the mill and walked to an area used as a holding pen for some of the mill's machines needing repair. The area bustles during work shifts but is deserted during shift changes. I waited for several minutes until I heard a noise in the dark shadows. A man motioned me to the side of a hopper. I couldn't see his face and his overcoat, with the collar up, was pulled around his shoulders.

"You come alone?"

"Of course. Just as Otto told me."

"You know that if you try to identify me, or if you are a government agent, I will shoot you. Do you have the money?"

I pulled several bills from my pocket and handed them to him. "This is the amount Otto told me."

He grabbed me by the shirt collar and pulled me behind the hopper. Holding me with one hand he frisked me with the other.

"I'm sorry, but I had to see if you were a government agent. No gun, no badge. I am satisfied."

He handed me a package that contained a gun and bullets, then turned and disappeared.

I didn't expect the purchase to be so frightening, but anything that might keep Katie safe was worth the risk. When I arrived home I did not tell her the whole story. I just gave her the pistol. She slipped it in the pocket of her apron. Perfect fit!

A few days later I was at work as Katie did her morning chores. She had flipped the mattresses in the rental unit and moved to our master bedroom, removing the bedding for laundering. Baby Ruža was asleep in her bassinet at the foot of the bed.

Since AB's threat she carried the pistol everywhere, but had fired it only once, in the backyard for practice. She didn't like the noise it made.

As the police later reported, the former tenant appeared to have approached the locked screen door, then quietly slit the screen and unlatched the door. He entered the residential side of the house, vacant except for Katie singing to baby Ruža, upstairs.

With her back to the bedroom door, she was totally absorbed as she hummed a song to her baby. She did not hear AB stealthily climb the stairs until a creak gave him away. Thinking it must be me, she called out, "What you doing home, Old Man?" She turned just as AB wrapped his arms around her, squeezing her breast with one hand, and holding a knife to her throat with the other.

Katie struggled to break his grasp but the Albanian had surprised her and his sinewy arms, too strong to allow her to twist free, held her fast. He spun her partway around and pressed his stinking mouth hard to her ear. The knife still tight against her neck broke her skin. His breath, foul from rotting teeth, cigarettes and whiskey, swept over her. AB had not bathed or shaved for several days. His whiskers scratched roughly on Katie's smooth skin.

His gravelly voice whispered as he held her. "Croatian bitch, I'm gonna work you over good and give you what you want. Then I'm gonna kill you."

He twisted her neck until she faced him, then pressed his foul mouth over hers. She tried without success to bite him while she slid her free hand down into her apron pocket, wrapped her fingers around the Mauser, and squeezed the pistol's trigger.

The gun went off with an ear-splitting blast that echoed through the large master bedroom. The bullet missed both her target and herself, ricocheting off the furniture behind AB. Everything seemed to be happening in silence and slow motion. Her adrenaline pumped so hard, she did not hear the shot nor feel the tiny kick of the weapon inside her apron pocket, but the noise stunned the Albanian enough that he dropped the knife, which skittered under the bed.

In the instant that the bullet was fired, a humbling change came over the intruder. He froze momentarily and his mien transfigured from the aggressor to a sniveling, shrunken coward. The impact of the bullet, though it missed him, transformed him into a hunted animal getting ready to flee for it's life.

The deafening report of the Mauser echoed through the room and hallway, rendering the occupants of the room momentarily deaf. AB eased his grip on Katie and opened and distorted his mouth, trying to get his ears to pop back to normal. The move allowed Katie an opening to step back, aim the small pistol at a spot between his legs and pull the trigger a second time. The pistol misfired.

Without the knife, AB punched Katie in the face, splitting her nose. He turned and ran out the bedroom door and stumbled into the hall.

Katie, eyes blurred and bloodied by the punch, and with adrenaline coursing through her body, wiped her eyes, followed him to the landing, pointed the gun after him and pulled the trigger a third time and a fourth.

AB shrieked as a bullet tore through his flesh. Screaming incoherently, the wounded Albanian careened to the bottom of the stairs and onto the porch, tearing the screen door from its hinges as he went. Katie fired two more shots. He disappeared, not to be seen nor heard from again.

Once AB fled, Katie stood for a moment, more than a little shaken. She staggered back into the master bedroom, sat on the edge of the double bed quivering and waiting for her ears to stop ringing. Her eyes were still blurred from the punch in the face. Trickles of blood ran from her nose, and from a nick on her neck where the knife's tip had punctured her skin. When her ears returned to near normal she finally heard little Ruža screaming in her bassinet next to the bed. Katie leaned down to pick up the baby and saw the bullet hole. Her first shot apparently had ricocheted off the furniture and tore through the bassinette just inches from little Ruža's head.

Seeing that her baby was safe, Katie realized what might have been, and clutched the child to her breast, trembling for several minutes until she heard shouting at the front door.

A neighbor heard the gunfire and grabbed the attention of the local beat cop walking near the mill gate. The officer rushed to the house, gun drawn. Seeing the screen door hanging like a limp rag doll, and blood splattered on the jamb and stairwell, the officer surmised the shooter fled but feared what he might find inside. He shouted for Katie.

A second policeman arrived. They cautiously climbed the stairs to find Katie still clutching her daughter and trembling.

As Katie calmed, the police officers listened intently to her story and investigated the scene; the holes in the wall where bullets had lodged, blood splatters along the stairs, and the hole in the bassinet.

At the mill, one of the supervisors pulled me aside. "Hey Pete, there was a shooting at your house."

I immediately dropped what I was doing and raced home, terrified at what I might find. Several neighbors had gathered on the front porch under the grape arbor. I elbowed my way through them, past the broken screen door and took the steps two at a time.

My heart pumped harder than ever as I looked in and saw Officers Kočka and O'Leary interviewing Katie.

"Are you ok?"

Katie nodded and when little Ruža noticed me, she stopped crying and I lifted her from Katie, holding the baby in one arm and hugging Katie with the other. Ruža closed her eyes and leaned against my shoulder and slept as I squeezed Katie tighter.

"Thank you for helping to protect us, Old Man," she cooed as she rested her head on my shoulder.

I listened to her narrative to the police while clutching them both as Katie spoke. Hearing her tell the two officers the details of the incident, I silently gave thanks that I'd bought the illegal pistol from Otto's cousin.

The two immigrant policemen walked this beat and were also regular patrons of Katie's payday poker nights. Both took part in her gambling games and drank her bootleg whiskey.

Kočka, the Czech, put his notebook aside. "Well, Katie, you know that I have to make a report whenever there has been a shooting. But since I can't find a victim I can't be sure whether there was a shooting or an accidental misfire. He winked at her and licked his lips. "If I just had something to calm my nerves, perhaps I could be sure it was an accidental misfire." O'Leary licked his lips, too, nodding in agreement.

Katie winked. "I'll be right back."

I held the baby while Katie went to the dugout behind the laundry room and pulled out two Mason jars filled with clear liquid. She returned, and handed one jar to each officer. They tucked the jars into their tunics and O'Leary said, "Accidental misfire. I'm sure of it. See you at the card game." Officer Kočka nodded in agreement.

19

The Accidental Entrepreneur

After the shooting and AB's disappearance, rumors flew about his life and background. Some said his body turned up in the Monongahela River. Others insisted he recovered, changed his name, and moved to Chicago. My workmate Otto told me he'd heard that AB had been convicted of murdering his wife in the old country.

Once the trauma was behind us, our lives continued on the upswing. I enjoyed my dream home, family, and tolerated working at the Clairton steel mill. That all changed when the Amalgamated Association of Iron, Steel, and Tin Workers called a strike. Owners shuttered the mills and strikers picketed the plant. Tension between the union and management ran high and several skirmishes erupted. The Serbian foreman who hired me now demanded I return the loyalty by joining the group of non-union workers to work during the strike.

"Pete, I've done a lot for you and your wife. I stuck my neck out for you and covered for you while you built your house, and you know that. Now I am in a bind. Come to work and I will make sure your rate of pay increases and see that you get promoted. We need good men like you."

Union bosses knew of management's efforts to seduce members into crossing the picket line. During a union meeting a steward made a direct threat. "Any man who crosses the line and becomes a scab will never work in a union shop again. Maybe he gets hurt, real bad. Maybe his family gets hurt, too, or maybe his legs get broke and he can't work no more. We know where each of you lives. Do not cross that line and put your family in danger. Stand with us and we will win the benefits we deserve. The union is strong. We will win!"

As he spoke he looked directly at me. I had always been a gentle man, not one to march in protest or defy either the union boss or the foreman. Both sides pressed me to make a decision; walk the picket line or cross it.

I explained my problem to Katie, and as usual she had an answer for me. "Old Man, I know you don't like to fight and don't want to walk the picket line. Why don't you go visit my cousins Zdenko and Branislav Brezović in Johnstown? You can come back after the strike is over."

I agreed, and left Clairton that evening, taking the train to Johnstown, seventy-five miles away. Their mills were working around the clock with no threat of a strike. Katie's relatives kept me until the Clairton strike ended.

After several weeks of union picketing the strikers finally settled and I returned home. Seeing my wife and child made me glad to be back and anxious to return to my daily routine. As I dressed for work Katie asked, "How was Johnstown?"

"I was cold the whole time. I forgot to take my sweater."

My mother-in-law, Stela knitted me a sweater when I first arrived at the Boxcar. Rain or shine, summer or winter, I never dressed without wearing it beneath my shirt. But I'd left for Johnstown in such a hurry to avoid a confrontation that I'd forgotten to take it with me, and caught a chill.

I slipped the sweater over my head, then pulled on my work coveralls and placed my foot on a chair as I laced the black steel-toed safety boots. "The Brezović family sends their best to you and your parents."

Katie packed my lunch bucket and handed it to me. I left the house in full steelworker attire, and began the five-block trek to the mill gate to begin my first day back to work.

A brisk fall morning greeted me as I walked from the house to the mill gate. A thick shroud of fog hung over the river, pressing against my body and every inch of exposed surface that surrounded me. On mornings like this the fog lay like a blanket, cloaking the river, creeping up the banks and beyond. A blue-white haze formed an illusion that hid all structures beneath its ghostlike body, and obscured the view from our bedroom picture window. Katie lost sight of me almost immediately as I stepped off the porch. I could tell she was happy to get me out of the house and out of her way that morning as she would be tending to her routine; baking, cleaning the rooms of the boarders, doing laundry, and other daily tasks.

The fog made the rest of the world invisible, but I was able to navigate the five blocks from memory, like a blind man who needed no walking cane. When I arrived at the gate and showed my identification badge, the guard examined it closely, and then checked it against a typed list. "You don't work here anymore."

I looked at him, puzzled. The guard spoke only English and I thought maybe I misunderstood him. Using my best English, I tried to respond. "What you mean? I be transfer? Who say?"

The guard, an Irishman who the men called Brady, did not speak my language, and of course, my limited command of English didn't help. "You call boss. He say you mistake."

Brady held firm, "You no longer have a job at the mill. Your boss can't help you. He's gone too. The union barred you from working for crossing a picket line during the strike. Scabs can't work here"

"I no scab. I no cross line," I insisted.

The union steward appeared at the gate with a list of names in hand, and repeated the mantra I knew by heart. "A firm union rule states that any union member who crosses a picket line will be barred from working in a union shop. Here is a list of names of men who worked as scabs during the strike.

He scanned the list. "Here is your name, Pete Novak." He pointed to my name on the list.

"Is mistake. I no cross line."

The three of us stood waited at the guard gate as other men were waved through. Another union official was summoned. The representative looked me directly in the eye and recited the union line, "Pete, one of our brothers positively identified you as a scab who crossed the picket line. There is no record of you walking the picket line during the strike. Did you walk the line?"

I shook my head.

"Then you must have scabbed. You're a scab and troublemaker. You may not work at any union shop from this day forward." He extended his hand. "Give me your badge."

My English language skills were limited to curse words and terms specific to the steel industry. I did understand some of the words of the union official, including 'troublemaker' and 'scab.'

I answered with bungled English. "I no be scab, sunamabitch. I no start no truble. I no cross line. Why you lie on me?"

The official stood firm. "Give me the badge, Pete. There is nothing I can do."

Further arguing would do no good. I did not walk the picket line so I couldn't prove I didn't cross it. My refusal to take sides during the strike cost me my job. I said, "Somebody lie on me. I no be scab," and handed over my badge to the union official. As I turned to leave, the fog began to lift from the river and a few rays of sunlight broke through. That usually signaled a good omen, but not today. Still clutching the lunch bucket, I retraced my steps home.

Katie seemed surprised to see me back so quickly. "What you do home, Old Man? Why you no go work?" She did her best to learn as much English as she could, but most opportunities for conversation took place with neighbors who also spoke Balto-Slavic languages, or steelworkers whose English language was nasty and off-color.

I answered in Bosnian. "The union man says I'm a scab. I didn't walk the picket line and somebody swore that I worked scab. They lied about me. I can never work in a union shop again."

Katie listened intently and when I finished she spat on the ground and spoke in English. "Piss on union. They bunch no good fuck bastid. You pay dues for nutting. I tell them go hell."

Katie's English vocabulary had indeed expanded and become more colorful.

My banishment from the mill turned Katie bitterly against unions. She knew her husband had not crossed the picket line, but she also knew that once a worker is branded a scab, there's no reversing the status, justified or not. She became so angry she ran out of English words and continued her rant in Croatian. "Let me tell you, that union is no damn good. They protect the lazy workers but refuse to listen to you. Either somebody lied about you and swore to it or the big shots just made it up. To hell with them all"

All of a sudden she went silent. She was still for several moments, as though meditating.

"What is it?" I asked.

"The voice inside me is saying something."

"What is it saying?"

"Not sure, but something good."

In an instant she left thoughts of the union men behind and vowed to do something to improve their life in America. The voice did not tell her exactly how, but she felt sure it would happen.

It was the first time I'd witnessed Katie interacting with her inner voice. I never understood it, but over the years it protected and guided her.

                    ~

Katie's appearance had changed considerably since our marriage. Her robust color glowed, and her figure blossomed; she had become a full-figure woman. She'd added nearly sixty pounds to her once-spindly frame since she arrived in America, cut her long black hair to make it more manageable, and walked with the air of a woman in charge.

She also inherited her parent's business sense, being both clever and frugal with family expenses. Her side income paid bills and purchased extras for the baby. Money from the moonshine, rent from the duplex, profits from the gambling games, and revenue from fruit and vegetables all went into Katie's budget. Still, without my steel mill income, the money stream became a trickle, and barely allowed us to survive. She did not have enough extra to do something she desperately wanted—to buy more rental property.

Katie did her best to balance the household budget without my earnings from the mill, but after my getting fired, the missing income made it a difficult task. We'd built the house by ourselves, adding segments as we could afford to pay cash for materials and within a year completed the building without having to mortgage the property. My famous garden fed the family with plenty of vegetables left over for Katie to sell to neighbors and to the local grocery store. Chickens and cows provided much of our food. Katie's ventures into bootleg whiskey and payday gambling nights also supplemented the budget, all of which allowed us to scrape by financially.

She didn't complain about her difficulty making ends meet nor did she tell me of her desire to purchase more property. She managed the household budget and it looked to me like she did more than an adequate job. I did not want to interfere.

Try as she might Katie was unable to figure how I'd saved enough money to purchase our property with my steel mill salary minus the rent and money sent to my family in Bosnia. Whenever she asked me about it I just shrugged.

She decided to visit her parents and ask their thoughts on matters of budgeting. When she got home did I ever get an earful!

Katie had not visited her parents in months. She neared the boxcar and saw Stela hanging laundry.

"Can the old washer woman use a pair of young hands to help?"

"Kata let me look at you. I am so proud of you. It has only been a couple of years and look at all you have accomplished."

She grabbed one end of a damp sheet and pinned it to the rope strung from the edge of the boxcar to a tree. "Thank you for the compliment, Mother."

The two women finished hanging the laundry then sat on a bench to visit. Ante joined them.

"Mama, I have gone over all our income sources again and again. I want to buy some rental property, but even with the money I've saved, I cannot figure how I can do it. You tell me the banks won't loan to us, so unless I can find another abandoned boxcar, how can I ever own rental property?"

Ante chimed in; "Why not use some of the money in the bank account?"

"Papa! Shush! Don't be a blabbermouth!" Stela hissed at Ante. But she spoke too late. Katie realized that her father had spilled the beans about something she did not know, so she pressed the issue.

"What bank account?"

The couple looked at each other. They must not break the trust or the promise they made to their son-in-law. A strained silence filled the air for several seconds until Stela broke the spell. "We promised Pete to keep a secret. That's all I can tell you. You are his wife and the two of you must settle this issue between you. Do not drag us into this any further. We have said enough to betray his secret."

As Katie walked back to our house she ran the numbers through her mind. "Of course! It only made sense that Pete had a secret stash to draw from when there was a budget shortfall." She smiled to herself. "That sly old closed-mouth devil."

She approached the house as I sat on the front porch having a smoke and watching the grape arbor, the baby at my side. "Old Man, we need to talk about money. Do you want to talk here or go inside?"

Not until that moment did the thought of my bank account enter my mind. I almost never thought about the money in the bank. It just never occurred to me to do anything but leave it where it was safe. I didn't have to manage money when I lived on the estate. I always had enough to do what I wanted. If I needed a little extra for materials or living expenses, I went to the bank. Otherwise I ignored my stash. My needs have always been humble. I patted the swing and motioned for Katie to sit beside me, then began, "I have much to tell you. I've kept much of my past to myself. There are things I have not shared with you. Now I have a wife and child. It is a good time to let you know."

Much of what I told her, Katie already knew or had guessed. I told of my mother's death while bringing me into this world, of the poverty in my village, of my indentured servitude, and the kindness Herr Richter and Marija showed me. I also expressed how considerate and important her parents had been to me when I first arrived and that I would be forever grateful to them and to her. I even shared how I had come to invent my slingshot.

By nature I am neither a talkative nor an outwardly emotional man, but my voice wavered, and I occasionally choked up while telling her these things. Finally, I told of the money Herr Richter had Marija sew into the coat lining, and that Ante took me to a German-Jewish bank across the river where I opened an account. "The money means nothing to me. I'm not even sure how much is in the account. When I walked across the state, I would have used it as tinder to start a fire if need be. Money is not important to me. You are important, and our daughter and the house and my family, and of course your parents. Not money."

By the time I finished talking, the conversation became the longest we'd ever had.

I did not reveal everything, omitting parts of the story about Hans' need for violence and sadism, and the part of my being a deserter and entering the country illegally. But otherwise I told her all about my past.

"Old Man, you don't think past tomorrow." Katie scolded me. "It's a good thing to keep money in the bank where is safe. I am not upset with you for not telling me, but my responsibility is to run household and balance the finances. What if you had been killed in a mill accident? What would happen to the money?"

I shrugged, "I don't know."

"Look, Old Man, you are a wonderful farmer and a terrific father. You are happiest when you're tending your garden, our home and daughter. Am I right?"

I nodded.

"What do you think if we use some of the money in the account to buy rentals? People need a place to live and they could pay us. We will have an income as long as there are people who need housing. You can tend to your home and garden and the baby. I will manage the rentals."

"It sounds like a good plan," I agreed. "Tomorrow I'll get some money from the bank and we can buy rental houses."

By the next day Katie had a plan firmly fixed in her mind. She had me dress in my best wedding and funeral suit and go to the German bank. I walked in, briefcase in hand, and Mr. Frank, the German bank manager smiled at me. "Good morning, Mr. Novak. How are you doing this fine day?"

He must have thought I planned to make a deposit. Instead I said, "I would like to withdraw some of my money."

He grimaced. "Of course. And how much do you wish to withdraw?"

"Ten percent."

The bank manager nearly had a stroke. Giving up ten percent of my assets was a blow to the bank but Mr. Frank, still intimidated by my large account balance, personally made the withdrawal.

"Herr Novak, Sir, please consider us for any future transactions."

"I will do that," I said, and left the bank with the same briefcase I'd used for my original deposit.

When I returned home and handed the briefcase to Katie, she emptied the cash into her purse. She left the house the following morning strutting like a woman on a mission, walking briskly up the hill and out of my sight, to the business section of the city and into a real estate office.

She returned and was a sight. I could barely contain my laughter as she reviewed her morning. Arms flailing, face contorted, she began. "Old Man, why do they let men who don't know English run businesses?"

"I don't know, Katie. You tell me, in English what you said and what he said."

"Ok, I go ene. I take out money so he see I serious. I say, haf cash and want for buy room house for rent workers.

"He say bank no lend for foreigner.

Her voice rippled through the porch and her hands were gesticulating like a choir leader. I couldn't help laughing so hard tears rolled down my face. The harder I laughed, the wilder her story telling became, stomping from one side of the porch to the other.

"I wave cash in hand. I say never you mind bank. I haf monies. How mush for buy rent place?

"He shake head and say me sumting in nudder language, but I hear he say banken no lenden."

"Then what happened?" I ventured.

Placing her hands on her hips, jutting one hip out, she said, "I pick up monies. Put in bag, and say him, 'stupid Ameddigan bastid!' And I come home. You want me say you on our language?"

"No, my dear. I understood every word."

She stood, angry, out of breath and perplexed while I sat on the porch swing. Even the baby was smiling. Katie thought for several minutes then bellowed in Croatian, "Old Man, can you talk Jew words? The agent tried to tell me something and I could not understand him."

She paused then said, "I don't understand it. I'm certain that our future will be in real estate. I showed the realtor my money but he just shook his head and talked in another language."

"If you are sure the man is Jewish, he probably speaks Yiddish. If he is a Russian Jew, much of his language sounds like Croatian."

"Not Russian," she said simply.

I suggested, "If he is German I could speak to him in his language."

"I think maybe he sounded German."

The next morning Katie dressed me in my wedding and funeral suit and she donned her best outfit, including a hat and jewelry borrowed from our neighbor, Millie. We rode the trolley up St. Clair Avenue to the real estate agent's office. The agent seemed taken aback at our appearance. Katie looked like a different person in her fine regalia, almost elegant, and her escort looked like a prosperous businessman.

I spoke first, in German. "Good morning, Sir. I am Peter Novak and this is my wife, Katerina. I'm here to help my wife understand the conversation you had with her yesterday."

The realtor seemed surprised when I spoke in a manner usually heard only among upper class Germans and Austrians. I had retained use of the language, despite not speaking much German during the past decade.

The young agent, in his best German, explained to me what he had tried to make Katie understand the previous day. "My deepest apologies if I offended you, madam," he said to Katie. Then he turned to me. "I was trying to explain to her that banks will not finance a mortgage for immigrants. She can buy a single house with the cash she carries, and make a decent profit by renting it out. But I have discovered that lending money to immigrants is a much more lucrative proposition. If she takes the money she has, and loans it to immigrants she can make considerably more than she would as a landlord, and with fewer headaches."

The man paused and introduced himself. "I'm sorry. My name is Albert Lhormer. I recently emigrated from Munich, where I worked as a banker. I discovered that many immigrants in the U.S. are unable to secure property loans. Banks here look at the person's appearance rather than their balance sheet or their drive to succeed. In order to purchase a house, they must save up, sometimes for decades, and pay cash."

Albert paused every so often while I translated his message for Katie.

He continued, "Since the local banks prefer to loan to Anglos or established business people, a large niche market has been created. Eastern European immigrants particularly are coming in droves but are handicapped by the inability to establish a relationship with the Anglo-run banks. The real money," Albert repeated, "is not owning property for rental, but loaning money to people unable to otherwise get a mortgage."

As I repeated Albert's words, Katie interrupted, "Old man, ask how lending money is a good deal to make money."

I asked and Albert patiently explained, "Interest is added to the loan. The property belongs to the lender until the loan is repaid with interest. If the borrower defaults, the lender gets to keep the property." He went on to describe the general workings of a bank.

I listened, clueless about the content of the agent's topic, and merely translating the banker's words. Katie concentrated intently and had me ask many questions of Albert, which the agent answered clearly.

When he finished, Katie had me ask him a direct question. "If money lending is such a good business, why isn't he doing it with his own money?"

Albert smiled. "Money lending is a government-regulated business. I am in the process of filing papers that will allow me to make real estate loans. My funds are limited to the savings I brought with me to this country."

Katie spoke again and I translated for Albert. "She would like to know if you would you consider a partner? We could put up some money. Katie knows the language of the borrowers."

Smiling at the bright young lady's proposition, Albert answered, "I agree, if Katie first develops her English language skills. I will hire her to work a few hours each day to come into the office, file, and learn English. If all goes well, and she learns Basic English in, say, six months, we can start our business together."

I translated. Katie nodded in agreement, but as they shook hands she held up three fingers and told me to tell Albert she would be ready in three months, not six.

For the next three months Katie came to the real estate office every day. When she returned home each evening, she gave me a full report of the day's events. It made for great dinner conversation.

She studied diligently; her intelligence and natural affinity for business shone as she learned the filing system and enough survival English to communicate with Anglos as well as her Slavic clients, although using severely broken and sometimes colorful English.

Over dinner she would practice her English as she regaled me with events of the day. "Today Albert say my English get better but sometimes I talk bad words. He say words in mill no good in business. I say tell me bad word and I make new one. He say me 'sunamabitch, bastid' is bad one and if I say 'sunamabitch, bastid' in office maybe I no able work there no more.

While we talking I filing. I look at number on paper and say Albert, 'Dis nomber, šezdeset i šest. How you say in English?'

"Albert say, 'Sixty-six.'

"I say him, Okay, when I get mad, I no say 'sunamabitch bastid,' I say 'Sunama-sixty-six.'"

"Albert laugh. He say 'Katie, you be do just fine.'"

The two immigrants developed and built their business by catering to other immigrants and even some Anglos, while Katie's English improved. Their concept might have been a first in Clairton, but in other parts of the country such loan businesses thrived.

As word among the Slavic community spread that Katie and Albert loaned money to immigrants, dozens flocked to the little office on the hill in Clairton. Others came from surrounding communities. Katie had a knack for languages and picked up enough of a dozen or so Balkan, German, and other European languages, in addition to English, until she was able to communicate with nearly all their clients.

I withdrew the rest of my money and put it into the business, but the cache still did not meet the needs of the community.

After the business had been in operation for nearly a year, Katie couldn't wait to get home to dinner to tell me of an elderly, well-dressed stranger with a perfectly trimmed full white beard and well-manicured moustache.

"Dis man, looking like gentleman, he come to the door and ask, 'Are you woman loan money to immigrant?'"

I interrupted her. "Tell me in our language, Katie. Your English is getting so good, and you talk so fast, I have trouble following you."

She switched to Croatian, "He wanted to know if I was the woman who loaned money to immigrants, and I asked why he wanted to know."

"The stranger chuckled. 'I already know the answer.' He extended his hand to me and said, 'my name is Henry Clay Frick. I am a businessman and have invested in coal, coke, and steel. I've been fortunate enough to do very well with hard work and shrewd investments. I would like to invest in your enterprise.'

"Albert heard the conversation and invited the man and me into the office. Frick explained his proposal and his plan. 'Europe is in a war that eventually will include American troops. When the war ends, prosperity will follow and people will have money to spend. Housing will be needed for returning soldiers, and businesses will need loans. The big banks serve the business community, but you have identified an area that is not being served by big banks.'

'People trust you and from what I hear you have done a good job serving them, but I am sure your resources are not unlimited, so here is my offer: I will provide you with a line of credit. You are now charging your customers seven percent interest. That is higher than the five percent the big banks charge, but your clients cannot get loans at big banks because they are considered high-risk borrowers.

'You only have so much cash to loan. Imagine how much more money you could make if you had an unlimited source of money. I will provide you with a line of credit and you will pay me three percent. That leaves you with a profit of four percent, less than you are making with your own funds, but you will be using my money and earning four percent on loans you could not otherwise make. Do you understand?'

"Albert understood perfectly. Frick's plan was perfect for us. Albert said he would explain the difficult to understand parts of the plan to me later but I wanted to have my say.

"I know 'bout you, Frick. You're a good man. You helped bust the union and fought with Carnegie. I'm ready make a deal, but I'll give you two percent, no three."

"Albert just sat, surprised that I understood Frick's proposal, and shocked that I tried to negotiate with him. Albert later told me he was sure I blew the deal and that Frick would walk out. But Frick smiled and said, 'little lady, I like your spunk. Two-point-five percent and it is a deal.'

"I wasn't sure exactly what 'point five' meant, but trusted that if the idea was bad, Albert would step in.

"We shook hands to seal the deal. When Frick got ready to leave, he said, 'Things are changing in America. I'm an old man and won't live to see all the changes but you two are the future. Smart business-women and immigrants will take the place of my generation. You will succeed and your success will make me richer than I am today. Your children and grandchildren will enjoy the benefits of your hard work and clever business sense. Never lose sight of the fact that any-thing is possible if you have vision and are willing to outwork the guy next to you. Get in touch with these people to set up a line of credit.'

"He handed each of us a business card, turned on his heel, and walked out the door.

"After Frick left, Albert explained fractions to me and said how my deal would make tens of thousands of dollars of profit over the years. He said, 'Katie, you are a natural at business. The luckiest day of my life was when you walked through that door.'

"I smiled and said to him in English, 'Yeah. Sunama sixty-six.'"

20

CHANCE ENCOUNTER

Katie and Albert prospered in the money lending and real estate business while I enjoyed taking care of the household chores in Katie's absence. Although still a young man of not quite thirty years, I worked happily in my garden or relaxed on the front porch between household duties. My respite included enjoying my pipe or a hand-rolled cigarette of Cutty Pipe tobacco between my lips. My joyous days included tending baby Ruža, and bringing her to the garden as my father brought me to the farm in Bosnia.

The rich soil along the Monongahela River, black and free of rocks, so differed from the dirt I'd wallowed in during my childhood. The ground in Clairton reminded me more of the rich soil of Germany. I sometimes thought that if I could only send the American topsoil to Stabandža it would increase the crop yield several times.

I loved those days, wishing I could live out my life just working in my garden and loving my family, and perhaps one-day, grandchildren and great grandchildren. I barely spoke English, but America was my home and my future. My family lived here and my wife's business thrived, allowing me to enjoy the things that were so important to me.

In my quiet moments I thought of the estate and wondered how Herr Richter got along without me. I worried about Hans, knowing of his very dark side. I knew Hans had killed and dismembered the boy in the forest. It seemed so unfair that Herr Richter, such a kind and gentle soul could have had a son such the opposite. I hoped Hans had matured and outgrown his wickedness. Perhaps he married and became a family man as I've done. I wondered if he pursued his studies seriously and avoided the war.

I thought about all that had happened in the years since my trip across the ocean and my marriage to Katie. As I daydreamed about the many people who crossed my path I felt a tug at my pants leg. Little Ruža was awake. I lifted her, kissed her, and then sat her next to me on the porch swing where we sang to one another.

I was as content as I could be as houseman and farmer. I even loved the river, polluted by the mills waste, and the dirty air that surrounded the lowland near the water. Filthy air and a tainted river meant a healthy economy. My Clairton property was paradise. Three acres of land and the house would have been a decent sized farm in Bosnia, or a small homestead in the rest of the Austro-Hungarian Empire. In the steel town of Clairton, my spread loomed much larger than the more expensive house lots on the hill.

I mixed the grapes from the arbor near the porch with those of a local Italian grape grower to make wine, and then sold the wine to steelworkers at the Payday Wednesday card games. I must admit that the games under my supervision earned considerably less money than when Katie ran them, but she more than made up the difference with her thriving Savings and Loan business.

My feelings toward the union leadership had mellowed and I donated food from the lush garden to the strikers during work stoppages. I became an upstanding citizen among the immigrants of Clairton.

As I sat on the swing with the baby, our neighbor Millie walked up the path in front of the house. "Old man Štokić passed yesterday. He's laid out up on the hill at Finney's."

"Oh, thank you for telling me Millie. Can you watch Little Ruža while I go to pay my respects?"

"Sure. That's why I came by. Go ahead and change clothes. I've got her."

Ivan Štokić, the man who first encouraged me to enlarge my house, had become a close family friend. Upon learning that he passed away I felt the need to visit with his widow and family. Ivan avoided the dangers of industrial accidents in the mill and after forty years of labor, retired with a pension. He died of lung disease at age eighty-seven. His viewing took place in Finney's Funeral Parlor located on the hill.

I rarely went up on the hill where most commerce, including Katie's business, took place, but did so this day to honor Ivan. I donned my fine wedding and funeral suit and left the baby with Millie, then walked up to the hill to the business district and to the funeral parlor.

"Mrs. Štokić, I am so sorry for your loss. The Štokić family is always welcome in our house. You have a wonderful family and I hope we will see you for many years."

"Thank you, Pete. He loved you like a son. I am an old lady. I don't have so many years before I see my Ivy again. Times have been good for us. We had a wonderful family together. Ivan was such a gentleman. He died in his sleep and I didn't know he was gone until he didn't come for coffee." She began to cry, then gathered herself. "But I have my three girls and my grandchildren. I am happy. I will see you at the mercy dinner?"

I nodded. "Of course."

After paying my respects to Mrs. Štokić and her family, I stopped by the real estate Savings and Loan office to see Katie. It was after noon and I hoped to spend time with her over a late lunch.

As I entered the office I watched Katie with admiration. She barely resembled the girl who crossed the ocean. Her command of the English language improved daily and her way with people, sharpened while working her side jobs at home, sparkled. She taught me about fashion. This day she wore a long black dress with a double stitched seam at the hips. A silver belt, cleverly wrapped around her ample waist accentuated the dress and gave her the look of a sophisticated woman. A strand of pearls encircled her neck complementing matching earrings. Her full red lips did not need to be highlighted by lipstick. Many women, immigrants and Anglos, envied her.

"You've grown up, Katie." I smiled at my wife. Albert stood behind her, and though he did not understand the Bosnian language, the message was clear. He winked and nodded in agreement. "Why don't you kids get out of here and get a bite to eat?"

Katie had not yet had lunch, so she took a break and we went across the street to the Crucible Hotel coffee shop. The Crucible offered the only hotel accommodations in town. Besides the thirty or so rooms, the hotel boasted the nicest coffee shop in the city. A silver and black sign that hung above the entrance announcing "Crucible Hotel and Café" shone brightly despite the foul air that bombarded it with particulates of mill residue. An Italian charwoman kept it clean. Her daily duty included wiping down the sign first thing each morning, except during bad weather.

The wooden floors, swept clean each night and waxed, shined. We entered the hotel lobby, and the waitress in the café portion of the hotel beckoned. Booths with upholstered benches and beautiful dark wood lined a wall to our right, welcoming customers who came in pairs. Across from the booths sat counter stools, available for patrons who came in alone or wanted just coffee or a quick snack. Toward the rear, tables with chairs made of twisted steel wire backs and round wooden seats awaited, covered with treated leather.

We found about half the tables occupied during the late lunch hour, including one occupied by two men dressed in rumpled, well-worn suits. The two might have been executives from the mill, or businessmen, or even union officials. They looked as though they must be in charge of whatever they did or wherever they worked.

I noticed one of the men, tall and thin, six-feet-two or so with thinning blond hair and pink skin, like a newborn's. The face of the other was blocked from view, though I could see he was portly and wore wire-rim glasses. He had wiry hair that started far back on his balding head and he chewed an unlit cigar. He reminded me of somebody but I couldn't remember who.

The two seemed to be deep in conversation, and whatever their discussion, it must have been important, as they had not touched the food that sat before them.

Katie and I sat in the last booth closest to the tables, and soon got caught up with our own conversation. "How is Ivan's widow doing?"

"Not bad. Her girls and the grandkids are with her. I think she's exhausted and still in shock. She asked me about coming to the mercy dinner."

"I'll try to get away, but make sure you go."

I nodded.

Katie sat with her back to the tables and I faced the men in suits. The waitress came to the booth to take the order. "Here's your coffee, kids. Usual for you, Katie?"

Katie nodded, "Ya." She was a regular and the staff knew her well. She added, "Bring my old man anudder coffee, too. He's don' be hungry."

THREE LIVES OF PETER NOVAK

We sat in the booth drinking our coffee, making small talk, and waiting for Katie's lunch to arrive. "I think I can get away from office for go mercy dinner," Katie sputtered in her fractured English, "just not sure what time."

Katie did not notice one of the men at the table staring at us. The portly man with the glasses and cigar stopped talking to his lunch-mate in mid-sentence and studied me. I tried to not make eye contact.

As he chewed the unlit cigar he said in a voice loud enough for me to hear, "I'm sure I know that man."

His tablemate answered. "You know a lot of people in this town. An old classmate, maybe, or a relative?"

"No," said the cigar chewer, "not from here. I know him from somewhere else. It has to be him. What a coincidence if it is."

The bespectacled man removed the unlit cigar from his mouth, stood, and approached the booth area. I tried to lower my head and look away.

His heels thudded on the wooden floor as he walked toward us and stopped where we sat, looked directly at me and said, "Hans?"

I froze. Unbidden calculations ran through my mind. I glanced at the man and stammered, in Bosnian, "Ne razumijem." I floundered, my face reddening. I now recognized the man who had spoken. Our last conversation had been in German, on the docks of Baltimore as we'd disembarked from the ship that brought me illegally into this country more than ten years earlier. It was Karl's voice. No question. Muted fears bumped into each other inside my head.

The man in the suit spoke in a friendly demeanor in German. "Hans, it's me, Karl, from the ship. Remember? We sailed together from Europe to Baltimore... must have been, what, eight or ten years ago? Your hair is darker and thicker, not like mine," he smiled, "but otherwise you look the same now as you did then."

263

Too stunned to respond, I did not move. Instead I focused on Katie as though in a stupor. Katie sat with a blank stare, attempting to process the scene. Her back stiffened. She shot a glance at the stranger that would wilt a wedding corsage, looked him directly in the eye and asked, "Vat you vant with my old man, you union bastid?"

Katie assumed the man to be a union official because he wore a rumpled suit. She had no love for unions since they banned me from working, and she did not appreciate them antagonizing me further.

Karl, taken aback by Katie's direct and firm question, did not respond.

I sat mute before Karl. Dressed in my suit I appeared to be the refined, educated German man with whom he'd had a chance meeting and brief shipboard friendship some ten years earlier. My wife, a nicely dressed ethnic woman, did not seem to have a clue of the happenings at the moment.

A rush of questions ran through my mind. Did Karl still work for the federal government? Who was the man with him? Why was he here?

If fate had smiled on me when I left Germany and met Karl, who unknowingly helped me enter the country illegally, surely fate it was about to now cause me pain.

Katie eyed the man in the suit, still assuming him to be a union official. She spoke to me in Croatian, "Old man, you go talk to your no-good bastard union man," then switched back to English, "I haf go back work."

She choked back her fury and left the booth in a huff before her lunch was delivered to the table. As she stood, her knee caught the tablecloth, rattling the coffee cups, sloshing the liquid and staining the cloth.

In an unusual display of affection, I stood and hugged Katie as she rose to leave, and kissed her full on the mouth. I thought it might be the last time I would see her and the baby.

21

Interrogation

Karl spoke quietly to me in German as people in the coffee shop began to take notice. In the ten years since we'd last seen each other, his command of the German language had improved, but was still far from perfect. I sat in the booth and stared blankly as he stood next to me. Karl finally asked, "You do speak German, do you not?" I nodded.

Sensing my discomfort and not wanting to arouse further suspicion, he suggested, "Why don't we move to my room so we do not cause a disruption here. There is a very important matter we need to discuss."

I nodded again and said nothing, but I knew Karl had found me out, and I would soon be arrested and deported. I entered the country illegally, avoided military service in Europe, ran from the Baltimore police, and broken who knows how many laws?

How in the world, I wondered, did Karl discover me? After all, I did exactly as Herr Richter instructed, burned all the travel and identification documents. I had been lying low for more than a decade. How could he possibly have found me out? Even my wife and her family didn't know all my secrets. Perhaps he'd discovered my name on the union rolls or the mill lists of employees.

As we left the dining area, Karl said to the waitress, "Be sure to add this gentleman's bill to my room tab. Tell room service to send up coffee and sandwiches for three."

Confused thoughts swirled in my head as we walked through the oak and glass front doors, along the carpeted floors, and upstairs to his suite.

I walked between Karl and the other man. My mouth went dry. I licked my lips and tasted salt from the perspiration.

Silently the three of us took to the stairs. My heart beat faster as we climbed. With each step, the stairs moaned under the musty carpeting. I clutched the glossy rail, worn thin from heavy use, until my knuckles turned white. Golden rays of sun caressed the wood and warmed my hand. I climbed like a stray lamb heading toward an unknown end.

With the turn of a key the door opened and Karl invited me to enter the suite that he and the other man had called home for the past week. Dark wood with ornate carving adorned the jamb around the heavy dark wooden door. Walls were framed with dark wood, some panels with paintings and others carved to depict vine fruit. Rich velvet curtains draped clear windows. A second room, with a heavy, iron chandelier served as a workroom. Papers lay scattered over every table and available space. As I surveyed the room I wondered if he used all that paperwork to track me down.

Karl showed me his badge, confirming what I already knew—that he still worked for the government and had somehow discovered my charade. I felt helpless as a fish on a grassy bank with a barbed hook through its mouth, hoping he would not send me back to Europe for punishment. At least if I were imprisoned in the United States, Katie and Ruža could visit me. The outcome of this meeting would not be good. Of that I had no doubt.

Looking back across time I thought my life was over, but at least I could take comfort in the knowledge that Katie's business was prospering. She could afford to hire help to tend the baby, do the gardening, and maintain the house and all the duties that I had enjoyed. Perhaps she would find an anxious, ambitious young boy to help as Herr Richter did with me.

On the other hand, I've never been one to weep over my circumstances. I've had a good life to this point, better than I could have imagined during my early years. Fortune smiled on me many times. I was prepared to take whatever consequences lie ahead.

Speaking heavily accented college-level American German, Karl said, "Okay, Hans, start from the beginning. Tell me what you do for a living, how you got here, and what your business is in this area. Tell me everything."

He intended the comment to be a friendly icebreaker between two old friends, to open a conversation. But I knew I'd been found out, so in perfect German, as Peter Novak, alias Hans Richter, I began to pour out my heart to the two government officials. The truth was a bad taste on my tongue.

"First and foremost, Karl, my wife knows nothing of what I am about to tell you. She is not involved in any way."

Karl rubbed his chin, adjusted his thick wire-rim glasses, and ran his fingers through his thinning salt-and-pepper hair, but said nothing and showed no emotion as I began to speak.

"My name is not Hans Richter. It is Peter Novak, and I'm no German diplomat. I'm not even German. I am an imposter. I'm simply a peon who came into the world in the hopeless poverty of a Bosnian village. My birth caused the death of my mother."

The two agents sat motionless. Karl nodded to Raymond, who began to take notes as I told my life story. "My belly was a constant companion to hunger in Bosnia, yet babies kept coming for my father and his new wife..."

When I got to the termination of my servitude, I described in minute detail the recruiter coming to the estate, the bribe to allow a substitute so Hans could travel abroad and avoid conscription, and how I used a duplicate set of Hans's documents to travel to avoid the army and sail to America.

"I boarded the ship with forged papers, and became terrified when we first met, fearing you might see through my disguise. I'm sorry, Karl, for deceiving you."

The conversation lasted throughout the afternoon. I paused only to drink several glasses of cold water, brought to the room by a hotel employee. The platter of sandwiches that Karl ordered went untouched.

I gave Karl every detail I could recall, even telling him of my slingshot. I wanted to be as honest and straightforward as possible, not because I hoped for more lenient treatment or a lighter sentence, but simply because I needed to unburden myself from the secrets I'd kept to myself for the past decade and weighed so heavily on my heart.

"I'm prepared to take my punishment for laws I've broken. But I beg you not to harm my wife or Herr Richter. She is innocent and he has been so good to me. It was only I who violated the laws of the countries. Nobody in this country, not even my wife, knows of my illegal status."

Karl and Raymond sat spellbound as my confession flowed. Raymond vigorously wrote notes throughout my confession.

When I finished talking I breathed a sigh of relief and again apologized. The two agents sat quietly for several minutes until, Karl asked, "Do you speak any English at all, Sir?"

I shook my head and responded in German, "No, I'm sorry. It was such a difficult task to learn the German language that, although I mastered it, I avoided all efforts to learn yet another one. The need was never pressing to learn American. Everybody I was with spoke the Baltic languages or German. I understand a little but speak almost none except for bad words I learned at the mill."

I stood and walked to the table to pour myself another glass of water from the pitcher, and Karl spoke to Raymond in English. I did not understand most of what he said at the time, but he caught himself and explained it to me in German. "I have a top-level clearance with the federal government and I've been trained to recognize imposters, spies, and fakes. Yet I had no idea when we met aboard the ship that you were not who you appeared to be, but instead an illiterate peasant boy. If you could fool me, perhaps he could fool others in a game where the stakes are much higher.

Karl smiled. "My friend, you have no idea the gift you have just given to your country. I now have a plan that could include you. It will help our government and if we are successful, not only can I make all your offenses disappear, I can include American citizenship for you as a bonus."

This time it was my turn to be stunned.

"I want you to go home and be as normal as you can. Say nothing of our meeting or my identity to anybody, including your wife. Can you do that?

"Yes, but I don't understand."

"You will soon enough. I'll be in touch. Do you have any questions?"

"Just one. How did you ever track me down?"

"That, Sir, was strictly Kismet. Fate. It was a stroke of good fortune and a strange coincidence.

For now, go home and wait."

Bewildered, I walked home in a fuddle.

22

PEASANT, SERVANT STEELER, SPY

"MOST SECRET. FOR YOUR EXCELLENCY'S PERSONAL INFORMATION TO BE HANDED TO THE IMPERIAL GERMAN MINISTER IN MEXICO BY A SAFE ROUTE."
The Zimmerman Telegram, January 16, 1917

The following day, after Katie left for the office, Raymond came by and knocked on the door. Instead of a suit, he wore common street clothes. "We have a meeting to attend."

"Give me a minute. Wait here. The baby is sleeping."

I walked to Katie's friend Millie's house and called through the open door, "Millie, can you watch Ruža while I go with a friend for a while?

"Sure, Pete. Go!"

Raymond and I walked up St. Clair Avenue to the Crucible Hotel and passed through the rear entrance and up the carpeted stairs. Nobody took notice of us. Once in the room, Karl gave me a history lesson. "As you may know, Germany has been at war for the past three years."

I shrugged. I'd heard bits and pieces but knew few facts about the war in my homeland.

"The Great War rages in Europe without American troops. President Wilson's Secretary of War, Newton Baker, calls it 'Europe's war.' Mr. Wilson kept us out of the war during his first term but privately he's changed his position. Our allies need our help, but the president is not willing to declare war without the support of the American people. My strategy, if successful, will help him get that support."

"Ok, I follow what you are saying, but still don't understand."

"Our friends, in Britain intercepted two German telegrams and turned them over to us. One announces that German submarines will sink all ships in the war zone, even merchant ships and passenger liners. The second one we call the Zimmermann Telegram.

"The Foreign Secretary of Germany, Arthur Zimmermann, wrote it in hopes the contents will persuade Mexico to help Germany by Mexico attacking America and keep us busy. Germany does not want America to enter the war against them."

"He wants Mexico to attack America? Why would Mexico even consider this?"

"Germany's ambassador in Mexico, by pledging money and materiel, will try to convince the Mexican president to attack the U.S. The Germans believe that if they can get Mexico to invade the US, our troops will be bogged down on our own soil, and not able enter the war against them. They don't know their telegram has been intercepted.

"As soon as he received the Zimmerman Telegram, President Wilson briefed me. I pleaded with the president. We need to enter the war and end it. He agreed, but to win the public's support, an event or incident is needed; something to justify a declaration of war to the American people and make sure the Mexican government will not attack us. The telegram offers that hope. Now do you understand?"

"I'm beginning to. But how can your knowledge of the telegram make a difference?"

"My task is to develop a plan and identify a team that will carry out a dangerous mission. The president chose me because I'm a career diplomat, have served three presidents, and I speak the German language. So does my assistant, Raymond.

"Raymond and I came here, to my hometown to work out the plan. I keep this suite for my work, away from Washington. It reduces the chance of information leaking. Washington can be an awful place to keep secrets. That's how I happen to be here. It was pure fate that I saw you. I'm as surprised to find you here, as you are to see me."

I began to smile for the first time. "And I thought you were here to arrest me for my transgressions!"

"No, my current project requires that an American spy pose as a German diplomat and courier. This 'German diplomat' will take a bogus message to the Mexican president, telling him of the Zimmerman Telegram but say it is a fake, and that a leak in German intelligence has been uncovered. We must convince the Mexican president that a small band of radicals has infiltrated the German diplomatic network.

"This 'diplomat' will tell President Carranza that a rogue messenger gave the fake document to the German ambassador to Mexico, Heinrich von Eckardt, who will innocently present the document to the Mexican president, and encourage him to rally troops against America."

"And you want me to be that 'diplomat,' right?"

"Precisely. You, as the 'diplomat' will tell the Mexican president that Germany's own intelligence agency has been compromised, then add 'Not only is the document a fake, but Germany has neither the means nor the inclination to support Mexico in such a folly as war against the United States.' You will also tell President Carranza that von Eckardt is unaware the document is a fake and that the German high command wants to let the scheme play out to identify the mole."

I sat staring blankly. I understood what Karl was asking me to do, but was flabbergasted at the thought.

"Once we are assured Mexico will not invade our southwest, the Zimmerman Telegram will be released to our press. The American public will be outraged at Germany, and President Wilson will have support to declare war."

I tried to understand the level of trust Karl had placed in me but still lacked the confidence that I could pull off this charade. I knew little of world affairs aside from the war that is taking place in my homeland. "Of course, I will help. But what can I do? How can I even consider taking part in such a grand and important venture? I'm just an uneducated peasant farmer and a laborer who has been banned from working in the steel mill. What skills do I have that could possibly be of value to you or the government?"

"Don't be so modest, Pete. On the table before you are files of every German-speaking American spy. Each has something to disqualify them for this mission. None fit the bill. When you came into the picture everything changed."

"What experience do I have for this project? I do not speak the language of Mexico and don't even understand much of what you said."

"Time is short but you will be well prepared. Raymond and I will be at your side at all times, and you will have a translator with you. Tony Velasco, one of my deputies, speaks fluent German and Spanish as well as English.

"Do not underestimate yourself, Mr. Novak. Your German language is still perfect, and you already have experience posing as a faux diplomat. I've seen how smooth you can be in that role."

I took a deep breath and paused for a moment of thought and self-reflection. "You are the professional. Do you really believe I can pull off this hoax? If you do, on what do you base your conclusion? I have no qualifications."

"In a nutshell, your qualifications are these: first, you look the part of a diplomat, or you will, once we make you over. Second, you speak perfect German, as a diplomat would. Third, your demeanor is calm and measured. When I think of the masquerade you pulled off during the ocean crossing, I know you are the man to pull this one off as well."

He could see I was still perplexed.

"Don't worry. I know that everything that I've said today is more than you can digest at the moment, but we'll go over this again and again until you understand perfectly. I wanted to outline the project to you because your role is crucial to our success. You will convince the Mexican president that the Zimmerman Telegram is a hoax. If we are successful, their government will be confused enough to keep from attacking our states in the west.

"Now, let's get to started. How do you feel about carrying a weapon?"

I thought for a minute. I couldn't believe I was actually buying into his argument. "I haven't shot a rifle in years and can't remember the last time I fired a pistol, but I do carry a weapon."

Pulling the slingshot from the inside pocket of my coat I held it up to him. "I use this now mostly for small game, but it can be effective against people."

Karl raised an eyebrow. "I was thinking of something a little more accurate and lethal."

I stood and went to a window of the suite and opened it. Across the street, perched on a pole, sat a crow. "See the bird on that pole?" I asked as I pulled a pebble from my pocket and centered it.

Karl and Raymond stretched to see the crow.

"I will hit the pole just below the bird."

Taking quick aim, I shot, and struck the spot squarely. The bird flew away.

"Well, that proves the accuracy of the device. But if our mission is compromised, you might need something more deadly."

"When I worked in the mill I brought home small ball bearings. I can assure you they can kill when they strike their target."

"The weapon makes no sound. That can be an advantage. I'll be sure to bring small ball bearings as ammunition for your device."

Karl continued. "We've already begun a thorough background check to assure that you have been totally truthful with us, but I believe you have. Once everything is verified, I will outline the specifics of our mission. But I must emphasize, nobody can know about this. You are sworn to secrecy. Go home. Tell your wife that you might have to leave for a week or so. Do you think you can arrange that?"

I nodded. "I have friends and rental property in Monaca, on the other side of Pittsburgh. I can tell her that I need to see them about some tenants. That is no problem."

"Good! We'll contact you as our plan is completed, and if you do this thing for your government, you will be well rewarded."

The two government agents shook my hand and sent me on my way. Karl and Raymond continued their work to counter the Zimmermann Telegram.

A few days later Raymond again hid in the shadows as he waited until Katie left the house, then came to my door. Millie stepped in to watch the baby and do household chores."

The hotel was beginning to feel like my second home.

"Hans… er, Pete, the agency has built a cover story and with you the primary player. You fit the part perfectly. You do not exist on any document in the United States besides steel mill and union records and those have disappeared. We were unable to find your marriage record.

"We don't expect it to happen, but if you are captured, all the Mexicans know about you is disinformation provided by my office. You are a phantom. There would be such chaos your identity would be virtually untraceable.

"I want to lay all the cards on the table before you commit to this mission. I'm confident nothing will go wrong. There is minimal risk, but anything is possible if the worst does happen, I promise you that your wife and daughter will be taken care of."

I thought for just an instant then said, "Karl, this country is my home. I understand there is a risk. But risks are part of life. Each day I went to work in the mill, an accident could have kept me from returning home. I'm prepared to make this sacrifice for my country."

"Spoken like a true patriot, my friend. Now, let me tell you what I've done since we last met.

"We rushed a research request labeled 'Top Secret—Urgent' through the Washington bureaucracy. It verified that you've been totally honest with us. But during their search of the alias Hans Richter, our researchers uncovered a chilling background. Let me read from this file.

"After being academically dismissed from Cambridge University in England, Richter relocated to Berlin in 1908. During his time in Berlin, a string of mutilations of young women took place. The case referred to in police files as 'Berlin's Jack the Ripper,' after the series of mutilation murders in London. Both cases remain unsolved, but the slashing stopped about the time Hans Richter became a member of the German Secret Police.

"The bureau expanded and the Secret Police was elevated to a secret intelligence agency called Department III-B. Hans Richter became one of its top officers, known by fellow police as *die Klinge,* or 'The Blade.' The term is a reference to the brutal interrogation techniques he conducted with the use of a scalpel. He now heads Department III-B.

"I am sorry to tell you of your former friend, Pete, but I want you to know that I will be as open and straightforward with you as I am with all my agents.

"The project is officially on and our team has just a short time to get you ready for the mission."

My cover story to Katie went into action. Her business had underwritten a mortgage on a rental property in Monaca, a two-hour train ride from Clairton. When the owner defaulted and returned to the old country, the property reverted to Katie and Albert's Savings and Loan Company. I volunteered to visit and evaluate the condition of the property. I would stay a week or so and visit with friends in Monaca and nearby Aliquippa. Katie didn't mind having me out of her hair while she worked on the booming business that occupied most of her time. We arranged for Millie to stay at the house and care for our daughter, with Katie at work and me away.

The night before I was to leave, Katie was unable to sleep. Her stirring woke me.

"Trouble sleeping, Katie?"

"Yeah. It is the voice inside me. Or maybe it's a dream. The message is mixed up. I'm confused but the voice never failed me. It told me you might run into danger on your trip. Old Man, you be sure you take your shooter, and be careful!"

"I'll take it and I'll be careful."

The next morning she tucked the weapon inside my coat and I put several ball bearings my vest pocket.

After Katie left for work, Millie arrived, and I walked down the hill to the train depot and boarded the train for Pittsburgh.

When I arrived, Karl, his assistant, Raymond, and two other men greeted me at the large urban station. Instead of transferring to a train for Monaca or Aliquippa, he directed me to a private parlor car owned by steel mogul Andrew Carnegie, but on loan to the government for special assignments. A beefed-up locomotive pulled the parlor car and a Pullman sleeper car. We boarded, and the train sped across the vast, sparsely populated countryside. Karl gave me a quick tour and showed off our surroundings.

"Here we have red plush carpeting, brocade couches, and gilt-framed mirrors to greet you. Fine china and gold-plated silverware grace the table. Hand-blown Murano glass chandeliers swing from side to side above this solid wooden dining table. Antiques worth half a million dollars decorate the car throughout. Look at the solid marble fireplace. Wintertime guests must appreciate it. The porter, also one of my staff, doubles as a chef."

He beckoned me to follow from the gaudy parlor car to a custom-built Pullman sleeper car. "This car is seventy-nine feet long, fourteen feet high, ten feet wide and weighs sixty-four tons. Look up and you will see the observation room. Three full size bedrooms, a separate dining room and kitchen, two bathrooms—two with showers and one with a tub. Notice the Pullman's extravagant interior; inlaid mahogany, ornate moldings, and stained glass. Before every trip it is freshly stocked with food, water, beer, and rye whiskey. The owner sure knows how to live. For now all of it is available to you. But ignore it. We're here to work

The luxury was lost on me in any event as we settled down in parlor car. The team prepared me for my meetings with the Mexican president.

My cover name, "Helmut Hahn," printed on official papers, showed me to be a German diplomat. Also on board, Agent Tony Velasco, a Spaniard linguist and expert marksman would serve as my interpreter.

The fast-paced and grueling briefing began immediately.

Karl initially had concerns that I would not be able to absorb the information. We sat facing each other and he tossed me questions in rapid-fire succession. "What's your name? Rank? Name the ambassador. Who is trying to pull off the charade? Why? What are the contents of the telegram?"

On it went, hour after hour. But I showed the same level of intensity and effort with Karl as I'd used doing language assignments with my old professor.

After three long days of travel, study, and rehearsal, the team felt "Helmut Hahn" to be up to the task.

We arrived in Mexico, and went directly to the office of President Venustiano Carranza. Formalities completed, interpreter Tony Velasco introduced me as Helmut Hahn, German diplomat and emissary. I immediately began the spiel I had rehearsed to perfection on the train.

'Emissary Hahn' began, "On behalf of the government of the German Empire, I deeply apologize to you and the noble people of Mexico for the need of this meeting, and thank you in advance for your valuable time. We have a grave problem on our hands that involves your country. Our intelligence sources have discovered that a spy has infiltrated our network and is trying to feed disinformation to your government. We have not identified the spy yet, but believe we know his plan. The spy hopes that information contained in a telegram will convince Mexico to attack U.S. forces along your border, and retake land that has been ceded to the United States."

I paused and Tony Velasco translated, then I continued.

"We have been in contact with American officials and are satisfied they have no interest in a war with Mexico or with Germany.

"The message in the telegram seeks a way to keep America out of the war in Europe by placing your country at risk. The telegram is a forgery. It is a desperate attempt by a disloyal group within our own German Empire to violate the conditions of war. The culprits will be rooted out and will be dealt with severely.

"If the plan reaches your desk, it will likely be delivered by Heinrich von Eckardt, German Ambassador to Mexico. If he approaches you with such a message it means the Ambassador has also been duped.

"The fake document is in the form a telegram with a forged signature of Arthur Zimmermann. That is all I am at liberty to say at this time. Do you have any questions, Mr. President?"

President Carranza listened without interruption then spoke to one of his aides who translated, "The president asks how we can be sure it is not you who are the imposters."

Tony Velasco's voice wavered ever so slightly as he translated the President's question for me. This was a question we had not planned for. No rehearsal prepared me to answer it. I stood on my own. The room became tense as all parties on both sides stiffened, except for Helmut Hahn.

"Sir, I understand that you might be skeptical by this late night meeting, but good friends and allies, as our two countries are, require a level of trust with each other. I offer you my credentials and my word. I beg you let your heart and your head be your guide and ask yourself if we appear to be German emissaries or imposters.

Adding backup information that the team had provided me, I continued to freelance. "I also ask you to consider these facts: First, my country has been at war in Europe for years. It is a costly war as I'm sure you understand. Second, our treasury is unable to fulfill our earlier commitment to provide gold necessary to stock the Mexican national bank.

"Third, evidence of the traitors and their plan was just recently discovered. We scrambled as quickly as we could to arrange this meeting with you in hopes of controlling the damage."

I stopped speaking. After his aide spoke my words, President Carranza sat for a long moment, then spoke to his translator. Before the Mexican could repeat the president's words to me, I noticed a glimmer in Tony's eye and took it as a good sign.

"His Excellency says that your argument is a strong one. We have no interest in war with our neighbors to the north. As a courtesy to your country we will let the scene play out as you suggest. His Excellency wishes you the best in finding your traitor."

Emissary Hahn bowed and thanked the president and the group left his office.

My heart pumped hard as Karl, Raymond, Tony and I crossed the courtyard. Racing across the cobblestones, we passed a man wearing a German-style suit that bore the lapel pins of a diplomat. He stared at me for a split second, trying to place my familiar face, then called out in German, "Who are you and what is your business here?

A shiver ran through me. The voice, the scar on his cheek and the disfigured nose that he'd worn since childhood confirmed it. There was no denying the German was Hans Richter. Word of the American scheme must have been leaked to the German Secret Police. Why else would he be here?

Karl stepped in front of me trying to shield me from his view, but it was too late. Hans looked at me, then at Karl. "I know who you are from your photo, Blackburn."

Hans stared at me for a long moment then shouted. "YOU! Boskur! It cannot be. How is it possible?"

Karl tried desperately to control the situation with a bluff. "If you show that telegram to the Mexican authorities you'll be executed as a traitor, Richter. Your war is a lost cause. Come with us and I'll grant you clemency and a good life in America."

Karl's eyes scoured the courtyard but he saw nobody else. He continued his bluff. "Germany is bankrupt and soon will surrender. Tomorrow the United States and Mexico will announce an alliance and enter the war on the side of your enemies," he lied. "Give up now. Live a good life on this side of the Atlantic while a war-torn Europe is in ruins."

Hans looked bewildered. He paused for an instant, then yelled, "It is you who will die here, not me."

Quick as a flash he drew a dagger from a sheath beneath his coat. It all seemed to happen in slow motion. In a split second, with one swift movement, Hans sliced Agent Velasco across the throat. The fine edge of the blade dripped crimson. He spun and shoved the knife up to its hilt into the heart cavity of Karl's assistant, Raymond Eichler. Hans struggled to remove the weapon from Raymond's body as the wound oozed out a large red splotch on his chest. Karl reached into his coat pocket, wrapped his fingers around a pistol, and fired a shot. The coat muffled the report of the pistol, and the bullet struck Hans in the ribcage.

The shot penetrated Hans's chest, but the coat softened its impact. The bullet caused only minor damage. As Hans turned and ran toward the presidential palace, Karl removed the pistol from his pocket, took careful aim, and squeezed the trigger again. The gun jammed.

Karl yelled. "Stop him! Do not let him get to the president!"

Raymond and Tony lay on the ground bleeding and unable to help. As Karl worked to clear the gun's chamber, I reached inside my coat and removed the slingshot and one ball bearing, pulled back the rubber, and released it.

Hans began to shout while running full speed. The spheroid struck the base of his skull. He stopped yelling, lurched forward, and made a gurgling sound, then stumbled, and fell. He looked back and attempted to stagger to his feet. Hans drew his own gun and aimed it directly at Karl and me just as the second ball bearing entered his eye socket and lodged in his brain.

The body of Hans Richter, bully, sadistic mass murderer, and heir to Herr Richter's fortune, lay dead, sprawled on the cold Mexican plaza stones.

The quiet war outside the presidential palace went unnoticed.

Karl and I lifted the blood-soaked Raymond, and I draped Tony across my shoulder. Both victims lost plenty of blood. We carried and dragged the two men across the street and into a waiting car, driven by our porter. He helped load them into the car and we raced to our train. By the time we boarded, all life had drained from Agents Raymond Eichler and Tony Velasco, the first American fatalities of the "The War to End All Wars."

23

PEASANT TO PATRIOT TO PEASANT

The speeding iron horse pulled the cars that carried the bodies of agents Tony Velasco and Raymond Eichler, along with Karl, me, and our porter. Barren landscape became green as we hurtled across America's heartland on our way back to Washington, D.C. with a whistle-stop in Clairton.

Once again I overlooked the grandness of the parlor car, this time in favor of a good night's rest. The motion of the train rocked me to sleep and the satisfaction of a job completed set me to dreaming. I dreamt about my wife and daughter, and how life had exceeded my wildest expectations. As I dreamed of the future, the first rays of sunshine peeked through uncovered windows and pried my eyes open, awakening me.

I took advantage of another comfort of the plush sleeper car, the shower. I liked the experience of "washing in the rain." After drying myself with large plush Turkish towels, I ignored the fancy diplomat suit that hung in the closet, soaked with the blood of the two dead agents, and instead dressed in my own clothes, laundered and pressed by the porter while I slept.

Making my way to the parlor car, I found Karl having hot black coffee with a thick steak and fresh eggs, over easy, as he read a report. Karl peered up over his thick spectacles, smiled, and asked, "Good morning, Sunshine. How did you sleep?"

"Like a baby."

"Well, baby, listen to this. Our intelligence team in Mexico reports our mission was a roaring success. Mexican Secret Service found the body of Hans Richter early this morning. Wait. Let me read the telegram to you. 'Early morning STOP body of German discovered STOP Mexican officials believe spy eliminated by German intelligence STOP.'

"So the Mexicans concluded Hans was the mole and German secret police killed him. They completely bought our story of the fake telegram. You did a great job winging it when President Carranza questioned you."

Karl paused as the porter set a hearty breakfast before me.

"I hope you like steak and eggs for breakfast."

I nodded as the porter filled my coffee cup.

"Pete, the president also wired me early this morning. He sends his thanks to you for service to your country and his condolences for our two casualties. Their deaths sadden me as well. Ray and Tony were good men and will be missed. Raymond has been with me for more than a year. I will visit his family personally and arrange for his wife to receive a pension for his service. I did not know Tony personally before this mission. We will bring them home to Washington and give them a hero's burial at Arlington.

Karl's tone became more solemn. "Pete, you handled yourself as well as any professional agent I've ever worked with. You were convincing and cool under fire. Nobody could have done a better job. Could I possibly interest you in a career with the government? The pay is decent and the work can be exciting, as you've discovered."

I looked at Karl and pulled a bag of Cutty Pipe smoking tobacco from my jacket pocket. "A fellow mill worker practicing his English first read the side of the bag to me. 'There is no purer, milder, better tobacco sold anywhere, at any price. When you get CUTTY PIPE you get the best.' I've been a loyal customer ever since.

"Remember when you taught me this?

Taking a pinch of tobacco from the Cutty Pipe bag, I slid a single Zig-Zag rolling paper from a booklet and placed the tobacco on it, then rolled it between my thumb and two fingers, slightly tapering each end. The tip of my tongue gently passed across the edge of the rolling paper, offering just a hint of spittle to keep it from unwrapping. My thumbnail flicked the redheaded tip of a wooden match. A spark, then flame jumped briefly and receded. I lit the cigarette and took a deep drag, exhaling blue-white vapor.

The sweet smell of my Cutty Pipe tobacco drifted through the rail car. I took a second drag, exhaled, then said, "I thank you for your good words. I am happy to help the government of this country that has been so good to my family and me. But I have to say no to your offer. I'm just a simple farmer. My own clothes suit me better than the stiff, uncomfortable diplomat suit. All this coming and going is not to my liking. I just want to get back to my home and family, and tend my crops and my animals. Katie does well with her business, and I want to live the rest of my days at home. Once this trip is done I plan to travel only as far as these legs carry me."

Karl smiled. "Well, you can't blame a man for trying to recruit a hero. I admire you, Pete. I even envy you. Your service is recognized and rewarded. Your citizenship papers are in order and your immigration status is no longer an issue. I saw to that before we left. If Katie chooses to become a citizen I will personally fast track her application.

"Our war with Germany won't take long, eighteen months…two years at the most I suspect. When the war ends, returning soldiers will marry and buy homes. Katie's business is in a position to prosper from that. I'll put her in touch with staff members to ensure that her Savings and Loan business is on the preferred lender list for government programs."

We sat chatting like two old soldiers. "Thank you, Karl. You are a true friend. What started as a deception has become…"

He interrupted. "…another deception. Your first one helped bring you to America, but this one was for the good of our country. To me, you will always be, 'Citizen Novak, American hero.'"

We both smiled at my new title: Citizen.

"If you ever change your mind about entering government service, let me know. A position will always be open to you."

We finished breakfast, and I rolled another cigarette. Karl raised an eyebrow, motioning the porter to remove the remaining items from the white satin tablecloth. He invited me to join him on the overstuffed leather lounge chairs.

Once settled, Karl picked up a fancy, expensive briefcase from beside his chair, and undid the dual buckles that held the top together. "Citizen Novak, I have a few items to remind you of the great service you did for our country. I had them prepared before leaving Washington because of my confidence that our mission would succeed. First, a letter of appreciation signed by President Wilson. Since it is written in English, I would like to read it to you in German to make sure you understand exactly what it says.

Dear Mr. Novak, The manner in which you conducted yourself on this highly important mission brings me a great deal of satisfaction. I have only enough time to write a line of acknowledgement but it is one of deep gratitude. I am certain that your devotion and assistance made us a stronger country. You are an American Hero. Cordially and Sincerely Yours, (signed) *Woodrow Wilson.*

"The letter is written on White House stationery. I also have President Wilson's official inauguration medals for you, Katie, and your baby. The engraving on your medal says, 'To Peter Novak, American Hero.'

"These are but small tokens of our appreciation for your service to our country." He carefully packed the items back into the valise and handed it to me.

I am a man of few words in the best of times. Tears welled up in my eyes as I shook Karl's hand and hugged him, "I have no words…."

"None needed."

Karl relaxed at the table and smiled. "Remember our trip from Europe? We were both so young. I had just entered government service and you must have been, what? Twenty, twenty-one?"

"Eighteen. My indentured servitude was ending and I was about to be drafted. I'm probably still a wanted man for draft evasion in Germany."

"Well, Pete, we checked on that as well. Your name does not appear in any German archives listing you as an evader or anything else that would put you at risk. Apparently your Herr Richter gave them a phony name for you. So Peter Novak does not exist in Germany or Bosnia. He is a stalwart American citizen."

I hesitated, and then asked, "Do you have any idea what happened to Herr Richter? Such a kind and gentle man."

"I'm sorry to tell you this, Pete. Our intelligence shows him drafted into the Navy as an officer and killed in action while serving on a U-boat, destroyed by the British Navy."

"Such a loss. He was like a father to me. I loved that man."

Tears again welled up despite my efforts to control my emotions. We rode the rest of the way in silence.

The VIP train bypassed the Pittsburgh station and stopped in Clairton just long enough for me to disembark. It was the middle of the night and Karl had another several-hour ride to Washington ahead of him.

I approached the house anxiously. It had been nearly a week since I left but it seemed like forever.

I set the new valise on the kitchen table. As I climbed the stairs to the second floor, I heard Katie stirring.

"You come in late, Old Man. I heard your train stop and go."

I kicked off my shoes and climbed, fully clothed, into bed. Katie rested her head on my shoulder. I gathered her in my arms and held her tightly. We lay together, neither uttering a word, watching the mighty Monongahela River through the picture window of our master bedroom.

"So where have you been, Old Man? Something's up. The train doesn't stop here this late," Katie cooed.

I waited a long time before answering. "Mrs. Novak, I have much to tell you."

(tape ends)

About the Author

Andrew Richard Nixon was born in Clairton, Pennsylvania to first generation American parentage of Bosnian-Serbian and Croatian ethnicity. His birth occurred during the height of the Second World War. He grew up amidst tales of "The Old Country," and struggles by his immigrant grandparents to assimilate into the American culture.

The author holds multiple degrees including Doctor of Education. His first book, *50 Shades of Grades, My Journey Through Wacademia*, is a hilarious memoir that has received outstanding reviews. *Three Lives of Peter Novak* is his first novel.

The author and his wife Patricia have lived in Las Vegas for the past half-century.

andynixonwordsmith.com
Follow *Three Lives of Peter Novak* on Facebook

Books are rated by their reviews. If you enjoyed this book, please visit Amazon.com or Barnes & Noble and leave a review. Thank you. ARN

Acknowledgments

I would like to express my gratitude to the many people who saw me through this venture; all those who provided support, talked things over, read, wrote, offered comments, and assisted in the editing, proofreading and design.

In particular I wish to personally thank the following people and organizations for their contributions to my inspiration and knowledge and other help in creating this book. First and foremost thanks to my favorite Reading Specialist, my wife Pat, who not only offered suggestions, but support and hot chocolate.

Readers and editors: Jenn Alexy, Jami Carpenter, Dinko Čelić, Carrie Ann Lahain, Joanie Jordan, and "The Thing at the Place" writers group.

Deborah Dorchak and Wendi Kelly of Blue Sun Studio, Inc. so graciously offered advice and direction on the process and mechanics of putting a novel together. Their coaching was invaluable.

Individuals and organizations that provided research information include the late Jim Hartman, who provided his personal resources and those of the Mifflin Township Historical Society, and Brian Butko and the Lincoln Highway News, Francis O'Neill of The

Maryland Historical Society, the Baltimore City Historical Society, and members of the Historical Novel Society, and authority on Northern Virginia history, author William Connery.

Bosnian and German language experts Jelena Misura, and Ralph Buechler provided selected feedback on spoken words of characters.

Family members, including my grandparents, parents, and siblings contributed their recollections of family lore. Many of their stories served as background information.

Last but not least: I beg forgiveness of all those who have been with me over the course of the years and whose names I have failed to mention.

Author's Note

Three Lives of Peter Novak was inspired by family lore, and stories passed on to me by my grandmother. She told of her journey from Eastern Europe to America to reunite with her parents and meet my grandfather. This is not their story but small nuggets of the tale are taken from her storytelling, and developed into a work of fiction.

Names, characters, businesses, places, events and incidents are either the products of the imagination, or used in a fictitious manner. Any resemblance to actual persons, living or dead, or actual events, is purely coincidental.

Many of the locations in the novel are actual places that did, and still do exist. Some events did or could have taken place, but the characters are fictionalized. Anti-Semitism existed in Europe, and facts of the murder of a Jewish university student in Prussia are taken from archives and newspaper articles of the time. The murder was never solved.

Stabandža is a village in Bosnia, a small rural community whose demographics have changed from those depicted in this novel. Šišljavić is a Croatian village set along the Kupa River. Clairton, Charleroi,

Elrama, and Elizabeth are Pennsylvania towns located along the Monongahela River. Monaca and Aliquippa are Pennsylvania towns located along the Ohio River. Street names in the story are actual Clairton street names. Several local family names have been used but characters that bear those names are all fictional. Clairton boomed and thrived for more than seventy years, until the demise of the steel industry in America. Clairton, Charleroi, Elrama and Elizabeth are part of the Monongahela valley that struggles to adapt to changing economic conditions.

Immigrant-owned banks and savings and loan companies sprang up around the time of the story, but the actual company portrayed in the novel is fictional.

The Zimmerman Telegram and President Wilson's reluctance to enter the war are historically represented based upon newspapers and articles of the time. Shortly after the fictionalized events portrayed in this book, America entered the First World War, then referred to as "The War to end All Wars."

Who's Who?

Names listed alphabetically by last name or first if there is no last name.

Adi, day laborer

Alric, gypsy

Sergeant Major Altenburg, soldier/recruiter

Andjela, gossip

Anton, Peter's half-brother

Baba/Kata/Katerina, Peter's wife

Andrij Babić, farmer

Newton Baker, U.S. Secretary of State

Gotthard Baldenburg, accused murderer

Berezovsky, renter

Arben Bizi, aka AB, Albanian renter

Karl Blackburn, American government agent

Bobo, bar patron

Fritz Boehm, student

Vasilije Božić, blacksmith

Brady, mill guard

Klaus Braun, language professor

Branislav and Zdenko Brezović, Katie's cousins

Michael Buchele, printer

Andrew Carnegie, steel mogul

Venustiano Carranza, President of Mexico

Simon Chottiner, lumberyard merchant

Stevo Čolić, coal miner/Ante's cousin

Darko, Ruža's brother

Danica, neighbor

Diedo, pronounced "Jedo," Slavic for "Grandfather"

Drago, Croatian translator

Father Drobak, Catholic priest

Serge Dukić, architect/builder

Džordž, (George) Peter's half-brother

Raymond Eichler, government agent

Archduke Ferdinand, heir to the throne

Francie, Peter's granddaughter

Mr. Frank, banker

Franz, day laborer

Henry Clay Frick, steel magnate

Mitzi Fritz, Tavern owner's daughter

Frizzy Hair, card player, aka Tahir Virkkula

George, Peter's grandson

Dieter Glock, butcher

Charles Goodyear, American inventor

Tomas Grgurić, constable

Grisnik, renter

Hadž, Bosnian card player

Helmut Hahn, diplomat, Peter Novak's code name

Little Hans, orphan

Emil Heller, student/murder victim

Hopp, Prussian policeman

Eda Horvat, Kata's chaperone onboard ship

Dženana Ibrahim, midwife

Mladen Ilić, friend/mill worker

Ismet, Bosnian card player

Stretch Jakovac, renter,

Janssens, mystery Belgian official

John, Peter's grandson

Jovanka, Ruža's friend/flower girl

Dragana Jovanović, Peter's godmother

Goran Jovanović, Peter's godfather

Little Jozo, Peter's half-brother

Kathy, Peter's granddaughter

Kočka, police officer

Kraljevstvo, (Royalty) name of Percheron horse

Branko Kukić, Kata's boyfriend

Albert Lhormer, realtor

Ludwig, day laborer

Herman Lutz, Mennonite boy

Mrs. Lutz, Mennonite mother

Magarac Njemacji, nickname meaning German Jackass

Baka Mara, Kata's grandmother

Marija, housekeeper

Marinović, renter

Maryann, Peter's granddaughter

Mijo, Peter's pal

Milan, Peter's grandson

Nenad Mikulić, vendor

Milinka, widow

Miloška, Nikola's second wife

Momir, carpenter

Mrozinski, renter

Netzke, Prussian policeman

Nikola Novak, Peter's father

Pedrag Novak, Peter's brother

Pero, Peter Novak's boyhood nickname

Peter Novak, protagonist

O'Leary, police officer

Oskar, day laborer

Otto, mill worker

Jozo and Miloška Pacić, Nikola Novak's neighbors

Ante Radić, Kata's father

Stela Radić, Kata's mother

Friedrich Richter, wealthy estate owner

Hans Richter, son of wealthy estate owner

Saša, neighbor

Gisela Schmidt, deceased elderly widow

Shevchenko, renter

Damir Šimundić, train passenger

Klaudija Šimundić, train passenger

Sonny, Peter's grandson

Austin D. Stevens, Allegheny County official

Pavle and Jelena Stojanović, Ruža's parents

Ruža Stojanović Novak, Peter's mother

Ivan Štokić, steel mill retiree

Fabijan Tadić, renter

Nikola Tesla, Serbian inventor

Tony Velasco, government agent

Vesna, Ruža's friend/flowergirl

Tahir Virkkula, aka Frizzy Hair, card player

Franz Friedrich Volk, Professor/translator of tapes

Heinrich von Eckardt, German Ambassador

Pop Vučen, village priest

Iva Vučen, priest's wife

Millie Vucanović, neighbor

Slobodan Vuković, steel mill foreman

Mr. J. W. Walters, banker

Wolfgang, gypsy

Woodrow Wilson, U. S. President

Arthur Zimmermann, German Foreign Secretary

Zora, gossip

Glossary

Baka—Grandmother

Boskur—Derogatory term for Bosnian person

Bošnjački—Bosnian

Burra—Howling wind

Danke schön—Thank you

Danke das du—Thank you for

Diedo—Grandfather

Djever—Bride's guard

Dobro Jutro—Good Morning

Dojilja—Wet nurse

Draga moija—My dear

Dušo—Honey (affectionately)

Frfljanje—Gibberish

Guten morgen—Good Morning

Hrvat—Croatian

Hvala ljepo—Thank you very much

Ja—Yes

Koliva—Boiled wheat with honey

Kraljevstvo—Name of a Percheron horse, meaning "Royalty."

Krone—Official currency of the Austro-Hungarian Empire

Krchma—Roadside kiosk

Kum—Godfather, title of respect

Kuma—Godmother

Kumovi—Godparents

Kumče—Godson

Magarac—Donkey

Magarac Njemacji—German Jackass

Mala praćka—Sling shot

Marché aux puces—Flea market

Mein—My

Monokel—Single eyepiece

Mužu—Husband

Ne razumijem—I don't understand

Nein—No

Pogača—Bread

Polizeibeamte—Policeman

Pop—Father, Priest

Preko—Totally

Rakija—Whiskey

Rezume ti—Do you understand?

Säbel—Sabre

Sarma—Cabbage leaves rolled around a mincemeat filling

Skup—Wedding festivities

Slava—Holy day

Slivovitz—Plum brandy

Sprechen sie Deutsch?—Do you speak German?

Srbski—Serbian

Ta—father (informally)

Willkommen heiben America—Welcome to America

Yak—Derogatory term for Bosnian person

Zajedničar—Newspaper of the Croatian Fraternal Union

Zdravo i dobrodošli—Hello and welcome

Ziveli—"To your health"

Zweite Sohn—Second son